A Crack In Everything

Catherine Ingram

Diamond Books
P.O. Box 10431 Portland, Oregon 97210
www.DiamondBooksInfo.com

ALSO BY CATHERINE INGRAM

In the Footsteps of Gandhi

Passionate Presence

A Crack In Everything

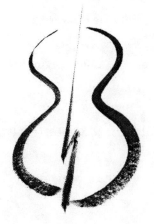

Catherine Ingram

Diamond Books

Published by Diamond Books
P.O. Box 10431, Portland, Oregon 97210, U.S.A.
www.DiamondBooksInfo.com

Library of Congress Control Number: 2006907991

ISBN 10: 0-9789193-0-0
ISBN 13: 978-0-9789193-0-6

First edition

Design by Gareth Jiffeau and Diamond Clear Technologies
Cover photograph by Hugh d'Autremont
Violin image by Maria Monroe
Set in Granjon

Printed in the United States of America

For my family

There is a crack, a crack in everything
That's how the light gets in.
—Leonard Cohen

1

Goddamnit! Alex shouted, though alone in his car. He was heading to his office in Santa Monica and the freeway had gone from a crawl to a stop. Ten lanes stalled in both directions at two in the afternoon. I can't believe I let Mandy talk me into taking her to the airport, he thought. "You never take me to the airport," she had whined that morning for the hundredth time. Well, from now on his response would be *never again.* What a stupid waste of time. The best and brightest from the entire world end up driving cabs in places like Los Angeles and he, who does not have a minute to spare, has to take her to the airport for the silly sentimental reason of saying good-bye *at the airport* instead of at home. And she goes to the airport *all the time.* One week she's shooting in New York, the next week in Paris. After that it's Milan or London or Toronto. The life of an actress/model. Mandy, like so many actress/models, was really a model who hoped to segue into acting when the short shelf life of being a model comes to an abrupt end at about age twenty-nine. At twenty-eight, Mandy was feeling the pressure. The other option was to marry a rich producer or director or anybody else with new or old money, or any other kind of money for that matter. And on that count, he was now feeling the pressure from Mandy. Christ, he was a living cliché. The rich young(ish) producer avoiding marriage to the model/actress. It could be a reality TV series if it weren't so worn out in reality.

He leaned on the horn in futility. Horns all around blared in turn. He briefly wondered how Ramu, his yoga teacher, would behave in this situation. Mister Serene, he called him. Yeah, who wouldn't be serene listening to new age music all day in your pajamas in a golden lit yoga room watching beautiful women in the downward dog position? If he were here in this car Ramu would no doubt be exhorting him to *breathe*. As if you need someone to tell you to breathe. As if you wouldn't be breathing unless someone from yoga class pointed out that you should. Oh right, *breathe*. What a truly novel idea! Why didn't I think of that? And that name, Ramu. What a hype. I'll bet Ramu wasn't known as Ramu in Norfolk, Nebraska, where he supposedly grew up on a farm. No, his use of *Ramu* was, of course Mister Serene's homage to the trends in pop music, fashion, books, movies, gurus, travel destinations, and acquired names for All Things Indian.

India. That hellhole on earth. Could he even think of a less likely place to emulate, to be the arbiter of fashion? Maybe Rwanda or somewhere in the former Soviet bloc. But no, India really wins out for filth, poverty, superstition, disease, and a runaway population living in the worst pollution he had ever seen. New Delhi made Los Angeles seem like Norway. He had once spent a month there years ago after his mother died. His sister, Joan, had talked him into a "sacred pilgrimage" with the lame idea of throwing their mother's ashes into the Ganges. They had smuggled the ashes into India in protein powder containers (it is illegal to import deceased relatives in any form without a lot of paperwork), but after filling up four containers and still having several pounds left over, his sister decided to take just under a third of the ashes with them and hope that there was no diminishment to the upgraded afterlife she had intended for their mother by dumping her remains in the holy river. Joanie, god love her. Now that his mother was gone, she was about the only woman he could really trust or respect, but she was a bit of a kook sometimes.

The lane next to him began to move at about two miles per hour. He distractedly gazed at the lucky creatures zooming toward their destinations when he noticed a bumper sticker on a passing Volkswagen bug that read, "SUVs Suck and People Who Drive Them Are Pigs." His black Lexus SUV seemed to be suddenly swathed in day glow calling out to his fellow prisoners of the freeway, "Look, here is one now. A disgusting SUV with a pig at the wheel." Of course, there were several other SUVs in the traffic jam at this exact moment. This was Los Angeles, after all. But he somehow felt it was beneath him to be lumped in with other SUV owners. He wasn't like the stupid people who owned SUVs but were not the slightest bit hip to the reasons not to own one. He knew all the reasons not to own an SUV, but he was not, in his mind, a typical SUV owner. He cared about the environment, he really did. And he was completely against the war based on his and his friends' beliefs that the war was all about the oil, about keeping it flowing so that Americans could have cheap gas and drive their big gas-guzzling cars and the fat-cat oil barons could go on with their looting. He knew all that. He gave money, lots of it, to environmental and anti-war causes and let Mandy drag him to galas and dinners and award functions for those causes at least once a week. But he had to admit that driving up to those events in an SUV was a little embarrassing, and he had been having some thoughts of late about buying a more suitable car for everyday use. He owned a Porsche 911 Turbo convertible, a fantastic machine that he loved to drive for fun and trips up the coast, but it wouldn't do for banging around town and handing off to Mexican parking valets. Mister Serene of course owned a hybrid, the new Toyota Prius Biodiesel. Runs on grass or something and goes about forty-five max on the open road. What a strange twist of fate that the coolest cars were now these goofy-looking featherweights that went the speed your grandmother drives, and the cars that were once the ultimate now brand you as a barbarian out to destroy planet Earth.

Well, he would have to find some middle ground on this one. He was certainly not going to buy a biodielsel or he would never live it down at the Thursday night poker game with the guys. Maybe he would have Linda, his personal assistant, do some research on new car deals right now. No, wait a minute. Bad idea. Women could not be trusted to investigate anything with a plug or a motor. He would have to do it himself. When would he have the time to visit a bunch of car showrooms? He badly needed some time off. What he really wanted was to get far away somewhere and stop for just a moment to plan a bit ahead. He had the feeling sometimes that he was running in place and that the scenery was beginning to blur. Mandy had been bugging him to take her to Italy—to all the romantic places there: Venice, Florence, Lake Como. But what fun would that be? First off, she doesn't eat. What would be the point of going to Italy and never having a meal or a glass of wine? Mandy's idea of a meal is some carrots and celery cut up to look like pasta with a drizzle of grapefruit juice and turmeric over it. She is big into *raw*. Her food groups come almost entirely from the gathering wing of our hunting and gathering ancestors. Italian cuisine, loaded with all the wrong kinds of carbs, would not make the cut of anything she would put in her mouth. And secondly, she is allergic to smoke so that would limit them from being anywhere *indoors*. She would probably want to just go on some expensive bicycle tour of the countryside. If he wanted to ride a bike in the great outdoors, he could do that right there in California.

Of course, Mandy and her model friends all looked great. That was one thing he had to give them for their obsession with health. They were all fit and thin. Really, really thin, in fact. Looked good in any kind of clothing. Mandy was a knockout whether in runway designer wear, sweatpants, or a thong bikini. But he had been noticing lately that the way she felt in bed was a little, well, bony. It was like being curled up with a tangle of wire hangers. There wasn't a soft curve on her entire body. She didn't even have breasts to speak of. Not that he was complaining since a lot of her girlfriends had fake ones, which he couldn't stand. Bolt-ons, he called them. He and the guys often had bets about which women had them since the surgical technology was getting better and it was harder to tell. But if you ever had to touch one, there was no doubt.

Anyway, he did need a break soon. He would have to think of where to go. First, he would buy a new car. Yeah, that's good. Next week, he would buy a new car and then he would figure out when he could take some time off and where to go. But at the moment, he had about six deals in the works and all of them required constant baby-sitting. In fact, he was now going to be very late for a script meeting with a writer and a director who were undoubtedly already waiting in his office. Well, let them wait. Part of the game of power in this town revolved around who waits for whom.

2

Aine knew she would die soon. It was not just the doctor's words of uncertainty about her latest tests in Dublin; he had been vague enough to convey a well-rehearsed hope. And it wasn't that the nurse in his office would not meet her eyes and made sure never to linger in a room with her without focusing on a medical chart. The evidence came from Aine's own body. It was in her increasing exhaustion no matter how much she had rested. It was in the smell of her sweat and urine, in the yellow of her skin, in the way small cuts took too long to heal. It was in the pain in her abdomen that had once come and gone and had now come to stay. No, Aine did not need the doctor in Dublin to tell her she was dying.

She stood in twilight at the cliff's edge near her home on the west coast of Ireland. She had been silently saying good-bye to the things of her world for some weeks. This night would be no different. The smell of seaweed. Whitecaps flashing like mother of pearl on the water at dusk. Calls of seagulls mixed with the wind. Sunset walks on the cliffs with Fiona…

With this last thought, she stopped herself. This was as close as she could come to saying good-bye to Fiona herself. For of all the beauty that Aine had released, for all that she had loved and let go, nothing she had known compared to her feelings for Fiona—her talented and sensitive daughter. Now the time had come for Aine to make arrangements for Fiona's care, and she would need to bring her clearest focus to this most important decision of her life. I cannot leave her with my family, thought Aine. They would do to her what they did to me. Aine suddenly felt a familiar weariness in her chest, a weariness that had intensified with her illness but had been there all along. This is what is killing me, she thought. It has been killing me since childhood.

She had fled her small-town Irish Catholic family at age twenty, and though she lived only a few hours' drive away, she rarely visited. The times she had gone back had been a test of her patience that she had usually failed. No matter how much she promised herself beforehand that she would ignore their provocations and their ignorance, it all became unbearable from the first moments of seeing them, from the first words out of their mouths. The cruelty of their Catholicism, the hatred of anyone who was different, the hypocrisy of their lives. Even the very rooms where they lived and breathed evoked claustrophobia. The small windowless kitchen, the paisley wallpaper in the living room stained several shades darker from years of cigarette and cigar smoke, the cheap knick-knacks and doilies on every surface of furniture. It was as if the pervasive dreariness of their surroundings represented the precise expression of their internal lives. She had tried to see that they could not help being who they were. She had tried to "forgive them for they know not what they do." But she was not strong enough. She was, in her own way, a product of their smallness.

Her thoughts went involuntarily to her uncle, her mother's youngest brother, the proverbial apple of her mother's eye. Uncle

Martin, who owned the local bakery and came home with them to dinner after mass every Sunday with fresh pastries. Uncle Martin, who was the only one who could make her mother laugh. She thought of the day her mother had slapped her across the face and said, "Don't you ever say anything like that about your uncle again, do you hear me, you lying girl? Don't you ever breathe one word of that nonsense to anyone." Aine had obeyed her mother and never again spoke the forbidden truth. She had endured her life there until the first opportunity to leave. But on the few visits to her family over recent years she had seen the way Martin's grown son Michael had looked at Fiona when his wife was out of the room. She had even noticed Martin himself, now in his sixties, with that familiar hunger in his eyes.

She pictured the school Fiona would attend if she lived with her family, the Catholic school she herself had attended. She remembered the grim nuns and having her knuckles rapped for slight infractions or missed homework and the way almost every natural joy of life was made to seem dirty. It could hardly be more dissimilar to the Waldorf-based school she and her small community had set up on the coast, where Fiona had thrived since the age of three. Fiona had never known an unkind word from a teacher. She had never sat in a straight-backed desk repeating the multiplication tables in unison with the class, fearful of a smack with a ruler should she falter in her recitation. She had never been sheltered from the company of boys her own age. Instead, Fiona had been encouraged from the time she was little to paint, draw, dance, sing, celebrate the solstices, and, when it was time and she was ready, to learn to read and study the basics of elementary education. But most of all, Fiona had been encouraged in her love of stringed instruments.

It had begun with an Irish fiddle. At the age of four she

heard a young man playing one on a street in Galway, and Fiona had been wonder-struck. Silently staring at the marvelous device, enchanted by its sounds, she stood perfectly still for twenty minutes, tightly gripping her mother's hand. When Aine decided that it was too cold to stand on the street any longer, Fiona had cried tears the size of marbles. A few weeks later, Aine bought an inexpensive used fiddle, and the love affair began. A parent at the school spent Tuesday afternoons over the course of a year teaching Fiona the basic hornpipes and jigs of fiddling, and she was off. She played when she awoke in the morning. She played during breaks in her school day. She played most evenings at home. She even slept with her fiddle at the side of her bed. Over the next few years Fiona's playing became the center around which most of the musical events and theatrical accompaniments occurred in her school. Local charities invited her to perform at their fundraisers, and she was often asked to join adult quartets at Galway county fairs and community gatherings in the summer, a sight that was sure to please the crowds. The young girl prodigy on the fiddle. But her real love was yet to come.

When Fiona turned nine, her mother took her to Dublin to see Vivaldi's violin concerto, *The Four Seasons*. Aine had saved for the trip over a six-month period, ever since she had seen notice of the concert in the bookstore where she worked. She had arranged for them to stay in Dublin with relatives of Moira Keaton, who, along with her husband Sean were fellow parents at the school and Aine's closest friends. She and Fiona had taken the train in from Galway, a journey of six hours counting the hour's bus ride from their home to the train station. They arrived in Dublin in the early afternoon. As they exited the city center station, Aine felt quietly excited, having lived and worked in Dublin for years after leaving home and having had her first tastes of freedom on those gray streets. But for Fiona, the big city was strange and foreboding, a noisy place where few people smiled and no one said hello, a very different place from her village or even Galway, the biggest town she had known to that point. She was happy to go directly to the house where they would be staying, a distance of several blocks, which they walked in the light afternoon drizzle, carrying their overnight cases.

That night, her mother hired a taxi to take them to the concert. Fiona had never ridden in a taxi and couldn't take her eyes off the meter.

"Mother, the numbers have the word *euros* and *cents* next to them, fixed right on that gadget, and they are rolling very fast. What does it mean?"

"That's what the taxi ride costs," Aine explained.

"Does that mean we have to pay that many euros just to ride in this car?" Fiona asked.

When Aine nodded, Fiona thought her mother must have shape-shifted into someone else, like the stories in Irish myths, in this case a city version who looked more or less like her mother but was behaving very oddly.

Ever since they arrived that day, Aine had been in a delightful regression to her twenties. She had once shared an apartment not far from where they were staying and had frequented the same local Spar shop on a nearby corner. Memories from that wonderful period of her life (was it wonderful or did it just seem so in hindsight?) drifted in and out of her awareness throughout the day and into the evening, creating in her a dreamy sensation of being in another time but also in *now*.

Fiona could not read her mother's mood but could clearly observe the facts at hand. Her mother was wearing perfume, a fancy black dress, and her special pearls. She had painted her face and lips and looked very pretty as she gazed out the taxi window, smiling for no obvious reason. And now she didn't even seem to care about this taxi gadget that was surely going to take all the money they had. How would they ever get back home? *Stop worrying*, Aine said, still smiling. *This is our holiday.* Fiona sank into the seat and tried to be interested in the enormous buildings, double-decker busses, and tattooed young people in all sorts of weird attire that passed before her eyes on the Saturday night streets of Dublin.

As strange as her day had been to that point, it was about to become stranger still. Within the hour, Fiona found herself in the most majestic room she had ever seen as she listened to the opening bars of *The Four Seasons*, played by the flamboyant Nigel Kennedy and the Irish Chamber Orchestra. In those first few moments, Fiona felt as if she had returned from a long journey, as if she were overcoming a homesickness she never knew she had. The violin reached deep into her body, her breath and the blood in her veins mysteriously connected to its strings. The notes themselves relied on her presence to dance in the air of the concert hall just as she, in turn, relied on their presence to continue to exist. Her own bodily rhythms somehow knew exactly what was coming next and ached to get there while mourning the notes that had only just passed and were forever gone, thus producing in the young girl an ecstatic mix of pleasure and pain. None of these feelings came to Fiona in words; they came only in the language of music in which her deft ear and heart were fluent. Her mother sensed that something like this might be happening and was not surprised when Fiona refused to leave her seat during intermission, preferring instead to let the sounds reverberate in her mind until the blessed moment when the concert began again.

They were silent when they left the hall that night. But Fiona noticed on the taxi ride home and on the walk to the train station the next day that the city of Dublin had become all at once the most beautiful and enchanting place on earth. After the concert, her mother purchased a CD of Nigel Kennedy playing Bach's violin concerto, recorded live in London. Within the next few months, Fiona would wear out the disk and require a new one, along with dozens of other violin concerti on CD. A few months later, her school held a bake and rummage sale two weekends in a row to help raise money for a violin. Several local businesses made donations, as did the bookstore owner where Aine worked. When Kevin O'Shea, a violinmaker in Galway, heard news of the young fiddle player in need of a violin, he offered to custom make one for her at a greatly reduced price. Fiona's patrons were thus able to purchase a beautiful violin that had been crafted on the design principles of the old Italian masters using selected tone woods. Kevin O'Shea presented it to Fiona in the school's small theater before the entire student assembly and many members of the local community.

Fiona did not disappoint. Her mother found a teacher just outside of Galway, a famous Italian recluse and former concert violinist, who no longer accepted students. Maria Girardi had been widowed four years previously when her Irish husband died in a fishing accident, and though she was still a relatively young woman, Maria had grown more and more eccentric, eventually refusing all company and arranging to have groceries and other supplies left on her doorstep once a week so she wouldn't need to go into town. It was rumored that she had family money and would one day return to Italy.

Aine sent Maria Girardi an audiocassette of Fiona playing the new violin along with a note explaining that her daughter, though skilled in traditional Irish fiddle, had never studied classical violin. Upon hearing the tape, Maria immediately phoned Aine to arrange for Fiona to begin weekly lessons at her home. For the next three years Fiona spent almost every Saturday with Maria Girardi. She had mastered the Bruch and Mendelssohn concerti as well as most of the Mozart and was now working on the Bach sonatas. She regularly held solo concerts at her school and in venues throughout County Galway. There had even been sightings at these concerts of Maria Girardi, who sometimes slipped into one of the back rows of a venue after the lights went down.

Aine thought about these things as she stood at the cliff's edge. She ruled out leaving Fiona with her family. And though she knew that the Keatons would take Fiona if she asked them, they were hard pressed to feed and clothe their own four boys. Plus, the Keaton lads were a rough and tumble lot. Loud, coarse, and always fighting, they were the biggest troublemakers in school.

Aine also felt it imperative that Fiona keep up her practice and concerts not only because she knew Fiona would need a passionate focus to get through losing her mother but also because she wanted her to have a career that would provide financial independence someday. She knew that the Keatons could probably not afford the time to drive Fiona to her Saturday lessons, even if Maria Girardi agreed to give them for free. She considered asking Maria to take Fiona but rejected this idea as well, feeling that, although Maria was a wonderful teacher and seemed to adore Fiona, her cloistered life and general disdain for the world were not the best environment for a child.

There was one other possibility. When the last rays of sunlight had been replaced by the first stars, Aine walked slowly home in the darkness, her feet knowing every stone and turn on the path as she silently composed a letter.

3

Alex pulled up at his sister's place in the rustic and semi-wild region of greater Los Angeles known as Topanga Canyon in his new BMW 740 il. The day was hot and dry, and he realized that his car would be covered with dust in less than an hour. Damn. I just had it detailed for two hundred bucks yesterday, he lamented to himself. Joan came out on the porch grinning her big sister smile and he immediately imagined his blood pressure lowering. God, it was good to see her. Why did they always let so many weeks go by without getting together when it was only a forty-minute drive? The hell with the dust. He would have the car done again tomorrow.

"There's that handsome devil brother of mine," she called out from the porch. "Are you hungry?"

That was another thing he loved about his sister. She liked to eat—and she was a great cook. "I made mom's lasagna and a rhubarb pie," she added. He made a mental note that he would spend an extra hour at the gym the following week as he ran up the porch steps to grab Joan and sweep her off her feet so that she would squeal. One of his most consistent pleasures in life for as long as he could remember was making his sister squeal. He swung her several revolutions until she screamed a satisfying number of times and set her down so that she would more or less fall backward onto the porch couch. He plunked down beside her, grateful that her large slobbery dog, Hamlet, was nowhere in sight.

"You will never guess who we got a letter from today, "she began in her usual dramatic style.

"A letter? You mean a letter delivered by the U.S. Post Office?" he asked incredulously.

"Exactly," she answered. "They still do that, you know."

"How quaint."

"But, guess who from," she repeated excitedly.

He really couldn't imagine anyone he knew who would write a letter as a means of communication to him and his sister. He certainly received plenty of legal drafts, copyright forms, tax documents, accounting documents, and so on through the U.S. Postal Service. And he got about three hundred emails a week, some of which could be construed as letters. But he hadn't received an actual hard copy letter in years. Who would write a letter to him *and* Joan? "Gee, Sis, is it from Mom? Is she writing us from the great beyond, thanking us for that schlep to India? Is she happy in her new condo in heaven?"

"Stop it, " Joan said playfully. "You're no fun, and since you won't try to guess, I'll just have to tell you. We got a letter from Aine! She is coming to L.A. in three weeks and wants to see us; specifically she asked if you could meet her for lunch after she arrives on Saturday. I plan to write back and invite her to stay here at my place. She's only around for the weekend."

Aine. He had to admit he was intrigued by the prospect of seeing Aine again. An Irish lass, smart as a whip, but kind of a brooding type, as if she was always thinking of something sad, even when she was laughing. Let's see, how old would she be? He remembered that she was about his age, so around forty, he'd say. Well, that's young for a man but getting old for a woman. But, who knows, she may have held up well. All that good Irish air and clean living. Maybe she still had that lovely quiet charm he was so taken with when they were last together, in fact, the only time they were together. She was a bright light of that India trip, a pleasant memory but a memory he had not visited in a long time. Nevertheless, he could recall it at will.

He and Joan had just checked into a little hotel on the banks of the Ganges in Benares. The place was run by two gay Indian guys, one of whom was painted up like a street dancer at Mardi Gras and wore a blonde wig, tight stretch pants, and a halter top. In the few hours since he first arrived in Benares, he had surmised that the entire city was actually a carnival where everyone was on acid. Only they weren't. The psychedelic carnival atmosphere was just ordinary life there. Hell, on the way from the train station he had seen a naked man covered only in ashes, which made his skin look pale blue. He had dreadlocks down to his ass and was walking with everyone else down the street, and no one batted an eye. So the guys at the hotel seemed fairly regular. The only other guest at the place was Aine. When Alex first saw her, she was sitting by the river's edge, reading a book, *The Doors of Perception,* by Aldous Huxley. He had read it in college and walked over to see if he could strike up a conversation. He now recalled her eyes as she looked up from her sitting position. Maybe that was what got him in that first meeting. Aine had eyes that had seen things. Or maybe it was that she had been living in India for eight months and seemed a seasoned veteran, one who could be a mentor in getting around that crazy place. In any case, the three of them became fast friends and spent every waking moment together, every meal, every walk along the river, every trip to the *bhang lassi* shop where they ordered hashish mango *lassis* and were stoned for what seemed like days on end. They went to Sarnath, the nearby village where the Buddha was supposed to have begun teaching, turning the wheel of *dharma*, as it was said. They flew to Kathmandu in Nepal for two days and held their breaths at seeing the Himalayan range for the first time from inside the plane. They spent night after night silently watching bodies being cremated at the *ghats* along the river. He had once seen a New Yorker tourist ad for India, which showed the Taj Mahal with a caption that read, "Only a fool could go to India and remain unchanged." Had he been changed by his experience there? Yes, he supposed he had.

Eventually he began spending nights as well as days with Aine. They fell into an easy romance, friends first. (He really should try that more often, he mused.) Aine was shy in bed, a trait he found endearing and one which he had rarely experienced before or since. Maybe it was India but his memories of their lovemaking seemed to produce more valleys of peace than peaks of ecstasy. He now recalled that there had been moments with Aine when he felt truly safe and at ease, not just the relaxation that comes after sex but a sense that he didn't have to prove anything.

Joan had always had nothing but the most glorious memories of their time in India and of their friendship with Aine. He knew that his sister was disappointed that they had lost touch with Aine and that she blamed him for that estrangement. He wasn't that great at endings, according to all the women in his life. It seemed so sticky and awkward to explicitly say what everyone in the equation already knew. I'm moving on; it's been nice. Or, I'm moving on or I would be forced to kill you. I mean, to have the big sad or mad ending works fine in movies but in real life it's a drag. He did admit the timing with the Aine thing was pretty bad, but he was in a bad way when it happened.

In the last week before their departure from Benares, they had prepared for the ceremony in which they would pour their mother's ashes into the Ganges. Alex went along with all of it for his sister's sake and was happy to have a few small projects during those last days there. Joan wanted everything to be just right. She had planned the entire trip around a particular date with an auspicious moon. They had to have certain kinds of flowers for the garlands that would be thrown in with the ashes and specific passages from the *Tibetan Book of the Dead* read at the appointed moment. Meanwhile, Aine, an ace at bargaining, having learned what things should actually cost (which was usually about one tenth of the first price quoted), had procured a rowboat for the three of them. They paddled out under a full moon in the month of October, and as they rowed Aine sang a hauntingly beautiful Gaelic song that she said had to do with loss. Then they all chanted a few Indian *bhajans* they had picked up in the previous few weeks, and when they had read all the right passages and sang their songs and said farewells, Alex began to slowly pour the ashes into the river while Joanie threw in the garlands. But, as it happened, a wind came up during the pouring and some of the ashes blew back onto Alex's white cotton *kurta*. He instinctively brushed at them and smeared the ash all over the front of his shirt in large black streaks. Joan quipped, "Well, you know how mom never liked to leave a party." They laughed so hard they nearly toppled the boat.

That night Alex dreamt of his mother for the first time since her death two months earlier. She was alive in the dream and in real time with them there in India. They were sitting in a *chai* shop, and she was laughing and teasing him about the ashes smeared on his *kurta*. In the dream, neither of them seemed to know or even wonder about the origin of those ashes. When he awoke feeling happy, it took a few moments to realize that his mother would never again drink tea with him, or laugh, or tease him in her sweet way, that he would never again see or talk with her, would never get to tell her all the things he wished he had, or that, though she always said he didn't listen to her, he was listening to her now, and the sorrow and remorse that he had managed to keep at bay for the previous two months engulfed him. He didn't want to talk about it with his sister or with Aine. And he didn't want to deal with another parting just then. He wanted to run, to be distracted, to be in motion. When Aine went out for her morning walk along the river, Alex quickly packed his bag and went to his sister's room to announce that he was leaving and would meet her in New Delhi at the hotel where they had stayed on their first night of arrival into India.

"What about Aine?" Joan asked in alarm.

"Sis, you know I hate saying good-bye. I left her a note. You can explain how I am," Alex told her.

"No, I can't, Alex, " Joan retorted angrily. "I really cannot explain how you are except to say that you are just like our piece-of-shit father."

Their father had left them and their mother when they were little. Ran off with a woman from the textile mill where he worked and was never heard from again. Their mother went to work in the same mill, putting in nine-hour shifts and taking care of two toddlers. She worked at the mill for the rest of her life and died before Alex had made it in Hollywood and would have been able to take care of her. Comparing him to his father was about the worst insult his sister could hurl at him, one that she had used only once or twice before. Alex walked to the door, his pack over his shoulder.

"I'll meet you at the hotel in Delhi; the flight is in three days so be there a day ahead," he said with his back to her. And with that he left Benares.

These memories hovered at the edges of his words as he said to his sister, sitting next to him on the porch, "Yeah, I could have lunch with Aine when she arrives. I'll send a car to pick her up."

"Alex, why don't you pick her up yourself?" Joan asked, in a tone that meant it was something he had better do.

Alex sighed, knowing he could not win this one. "Okay, Sis. I'll go to the airport myself. Despite my recent vow to never drop or pick anyone up there again, for you, I will pick Aine up at the airport. Let me see the letter."

Alex quickly scanned the letter with the curiosity of an old flame looking for clues or hints as to why Aine might be coming to visit. Finding nothing to fan that flame, he handed the letter back to his sister. "Call my office with her address and flight info. I'll have my assistant overnight a reply to her letting her know that I will pick her up, take her to lunch, and deposit her here with you for the weekend. How's that?"

"Good boy," Joan said, prompting Alex to retaliate with pokes, jabs, and tickles until she squealed.

4

"Fiona, how would you like to visit America? I have tickets for us to go there for a weekend soon." Aine tried to sound as casually buoyant as she could while she prepared their dinner, cutting cauliflower into bite-sized pieces.

If Fiona could have given voice to her feelings, if she could have articulated the shock that these words produced in her, she would have screamed, "What are you saying? What could you possibly be thinking?" America was the last place on earth that Fiona wished to visit, and as far as Fiona knew, Aine had always felt the same. The proposition was another in a series of her mother's disturbing actions of late.

For instance, her mother often seemed to be daydreaming, just staring into space. On their walks on the cliffs at sunset she would sometimes stop and gaze at the sea while Fiona was talking, not paying as close attention as usual, not asking Fiona questions about her day. Even the walks themselves, once their daily habit, were becoming less frequent. After getting home from work, her mother would instead stay in her bedroom with the door closed until it was time to make dinner. And the trips to Dublin her mother had made in the previous few months without her, though she had begged to go along in hopes of seeing a concert, were puzzling. Did her mother have a boyfriend there? She had said that she was buying books for the store, but if that were the case, why wouldn't she take Fiona with her? And now this absurd suggestion to visit America.

Because Fiona couldn't say all the things that were in her heart, she spoke with a crack in her voice, "What about Italy? You said we would go to Italy when we had enough money. You promised."

Ever since Maria Girardi first told Fiona about Italy, Fiona had begged her mother to take her there. Italy, seen through Maria Girardi's eyes, seemed to Fiona to be the only place on earth that anyone would ever need or want to go.

Maria Girardi had been raised in a large musical family in Rome and began playing violin at the age of five. By age ten, she was spending summers at the Accademia Musicale in Sienna studying with the renowned Renato De Barbieri as his youngest student. When she turned eighteen, she began touring as a soloist with major orchestras, first in Italy, and eventually throughout Europe and most of the world's major cities. Because she resembled Maria Callas as a young woman, many of the posters and concert program covers featured her face in profile, head inclined to her violin, thus making her a recognizable star among the concert-going public.

But after twelve years of touring, Maria Girardi had had enough of airplanes, hotels, and accolades to last the rest of her life. She was thirty years old and ready to retire. Maria Girardi had seen the world and was not too happy with the picture. Although her own situation was fortunate, she viewed humankind (a misnomer if ever there was one, she thought) as a rapacious freak show. She had witnessed appalling scenes of poverty, disease, and squalor and was hyper aware of the pressures those wretched circumstances put on human decency, but she also knew the cruelty and selfishness of the privileged, who had no excuse other than being human. She had grown to feel that the species itself was the problem. It was flawed at the core—mean and stupid—and the sooner it killed itself off, which it seemed hell bent on doing, the better. She liked the idea of all the other species having the earth to themselves without the murderous humans around, and she imagined the other animals and plants breathing a collective sigh of relief on the day *homo sapiens* finally annihilated themselves. She found comfort in music rather than society. Nevertheless, there were some among her species that Maria Girardi could tolerate and even a few with whom she experienced genuine delight.

She met her husband on a spring night in London. He came backstage after a concert and without small talk or flowers introduced himself—Patrick O'Shaunnessy—and asked if he could take her to dinner. By that time in her career she had a rule to never socialize with strangers, having learned the hard way that such engagements were typically either boring or irritating. But to her surprise, she said yes to this particular stranger because she could see that he would be neither. He was dressed in an Irish wool sweater that smelled of the earth, and when he spoke it was as if he was singing. They talked at the restaurant until closing time and then walked to her hotel in the West End. On the street outside the lobby she extended her hand to say good-bye, but he instead took her whole torso in his arms and kissed her lightly on the mouth with a laugh that already sounded familiar to her. She promised she would be in touch when she came to Dublin in the following few months, but what she was really thinking was that she was going to marry that man.

And she did. She had known a lot of men in the past and

was clear on exactly what she wanted. An emotionally intuitive man who could also put up a roof beam. A man who could recite poetry or sing a ballad for any occasion but who would fight to the death for anyone he loved. A man who delighted in the arts and was equally enamored with nature. In short, she wanted a sensitive macho man of great intelligence, humor, and refinement. And these were hard to find. When she married Patrick, Maria Girardi experienced the fulfillment of a long-running secret hope. She had been waiting for Patrick all her life and could now get on with the business of living.

Although his family lived in Donnegal, Patrick and Maria bought a place in Galway, a distance of several hours' drive from where Patrick had grown up. He had been based for the previous six years in Dublin, working as a pilot for Ryanair, but had longed to return to the countryside and thought Galway would be an agreeable mix of rural life and culture for the two of them. Maria Girardi entered the local music scene as a star, giving solo performances on special occasions at the Galway Opera House as well as lessons to the most gifted students of the country, who came from all of Ireland to study with her. Patrick obtained work as a pilot with a charter flight company that serviced Ireland's west coast.

Maria Girardi came to love the craggy west coast of Ireland with a passion that surprised her. She and Patrick would sometimes fly the short hop to Inishmor, one of the Aran Islands lying just off the coast of Galway. Inishmor, a place where people still spoke predominantly Gaelic, contained some of the most ancient Christian and pre-Christian remains in Ireland. Patrick and Maria would rent bikes and ride to the spectacular Iron Age fort ruins on the island. On summer evenings they would dine with locals at an improvised restaurant consisting of a small house whose living room had been turned into a dining area and whose chef, strangely enough, hailed from Jamaica.

Maria also loved the city of Galway, her new home. With its sixteenth and seventeenth century stone buildings and its lively streets and markets, she was sometimes reminded of her homeland, at least in spirit. She would spend hours in the local book store or linger for an afternoon at her favorite yarn shop when a fresh supply of wool had arrived. She would walk home along the River Carrib, which ran through the town on its way to the sea, stopping sometimes to speak with passersby. Even the winter didn't seem to bother her, and she and Patrick looked forward to the lights and festivities of Christmas and the famous Galway jazz festival in February.

Four happy years passed until the day that Maria Girardi got word that Patrick had drowned.

Her family begged her to return to Italy. She went there for a few months after the funeral but couldn't bear the brightness of her native country, the happiness that pervaded its streets and cafes, the tributes to love in its songs and art. She couldn't bear the joyful music of her familial home for it denied everything she knew about existence. She returned to her place near the sea in Ireland and at the age of thirty-five, Maria Girardi turned her back on life.

Five years later, the tape of Fiona's novice attempts at violin arrived in the post. From the moments Maria Girardi first heard the cassette, she was transported to her own childhood. There was something in the playing, in the lingering on certain notes, a delicacy of the bow on the strings that told Maria Girardi that the student she had once prayed would come into her life but had given up on long ago had now arrived. The past few years as Fiona's teacher had only intensified those sentiments. She and

Fiona of course shared a remarkable gift for music, but it went much deeper than that, for Maria Girardi recognized the range of Fiona's sensitivity in most matters of life as almost identical to her own. Fiona's thinking processes and views, her likes and dislikes were so parallel as to be both thrilling and disconcerting. This unusual child became a way for Maria Girardi to touch the world again. She imagined Fiona as an artificial limb for her own brokenness, able to pick up objects, open doors, shake hands at the market, perform on stage; able to be around people and ignore all the things that those same people might do at other times; the molestation of children, the cruelty to animals, the spouse and child beatings, the lies, the exaggerations of their accomplishments, the cheating on their friends and lovers. Fiona could help her to forget the fact that even when one found a good thing it could be snatched at any moment, gone forever. The girl represented a possibility for Maria Girardi to return to an innocence long forgotten. Did she even want this? Could she risk the hurt that innocence inevitably entails?

She had said yes to taking Fiona as a student when she received the tape that day. Through guiding Fiona's training in violin, Maria Girardi began a tentative communication with the young prodigy that would transform them both. In the sparse white music room of her Ireland home, overlooking a distant, mostly mist-covered sea, Maria walked Fiona through the vivid colors of her childhood so often and so thoroughly that Italy became the setting for most of Fiona's dreams. She told Fiona of the beautiful marble concert halls she had played there and of her subsequent travels to most of the capitals of the world. Maria Girardi left out all details of sadness and disappointment about her life. There are things that are better kept from the young. But whenever Maria spoke of the places and people she had known and loved, her brown eyes glistened, and in those moments she felt whole.

Fiona shared her dreams of Italy with her mother who made them her own as well. Someday they would visit Cremona, the violinmakers' capitol of the world, where they would go to the Museo Stradivariano and the Museo Civico, which housed among other notable violins a Stradivarius made in 1715. They would visit Rome and see the Sistine Chapel, the Colosseum, and the Spanish Steps, and they would walk on the street where Maria Girardi grew up. They would go to Florence to see the Italian art in the Uffizi Gallery and Michelangelo's David at the Galleria dell'Accademia and on from there, only a day trip away, to Sienna, to see the Accademia Musicale Chigiana where Maria had studied in the summers of her childhood. They would ride down the Grand Canal in a gondola in Venice and attend an opera at the newly refurbished Teatro La Fenice, Venice's premier opera house. All of these places held an enchantment for Fiona that sent her repeatedly to the large format book of photographs of Italy that Maria Girardi had given her for Christmas one year. Fiona had also purchased the *Lonely Planet Guide to Italy* and memorized all pertinent travel details of the cities she intended to visit. For example, if they went in spring, they could be in Venice for Carnevale just before Ash Wednesday when Venetians dress in spectacular costumes and masks and parade the streets for days. If they went in summer, they could attend the Todi Festival in Assisi, a mixture of classical and jazz concerts as well as theater, ballet, and cinema. But most of all Fiona wanted to see the light of Italy, the special quality of light, to which Maria Girardi had so often referred and which she said existed nowhere else.

How could her mother plan a trip to anywhere other than Italy? And how could she think Fiona would want to go to

America of all places? America, Fiona believed, was a horrible country, the bully of the world. A dangerous and mean place where people carried guns and killed each other and everyone cared only about money and it didn't matter that thousands of people lived on the streets. She had only seen America on television or heard about it from people who had visited, but it was enough to know that it held no interest for her.

"Fiona, I know you've had your heart set on Italy for a long time," Aine began, carefully choosing her words, "but there are some people in America that we're going to see. They're old friends of mine, and I want you to meet them."

"I don't want to go," Fiona said. "I can stay here with the Keatons or with Maria Girardi."

The plea in Fiona's voice tore at Aine's tired heart, and for a moment she didn't think she had the strength to carry out her plan. She suddenly felt she needed to lie down. She needed to sleep a little and perhaps things could somehow resolve themselves without her. But from somewhere deep in her reserves of love, she said to her daughter, "I want you to trust me. It's important that you come with me to America. I can't tell you more than that right now, but I will explain in time."

Aine had rarely spoken in such serious tones to her daughter, and Fiona sensed that there would be no negotiating whether or not she went to America. Foregoing dinner, Fiona went to her room and picked up her violin. As the bow touched the strings, the violin screeched and wailed and made the harshest sounds that a violin had ever been known to produce, for Fiona let her heart guide her hand and speak its frustration and foreboding through the instrument. And her mother, standing silently in the kitchen, though not as musically astute as her daughter, understood the meaning behind every discordant note.

5

Alex waited in the large hall adjoining the customs area at LAX. Not only had he driven to the airport, he had parked the car and gone into the terminal instead of waiting curbside near baggage claim. This was really beyond the call of duty, and he had already left a message for Joan apprising her of his heroism. But hell, the timing had worked out pretty well, especially since Mandy was away. She had gone off to some Hindu chanting retreat in Santa Barbara led by a guy named Vishnu, who was actually a middle-aged Jew from Brooklyn. She had begged and pleaded that he come with her, saying that it would be so good for him, the kind of meditation he could get into because there was action (he hated the kind where you had to sit still and be totally silent). In the chanting version, there was plenty of music, dancing, and sometimes some old rock and rollers accompanying Vishnu, which gave the whole thing a bit of life. He had been to a couple of these events at the yoga studio there in town but had no intention of spending an entire weekend with a bunch of airheads who had the annoying habit of locking you into Long Meaningful Stares if you happened to catch their eyes and who feigned a smug enthusiasm for existence, as though they had it all figured out and it was all *perfect*. To get her off his back about it, he had bribed

Mandy with letting her take his Porsche, a decision he was already regretting but at the time was the only thing he could come up with to avoid going himself. He pictured her now, driving up Pacific Coast Highway with the top down, his CD player blaring Indian *ragas* and Mandy in one of her chant trances, barely paying attention to the road.

As this unpleasant image faded from his mind, he became aware that people were beginning to exit from Customs into the receiving hall, and, with an imperceptible quickening of the heart, he scanned the crowd for Aine's face. Moving back deeper into the hall, away from where the new arrivals were entering, he figured he would have more time to find her and would also have the benefit of getting a good look at her before she saw him. Clusters of travelers spilled into the room, and suddenly, there she was. Disappointment overcame him. Even from this distance he could see that she looked terrible. Good lord, didn't they have cosmetic surgery in Ireland? Probably not. Even a little sun would have helped, but maybe they didn't have that either. But hang on, he thought, who is that beautiful young thing with her? Maybe this day would be salvaged after all. Oh, Christ, it's just a kid. What the hell am I thinking? I really have to back off on those Chinese herbs for libido; I don't care what Mandy says about her "special needs."

He made his way through the crowd to Aine and the young girl. "Aine, welcome," he said with outstretched hand, "wonderful to see you." Aine took his hand and smiled at him with that steady gaze that had once slayed him.

"Alex, it's good to see you. Thank you so much for coming for us. This is my daughter, Fiona."

Alex now turned to Fiona and within a few seconds he began to feel dizzy. His vision became blurred and he was having trouble standing. For when he saw the girl up close, he saw the face of his mother as a young woman. *Oh my god, oh my god.* His faculties of assessment leapt ahead of his emotions and were already processing the implications. How many years ago was I in India? Twelve, or was it thirteen? It was the year his mother had died; that made it a little more than thirteen years ago. Oh god, please let this be some bizarre coincidence. With difficulty in breathing, he managed to say to Fiona, "Nice to meet you. And how old are you?" This typical question, so innocently asked of anyone under the age of twenty, now contained the most calculating significance.

Fiona answered, a little unsettled by the nervousness of this stranger and the way he was looking at her as though she had just dropped in from outer space. "I'm twelve and a half."

Alex swallowed and tried to put the math out of his mind. Surely, this is a fluke. If he were the girl's father, why would Aine have waited until now to let him know? No, this is some coincidence. Aine must have had another affair around the same time. But with someone who looked like his mother? Damn! No, this doesn't make sense. Can't be.

Aine and Fiona were traveling with only carry-on luggage. Alex took Aine's bag and led them to the parking lot, making small talk along the way. They loaded their things into the car and Alex roared out of the airport, down Lincoln Boulevard and onto the coast highway to Malibu, where he had reserved a table for lunch at a lovely Italian restaurant called Tra Da Noi. During the drive, Alex distracted himself from his previous uneasiness by pointing out landmark sites and talking about the history of Los Angeles and how the developed areas they were presently seeing were once fields and groves and marshes.

"So, Aine," Alex turned to her, next to him in the front

seat, "I was just working out the math and I figure it has been about thirteen years or so since we last saw each other."

"Ay, it has been about that."

As Alex returned to his role as tour guide, pointing out surfers on waves that were breaking not far from the highway, he was unaware of an icy silence emanating between mother and daughter in his car. In the discovery of when her mother and Alex had last seen each other, Fiona now suspected that this man—this chattering man who seemed more like one of the boys in her school—was her father. The more she studied him, even from the partial angle she was afforded in the back seat, the more she felt she was right. The color of his skin, the wave of his hair, the shape of his ear and jaw. Fiona suddenly felt jittery and afraid. She wanted to scream and get out of this fancy car, fly high away from this horrid place of bright sunshine where the ocean meets a hundred miles of concrete and everyone drives as if their hair is on fire. She wanted to pour her fury onto her mother sitting calmly in the front seat and acting as though this day was like any other. She wanted to know why her mother had brought them here, and she now suspected that, whatever the reason, it would change her life. If this man was her father, why did her mother wait until now to put them together, and why didn't she explain any of this before coming? Fiona would have liked to let these worries burst from her lips in loud staccato blasts, but she was well trained in rules of comportment and would remain silent, stewing in the backseat, hating her mother and fearful of what this trip might portend.

Aine, of course, sensed her daughter's distress. It was expected; she had thought everything through for many weeks. She wanted Fiona, Alex, and Joan to simply meet each other, and she wanted to read the chemistry of that meeting on all sides before taking any further steps. She knew this was a long shot, but it was the best one she had.

For some time Aine had followed Alex's career through searches on the web. Using the computer at the bookstore where she worked (she and Fiona did not have one at home) she tracked Alex's increasing success in the movie industry, first as a production assistant, then as an associate producer, and eventually, an executive producer with a film company of his own. She had seen a few photos of him in the society pages of various newspapers and magazines online, always with beautiful women in glamorous settings. She read trade articles of deals he had in the works and of blockbuster hits that had shown returns in mind-boggling numbers. In short, Aine knew that Alex was rich. She also remembered that underneath the ambition of the young man she had known, a young man who had to be responsible too early in life, was a tender soul who had deeply loved his mother and sister, and who, she hoped, would love his daughter as well.

Aine was also counting on Joan, and here she felt more on solid ground. Joan would choose feelings over practicalities, love over convenience. From the moment they met in India, Aine and Joan recognized each other as kindred spirits, and Aine had since regretted that she had not been in touch with Joan in the intervening years. On the day that Alex left, Joan and Aine cried, walked by the river, and vowed to be friends forever. Joan had tried to explain her brother's behavior and his resistance to any kind of loss, his habit of running to stay ahead of his feelings. Aine understood as best she could at the time, no stranger to running from loss herself. She went with Joan to the train station the next day and promised she would write when she returned to Ireland.

"Here's my address in Topanga," Joan had said, giving her the slip of paper. "I'm not going *anywhere*, so write as soon as you get settled back in Ireland."

A month later, Aine felt sure she was pregnant. She had missed her period, her breasts were swollen, and the smell of cooked food emanating from the street vendors nauseated her. She craved only fruit. Realizing that she had better return home and make a nest for herself and her baby while she still had some savings, she flew from India to Shannon airport, which serviced the western half of Ireland. She had a friend near Galway, Moira Crowley, now Moira Keaton, a woman with whom she had worked in Dublin and who had since married and moved to the west coast. Moira had several times offered to help her get settled should she decide to move to the west, and Aine could think of no better place to begin a new life.

Whether it was a considered decision to exclude Fiona's father from her life based on the complication of distance or a youthful reaction due to the hurt and indignity of how she had been left, Aine had no intention of telling Alex about Fiona, which meant that she couldn't tell Joan either. And so they disappeared from her life as quickly as they had entered, though they continued to live on in her thoughts. Whenever Fiona asked about Aine's relationship with her father, Aine tried to be as honest as she could while giving as few details as possible: they had met in India, knew each other only a short while, and had lost touch. Fiona had mentioned her father only once in the past couple years: "Do you think my father is musical," she had asked.

Alex parked the car and escorted his guests to a nearby restaurant where the maitre d' called out from across the patio, "*Tutto bene*, Alexander! *Boun giorno*." Hearing these cheerful Italian words, Aine snuck a peek at her daughter who glared back in sweet revenge, assured that the universe was helping to punish her mother by reminding them of Italy.

They were shown to a table under a large umbrella on the

patio. For the next hour and a half, Alex regaled them with stories of Hollywood and his various adventures and exploits in the film industry. He dropped names of stars which he felt should have impressed anyone who cared at all about film and shared little anecdotes in which these world-famous luminaries had relied on him or been fired by him or had made a ton of money from being in one of his films. He even told the story of having lunch at this very restaurant with one of the world's biggest female celebrities who had cried as she begged him for a role in an upcoming film, a role that he didn't think suited her but one which she so desperately wanted that she was willing to take an impressive cut from her usual fee.

At some point, he realized in horror that he was uncontrollably bragging and must seem to his lunch companions to be terribly insecure, but he couldn't stop himself. As if suddenly afflicted with Turrets syndrome, words gushed out of his mouth with no modifying censor, no social decorum, no internal modesty that says, *enough about me*. Why am I doing this? he wondered, but his wondering was akin to a weak voice across a large tarmac and had no effect on his behavior until the end of the lunch when he was paying the check and managed to ask Fiona, "Do you like music? The Badlands are playing tonight at The Hollywood Bowl."

"Who are they?" Fiona asked.

"They're the hot new hip hop group in town. All the kids your age are into them."

Aine pre-empted any further discussion along these lines, not quite trusting Fiona to be polite much longer: "Fiona loves music, Alex. She plays the violin."

Alex studied the girl's face for any hint of her artistic tastes. Violin, huh? Wouldn't you know it? he thought.

"Sounds fun," he said, again horrified by having lost all capacity to respond to a simple statement without seeming like a jerk. Damn, I will be glad when this lunch is over, he thought. Aine is barely speaking, just sits carefully observing as I hang myself in a display of egomania. And everything about the girl is unsettling, especially that beautiful face, last seen on my mother.

They walked back to the car and Alex drove them along the coast and up Topanga Canyon Boulevard into the hills leading to his sister's house, speeding all the while and avoiding conversation lest he relapse into his newly developed Boasting Syndrome. Instead he put on Keith Jarrett's *Koln Concert,* jazz being in his mind perfectly acceptable for someone with possibly highbrow tastes, such as Fiona. And though he had no way of knowing, his instinct paid off. Pretty interesting piano playing, thought Fiona in the back seat, hearing the sound through the ten Bose speakers in the car as if in her own private auditorium. She'd have to get her mother to buy this CD for her when they were speaking again.

6

Joan had cleaned the house and confined all animals except Hamlet to the rickety back porch by locking the screen door, which led out to the backyard. Two cats and three dogs, all of whom she had rescued from the local shelter over the past two years, now shared this precarious real estate in Joan's effort to keep the rest of the house reasonably presentable. She had not cleaned in several weeks, and it had taken two days, three if you counted the day it took for the loads of sheets and towels. Although Aine planned to be there only for the weekend, Joan wanted the house to be as clean and welcoming as possible and secretly hoped Aine might be persuaded to stay a bit longer.

She had also been cooking for several days. Soups, casseroles, and sauces made from organic produce from the farmer's market lined the shelves of her refrigerator in beautiful earthenware bowls; and freshly baked brownies, the smell of which scented the entire house, waited on the kitchen table on a platter surrounded by marigold flowers, a tribute to their time in India. She ground coffee beans that morning and had the pot ready to go for when Alex and Aine arrived.

Joan also had a secret hope that something would ignite again between Aine and her brother. What a dream come true that would be. She would finally be able to relax, knowing that her brother was with a good woman and might perhaps start a family. Aine could have at least one or two children before the cut off date. Well, at least one anyway. Their mother would have definitely approved of this match. A good wholesome Irish girl who knew Alex when and loved him for all the right reasons. Anyway, she was getting ahead of herself. But it certainly would be nice if Alex chose someone he could talk with, someone who would take care of him and love him with the love of a real woman instead of a petulant child. She was weary of his string of young spoiled beauties, whose beauty quickly faded when you got to know them. And this latest one, Mandy, though not the worst of the lot, was still a superficial twit.

Her own love life had kind of dwindled to a full stop. A few years back, she had taken up with a guy in the neighborhood, a real Topanga character she had seen around town forever, who had gotten a job as a cook at the Mexican restaurant she managed, two miles from her house. They had fallen into the habit of going to her place for a beer after closing. One chilly night by the fire, a week into this routine, he leaned over and kissed her, and they ended up making love until dawn. Somehow he moved in, like one of her stray animals, and they settled into unofficial domesticity. But after a year he became restless, quit his job, and went to Costa Rica to surf. When he returned four months later, he moved back into his old place and called her once to let her know. She would run into him at the post office, the video store, or even the restaurant, and they would chat, but nothing would come of it.

Her true love, really, was Hamlet. How strange to have a dog as one's primary life companion. She had rescued him eight years earlier from an abusive couple who lived in her neighborhood and had thankfully moved away. He was just a puppy then and would often come to her back door at night when she got home from work, crying, shivering, and obviously hungry. She would bring him in, cuddle with him, and give him milk and mashed bananas. They would curl up in her bed and he would sigh before falling fast asleep. A little ball of fur tucked into the curve between her breast and belly. The next day she would bring him back to his owners who, when they weren't busy screaming at each other, would shout obscenities at the puppy and once even kicked him right in front of her, an act which provoked Joan to threaten them with the authorities. But as much as she wanted to turn them in, she also feared for the puppy's life if she were to make trouble for them. One late afternoon—it was a Monday, one of her days off—they showed up in her driveway, their van loaded with everything they owned, and pushed the puppy out of the car. "You can have the little monster," they shouted. And off they went. Hamlet had been her best friend ever since. He had grown to an enormous size and was a credit to his name, a prince of a creature—sensitive, protective, and dignified.

Her love of Hamlet had prompted Joan to begin rescuing animals. She found an animal shelter in the San Fernando Valley about a twenty minute drive from her house and began to frequent the place several times a month, first volunteering and eventually taking home some of the animals whose time in the shelter had expired and who were about to be euthanized. She would keep the animals until she could find homes for them; consequently there was always a menagerie of cats, dogs, and once an iguana living at her house. The patrons of the restaurant and her wide circle of friends provided a fairly constant supply of potential adoptive homes for the strays, and her brother, god bless him, had come through with funding for the shelter to expand their facility and thereby keep animals for longer periods instead of having to euthanize them after just one week.

Joan was in the back of the house, putting flowers in a vase in the guest room when Alex, Aine, and Fiona arrived. The three of them were already in her kitchen by the time she heard them, heralded by a couple barks from Hamlet. Joan came rushing into the kitchen and was slightly disoriented to see not two people but three awaiting her. She threw her arms around Aine, and the two of them laughed and cried for all the years that had passed. But Joan's tears also contained a more present sadness. She knew immediately on seeing her that Aine was not well, that the way she looked was not simply the result of jet lag. And now with her arms around her, she could feel the frailty of Aine's body, as though she were holding a stem of fine thin china. In those moments she tried to picture Aine as she had last seen her. True, she had not been a great beauty, but she was attractive in a quiet way with blue eyes and light hair, pale flawless skin, and a womanly body. Now she was stooped, her hair mostly gray, her skin the texture and color of old parchment, and she was far too thin. She is very ill, thought Joan.

When they released each other, Aine introduced Fiona. In one long look at the girl, Joan knew that she was Alex's daughter and therefore her niece. Like her brother, she immediately noticed the resemblance to their mother, but Joan also saw the striking resemblance to Alex himself. They both had that rare and beautiful combination of coloring: tawny skin, green eyes, and dark hair. The bone structure of the face, the shape of the mouth, the wavy thick hair, the long lanky body—all identical. It reminded Joan of seeing photographs of a young Elvis Presley next to current photos of his daughter Lisa Marie. The genes don't lie. Joan instantly assessed the two important pieces of information before her. Aine is very ill. She has shown up after all these years with a daughter who is clearly the offspring of Alex. The implications were clear. Aine might be dying and would want them to somehow be part of the girl's life. Boy, this weekend was certainly not going to turn out as she had imagined it.

All of Joan's ruminations on these subjects took place in the span of a few minutes while she busied herself with making coffee and serving brownies. She tried to catch her brother's eye several times, but he seemed in a world of his own, behaving like a gawky schoolboy and making small talk that fell flat each time he opened his mouth. He was rarely this socially inept, and Joan suspected that he must be thinking along the same lines as she about their young guest.

After coffee, Joan and Fiona took the overnight cases to the guest room, which gave Aine the opportunity to speak to Alex.

"Alex," she began, a force of intention forming in her every syllable. "Would you have dinner with me tonight somewhere nearby? I need to discuss something very important with you."

As she said the words, part of Alex's awareness seemed to know they were coming before the sounds touched his eardrums. It had happened once before when his mother died. Hearing the words, it was as though he were watching himself hearing the words, and moreover, as if he had already heard them. The dizziness he had experienced at the airport returned briefly, and for a moment he couldn't think of what to do when someone asks a direct question and stands before you in expectation of an answer. For, although the most accessible part of his awareness had been pretending all day that there was nothing unusual going on, the preponderance of his awareness, harder to reach but infinitely stronger, was braced for the fact that his life was about to change.

"Um, okay," he said, trying to sound casual, hoping irrationally that keeping a light tone about the evening might help it turn out that way. "I guess I could go home and come back later, say around eight. There are a few cafes here in Topanga. We could go to one of those."

"That would be fine," Aine said, just as Fiona and Joan came back into the room.

Alex said his good-byes to the three of them and rushed to his car, frustrated that there was no way to have a private talk with his sister prior to that night. He drove out of the canyon a couple miles, pulled over to the side of the road, got out of the car, and pacing beside it yelled, "Fuck!" to the sky.

7

Aine was by now exhausted and in extreme pain. She had not slept for twenty-four hours, and the emotions of the day had taken what few reserves she had. "I need to lie down for awhile," she said to Joan and Fiona. "I'm feeling the jet lag."

Joan had no need of any explanation since she could see that Aine was about to collapse. "Of course, you should get right to bed," she told her guest.

"I'm having dinner with Alex tonight here in Topanga. Would you wake me at seven so I can get ready? I'm sorry not to spend more time with you today, but let's plan to have a good talk tomorrow when I have revived."

"Absolutely," Joan said. "I've taken the weekend off so there is no rush. Fiona and I will take Hamlet for a walk in the hills. You just rest, and I'll wake you at seven."

Aine showered and went to bed. Laying in the quiet of the guest room, she drifted into a hazy half sleep that was not as restful as her body required. She worried that she may have made a huge mistake, gambling nearly all her money and the last of her strength to come to America for the conversation she would be having with Alex in a few hours. He was very changed since she had last seen him. Back then he seemed easier to talk with, lighter, more reflective. Of course, Aine must have seemed to him quite a bit lighter in those days compared to her current state. Nevertheless, in the previous few hours she had also seen moments of the goodness she had known in him. She even found his attempts to impress them at lunch somewhat touching.

But Fiona had not taken to him at all. Aine had hoped that the DNA in the two of them would recognize itself and override incompatible personality traits, an unreasonable hope given how Aine felt about her own family. What if this simply didn't work? What if Alex said no? Perhaps she should have just taken Fiona to Italy this weekend. She would have fulfilled that promise to her and they might have had one last glorious time together, which Fiona would have remembered for the rest of her life. She had risked everything for this current plan. Shivering and sweating simultaneously, Aine turned her thoughts to Joan. She was as Aine remembered—kind, warm, and gracious. Fiona seemed immediately comfortable with her. Aine tried to calm herself with the knowledge that at this moment Fiona and Joan were out walking together and that perhaps her daughter was enjoying herself.

The hills around Joan's house were dry, the color of wheat. Fiona had never been in that kind of landscape, having never been out of Ireland and being used to either the blue green terrain of the countryside or the stark rocky coastlines of County Galway. The breeze, which contained tendrils of warmth, and the golden colors of the hillside gave Fiona the impression of bread baking in a gigantic oven in the sky. She suddenly missed her violin and wished she could sit on a patch of this golden grass and practice the Bach sonata she had been studying before leaving home. Instead she contented herself with playing it in her head.

Joan interrupted Fiona's reverie with a question: "Fiona,

did your mother ever tell you about her time in India?"

"Ay," Fiona responded. "She often speaks of India and of the time she lived there. That's where she met my father, but they were never in touch after that so I've never met him."

A strained silence passed between them, both of them searching for information from the other.

"Did she tell you that Alex and I were with her in India for a month when we went there to put my mother's ashes in the Ganges"

"No, I only found out today when they were talking in the car," Fiona said carefully. "What kind of dog is Hamlet?"

Mindful of Fiona's wish to change subjects at this point, Joan picked up a stick and flung it as far as she could while Hamlet, delighted to be included at last, ran happily to fetch it. "Hamlet is a mutt. We think he's a mix of St. Bernard and Great Dane, which is why he's so big," Joan replied and proceeded to tell Fiona about how Hamlet had come to be her dog.

On hearing the story of Hamlet and the cruelty he had endured at the hands of his previous owners, Fiona began to cry. But though Hamlet's early days were certainly sad enough to warrant such a response, her tears were coming uncontrollably and for reasons she couldn't explain, even to herself. She tried to stop but the crying would instead erupt in great gasping sobs. Joan knelt down and put her arms around the distraught girl, stroking her hair and saying words of comfort that assumed no knowledge of why this was happening. "There, there, my dear. It will be all right." Hamlet came over and licked Fiona's face until she began to calm down. The three of them dropped into sitting positions on the golden grass, Joan's arm around Fiona on one side and Hamlet resting hip to hip with her on the other. They sat silently like this for nearly an hour. Then, as the brilliant reds of sunset crept over the sky, the three of them stood to go.

"How would you like to help me make dinner?" Joan asked. "Have you ever cooked Mexican food?"

"I've never even eaten Mexican food," Fiona said, smiling for the first time that day and revealing a dimple that corresponded exactly with the one on Alex's face. Definitely my brother's kid, thought Joan, as they walked back to the house.

That night Alex came for Aine exactly on time and took her to what was considered the best restaurant in Topanga, The Inn of the Seventh Ray, a throwback to the old days when Topanga was mostly a place for hippies and bohemian artists. It now catered to a mix of holdouts from that time (such as Joan and her friends) and the rich urbanites who had discovered Topanga in recent years as a place to live a country lifestyle within greater Los Angeles. The décor was meant to convey a world of enchantment with strings of white lights on the hedges, gas lanterns, standing heat units throughout the outside seating area, and candles on every table.

Alex and Aine were seated next to a creek, which ran through the restaurant's property and provided a pleasant ambience of sound. The large standing outdoor heating elements provided a remarkable amount of warmth. It would have been the most romantic of settings if not for the somber conversation underway.

"Alex, I don't know a better way to speak about this than to just say plainly what I have come here to say," Aine began. "Fiona is your daughter, and I want to discuss with you the possibility of your caring for her in time, as I am not likely to live much longer." She paused for a moment, then continued. "I know that this comes as a great shock, and I can only say that I made decisions long ago which, had I known better, I wouldn't have chosen. I am genuinely sorry for that, but we'll not have time to dwell on recriminations and past hurts. I can assure you that I am aware of the dreadful situation in which I have put all of us, especially Fiona, who, despite a maturity beyond her years, is just a child. I realize that you'll have to think this over, and, of course, I'll accede to your wishes and would have no interest in any legal intervention. But we'll need to make decisions very soon. I want you to know that although you may not have had much of a chance today to get to know her, our daughter is an extraordinary person who, I feel, would be a gift in your life. I'm just sorry that I've waited so long to share her with you."

Alex realized he had been holding his breath and could now hear Mister Serene's voice in his head. *Breathe, breathe.*

He looked at Aine and saw her clearly for the first time since her arrival that day. Oh my god, she *is* dying, he thought. How had he not noticed how sick she was? In the flickering candlelight she already looked like a corpse. For a moment his feelings were of pure compassion for the woman who sat across from him, the beautiful lover he had once known, a woman who would soon be leaving everything of this world behind. Too young to die, he thought, but then again, what evidence is there that dying should be only the province of the old? After this brief foray of consideration for Aine, his thoughts of concern turned quickly to himself. Damn, what a mess this was. He had no place in his life for a twelve-year-old girl.

"Aine," Alex began with a sigh, "I cannot tell you how sorry I am to hear that you are so ill. You know, there are lots of alternative treatments for every kind of so-called terminal disease, and we could…"

Aine interrupted him. "Alex, forgive my being terse about this, but we have very little time. I appreciate your suggestions for me, but I think it best that we stay on the subject of Fiona."

"Okay, okay," Alex said, clearing his throat. "You said that I could have some time to think this over. It's just that, it's a bit sudden for me to discover that I have a daughter and that I might now have to be her primary caretaker. I can certainly provide for her financially, and I'll try to come up with some sort of plan to help her. Maybe I can find a good school for her, a boarding school in Europe, or anywhere she wants to go."

Aine made an effort to stay calm. "I don't think that after losing her mother it would be the best thing for Fiona to be sent away to a place where she has no friends or family."

"What about your family?" Alex asked but regretted the question as soon as he spoke, as the memory from their time in India when Aine told him about her childhood streaked across his mind. "No, I guess that's not a good idea," he quickly added.

They sat silently for a moment, looking in opposite directions, as if in the lights from the lanterns of The Inn of the Seventh Ray there might appear another option, one they had not considered, the clear solution to save the day. But despite the general enchantment of the place, no such answer appeared, and they remained in an uncomfortable silence for the rest of the meal, Alex merely picking at his food and Aine drinking only water.

"Perhaps we should talk this over with Joan," Aine volunteered after a time.

Alex brightened immediately. "Yes, let's go there now. Joan will be up. She's a night owl. Joanie will help us figure this out."

And with that, Alex paid the check and drove them back to Joan's house.

Joan and Fiona had spent the evening mostly in the kitchen where Joan had taught Fiona to make guacamole, salsa, and bean burritos using all fresh organic ingredients and lots of cilantro, an herb Fiona had never seen. It was the most exotic meal of Fiona's life, and shortly after eating she showered and fell asleep on the couch by the fire, which they had built on returning from their walk. Fiona could not get over the temperature drop from the warmth of the day to the dry cool of the night, nor could she imagine the strange creatures Joan had called *coyotes*, which howled in the hills that surrounded them. What a wild place this is, thought Fiona as she drifted off to sleep. It was totally different from what she had heard about Los Angeles. She was now in dreamland, covered with a homemade quilt, fireglow on her face, and Hamlet snoring next to her on the floor by the couch. When Aine returned from dinner and saw that scene, she fought back tears. Joan would come through.

The three adults took up chairs around the table in the kitchen, Aine with a view of Fiona in the next room. In low voices they filled Joan in on what they had discussed at dinner. Joan kept her poker face throughout, never letting on that she had figured it out hours beforehand and asking questions that kept the conversation moving forward. "When will Fiona be told about this?"

"I had hoped to have something in place before telling Fiona," Aine replied. "It's going to be bad enough for her to hear about what is happening to me, but on top of that, to have no clear idea of where she'll be going to live would be too terrifying. I wanted to work it out first before telling her."

A wise decision, thought Joan. Looking at Alex and then back at Aine, Joan announced with unequivocal confidence meant especially for her brother, "When the day comes, we will take Fiona and give her all the love we can. Don't you worry any more about it, Aine. She will have a loving home."

With that, the tension that had plagued Aine's days and nights for months released itself into sobs. Not wanting to wake Fiona, Aine rushed onto the porch and, shivering under a canopy of stars, she let the tears flow. They flowed as though their well were infinite, no longer for herself or for Fiona, or even for humanity. They flowed for all the creatures who lived in time.

When it finally grew quiet on the porch, Joan came out, wrapped Aine in a shawl, and guided her back into the house. As Alex sat stunned at the kitchen table, Joan led Aine to the guest room, helped her into her nightclothes, and tucked her into bed. "We will look after Fiona," she whispered to her friend. "Now, you get some rest." Within minutes Aine fell into the deepest sleep she had had for months.

Joan went back to the kitchen to face her brother, who said in a tone of resentment, "I wish you had talked with me before making that offer, Joan."

"There was no need," Joan replied. "I had already decided that if you wouldn't take the girl, I would."

"But I hadn't said that I wouldn't take her. I just wanted time to think about it."

"What was there to think about, Alex?" Joan asked. "There is a child—your child—who is about to be motherless and homeless. And besides, there is no time."

"Maybe we should at least have a paternity test before we jump into this, Joan."

"Don't be ridiculous, Alex. First of all, Aine would never lie about something like this, and secondly, did you get a good look at that girl? She's your clone."

"Well, if you are so ready to take her, how are you planning to care for her?" Alex countered defensively. "You work nights. There are no good schools up here, so that would mean getting her into the valley or Santa Monica early every day, hours before you usually get up. Maybe it's time for you to take my offer to quit working and let me take care of you financially. I mean, take care of both of you."

"Alex...I am hoping that you will come around to seeing that being a father to this beautiful girl may be the best thing that ever happens to you. I think she should live with you. I'll be very much involved in her life, but you are her father. If you are unwilling to do this, and to do it well, then I'll raise Fiona and take you up on your offer of financial help so that I don't have to work."

As always with his sister, Alex felt that he was lagging behind in fundamental understandings about life. He had to admit that she usually turned out to be right in matters of the heart. But this was all just too much. How had this day, this bright and ordinary day when he woke up and drank his coffee and read the paper in the garden and made a few phone calls before going to the airport to meet an old friend, how had it gone from that to this: discussing with his sister the future of a daughter he never knew he had, said daughter sleeping just a few feet away?

He thought about how most extraordinary events and life-changing moments have intruded on what were otherwise ordinary days. The car accident that cripples oneself or another, the tsunami that comes onto a beach full of sunbathers, the chance encounter that leads to a love affair. People are just going about their business and then something happens that veers them onto an entirely different course, for better or worse. This is how it goes in life, so why was he in a state of bewilderment about how quickly his life had changed on this day? He looked over at Joan, so clear and certain in her decision, and remembered the day that Hamlet was dropped on her lawn. "Love turns out to be very simple," she had said at the time.

"Help me get Fiona to bed," Joan commanded her brother. He dutifully lifted the sleeping girl off the couch and carried her into the bedroom where he carefully put her onto the bed as Joan tucked her in next to her sleeping mother.

Driving home that night, he reviewed some of the moments with Fiona throughout the day. She certainly was a beauty—and quiet-smart, like her mother. How about during lunch when he was telling them about the staggering amounts he had paid the top actors in a recent film and Fiona had calmly asked, "Why do people get paid so much money for pretending?" He had explained that the public puts a high value on being distracted. "Distracted from what?" she had asked. It had stopped him for a moment and made him think, but he answered as honestly as he could: "From themselves."

As sleep overtook him later that night, unguarded feelings floated to the fore of his consciousness. He relived carrying the sleeping Fiona to Joan's guest room, and a shudder ran through him and out, ending in an involuntary body spasm that almost woke him. He had never experienced anything like holding that child—his child—in his arms, and even in this twilight of consciousness, he felt at once fiercely protective and helplessly vulnerable. He was a father. Imagine that. He was a father.

8

On Sunday, their second and last full day in Los Angeles, Joan and Aine spent the morning talking and drinking herbal tea on the front porch while Fiona slept. Then Alex came and drove them all to Zuma Beach in north Malibu for a picnic by the ocean. Afterward Joan, Fiona, and Hamlet went for a walk while Alex and Aine stayed behind and discussed what was ahead.

"How will this work?" asked Alex. "Should we have her move here before you, uh…you know…before the end?"

"No, I don't think that is a good idea," said Aine, staring at the sea. "I think that wouldn't give her closure. I know her; she would always feel that she should have been there. It's best that she stay with me for as long as possible, even to the end."

Alex nodded. "Joan and I will come to Ireland whenever you want." With that they spoke no more about it, and the rest of the day passed quietly. Alex dropped them back in Topanga and went on his way, not staying for dinner, which was just as well since Aine needed to lie down. Once again, Fiona and Joan cooked together in the kitchen, this time a simple lentil soup and salad.

"I hear you are quite the violin player," Joan said.

Fiona was thrilled to talk about music. She had not gone this long without playing her violin in the four years she had owned it and speaking about it was a way to miss playing a little less, or maybe to have the missing grow so big in her that there was nothing left to notice it. In any case, she told Joan all about her early life with the Irish fiddle, about the concert in Dublin with Nigel Kennedy, about how her community had purchased the wonderful violin she now had, and how Maria Girardi, the most brilliant master teacher of violin in all of Ireland and maybe all of Europe, was her teacher and she was her only student.

"Wow," Joan exclaimed. "I can't wait to hear you play!"

"Well, you probably won't be coming to Ireland, and our next trip is going to be to Italy, so it may be a long time," Fiona said, matter-of-factly. "But we can send you a tape, if you'd like," she added. Joan just nodded and with her back to Fiona, closed her eyes for a moment. This poor girl was about to hit some of the worst rapids of life, and there was nothing anyone could do about it.

The next morning, Monday, Alex phoned to say good-bye and Joan drove Fiona and Aine to the airport. Once on the plane, Aine closed her eyes as though asleep because the energy it took to keep her eyes open was more than she had. The exhaustion from the months of worry, constant pain, and the transatlantic trip had taken the last of her strength. She could die right in this seat, she thought; but she wouldn't. Having no reserves of biological life inside her, she would go the last leg on willpower, for there were two more things she had to do before dying. The first was to tell Fiona. When would be the right time? Here on the plane? No, she was too spent to open her eyes, let alone have that particular conversation. Should she tell her on the train ride home or wait until they were in their own house where Fiona would feel safe? She would need to do it soon as she couldn't keep her illness from her daughter much longer. With these thoughts in mind, Aine dropped into unconsciousness and could barely be roused ten hours later when they arrived in Dublin.

Fiona had become increasingly alarmed during the flight. She had not been able to wake her mother when the food trays came around, and when she could not rouse her after they announced that the seat backs had to be put forward because the plane was about to land, Fiona called for help from the flight attendant, who had to forcefully shake Aine and who asked Fiona if her mother was ill.

As they had only carry-on luggage, they went directly out of the airport and to the taxi stand. By this time, Aine could barely walk and had to give much of her weight to Fiona's free arm. Once inside the taxi, Fiona, who by now was nearly in panic, asked, "Mother, should we go to the hospital?"

"No," Aine replied. "We should go home. Please take us to the central train station," she said to the taxi driver. Once on the train, Aine could no longer put off the conversation. On the five hour journey across Ireland, Aine, her breath and words coming in fits and starts, explained the unthinkable with as much detail and sensitivity as was possible in telling a young girl that her mother would soon be gone from her life, that she would be living in another country, and that she would be handed over to people she had only just met.

As her mother spoke, Fiona's mind raced to the refuge of disbelief. This was just a bad dream. She would wake soon and the entire last week would be forgotten and they would go back to their lives and her mother would go to the bookstore in the mornings and she would go to school and to her lessons with Maria Girardi, and at the end of the day she would walk with her mother along the cliffs. But as much as she tried to focus on these pictures, the visceral reality of the present eclipsed them. For the vision of her sick mother in the here and now would not allow disbelief a foothold in her awareness.

Fiona could not speak. She couldn't even cry. She was overcome with a shock and despair that no expression at her disposal could communicate. She stared into space but saw nothing. Her mother was too tired to hold her in her arms but instead guided Fiona's head onto her shoulder and then rested her own head on her daughter's. They spent the last half hour on the train in this way, Fiona in a despondency that could find no outlet for release, and Aine, who had prepared for these moments in her mind but had no way to prepare for them in her heart.

9

Mandy's weekend in Santa Barbara had been fantastic. Some of her friends from yoga class had also attended the retreat, and they had chanted and danced late into Saturday night. The next day they all reported feeling spiritually recharged and, though no one said in so many words, they felt they were better people for having sung those Hindu *bhajans* with such devotion. Mandy had topped off the retreat with a trip to a nearby spa late Sunday afternoon where she had been exfoliated, massaged, and slathered in therapeutic oils for hours and had then bathed in rosewater and climbed into crisp white six hundred-thread-count sheets for a good long sleep. She spent the next morning by the pool, drinking ginger lemonade with sprigs of mint and eating pieces of coconut drizzled with fresh limes.

She was now zooming along the coast highway in Alex's $100,000 Porsche, top down, her blonde hair exuding intoxicating wafts of lavender and jasmine in the wind around her face. God, life was good. She felt beautiful and fresh, cleansed in body and soul, and she couldn't wait to dazzle Alex with her buffed and shining self. Most of her sexual thoughts were, in fact, pictures of herself in various provocative positions, with Alex in a supporting role. But, never mind that; she loved sex and so what if she loved how she imagined she looked having sex. That was part of the fun of it. She dialed Alex's office from the phone in his Porsche and left a message for him to meet her at his house at noon. She thrilled at the idea of a midday tryst during the workweek, especially on a Monday. There was something vaguely illicit about it.

But Alex had not gone to his office that day at all. He was shirtless and in khakis with no belt, hair disheveled and sprouting a two-day beard, pacing on the lawn, his Mexican groundskeepers instinctively keeping their distance from him. He had hardly slept the previous two nights and felt like shit. His life had gone to pieces over the weekend and his thoughts were all over the map about what to do. Could he hire someone for the day-to-day care of his newly acquired kid? Drive her to school, shop and cook for her, take her to play dates or whatever kids her age were into these days? He knew that there were people who do that sort of thing as a job—*kid minders*, he guessed you could call them, the term to be distinguished from *nannies,* which, it seemed to him, usually referred to people who looked after younger children. He certainly knew plenty of people with kids around her age that he could ask for referrals. He would now have to enter that mysterious world of parenting: homework and extracurricular activities and setting limits and spending quality time and talking about all these thrilling subjects at social engagements like those friends of his who were parents and who seemed hopelessly fascinated with the debate about which were the best private schools in the area.

And what the hell was he going to do about Mandy? She will flip! She had been needling him to marry her, hinting that it would soon be time for her to start thinking of children, implying that if it were not with him, then it would be with someone else. He had not seen what the big rush was, and they had sometimes been testy on this subject. But Mandy knew better than to push him and no doubt was biding her time to strike at a perfect moment. While searching for some dental floss at her place one day he had noticed her collection of books on these subjects discreetly tucked away under the bathroom sink; books with titles such as *Got Him!: Letting Him Think Marriage was His Idea*. He had almost felt sorry for her.

His assistant phoned and said that Mandy wanted to meet him at his house at noon. He knew that could only mean she wanted sex; it was a sort of code between them since she had always liked the idea of sneaking away in the day, like playing hooky from school, "but playing nooky instead," she had joked. He would be obliged to meet her "special needs," which consisted of at least an hour of foreplay during which Mandy's dedicated yoga practice paid off in impressive displays of contortion. But with his world disintegrating he was not really in the mood for a whole hour of sex. On the other hand, what better way to relieve all this tension? He would have to decide when to tell Mandy about Fiona. If he were to tell her before sex, she would likely not want to go through with it and they would instead have a tedious Big Talk, which would involve tears and threats on her part and extravagant promises on his. If he waited to tell her after sex, she'd be truly furious and accuse him of manipulating her. In either case, it would end badly. He decided to see what would happen when she arrived. Play it as it lay, so to speak.

Mandy pulled into the driveway a bit before noon. Wearing a white tank top, short cut-off jeans, and sparkly, jeweled sandals (from India, no doubt), her lanky thin body tan and toned, she was a vision of health in its prime. He was walking out to greet her when she bounded up to him, threw her arms around his neck, and said, "Let's go to the bedroom. Don't say a word. Just take me there right now."

Well, what could he do? Surely she couldn't hold it against him if he waited until after they had sex to tell her about his weekend since she had forbidden him to speak.

Meanwhile, after dropping her guests off at the airport, Joan headed to Barnes and Noble in Santa Monica and purchased a dozen self-help books on teens, such as *Don't Sweat the Small Stuff for Teens* and *The Primal Teen: What the New Discoveries about the Teenage Brain Tell Us about our Kids*. She also picked up several titles for dealing with loss, such as *After the Tears, A Gentle Guide to Help Young People Understand Death*. The last book she purchased was *The Violin Explained: Components, Mechanism, and Sound*.

Although Joan had always relied on her instincts in dealing with living things, she felt she needed a crash course in understanding a soon-to-be teenager. She hauled her stack of books to the counter and paid for them with the credit card Alex had given her "for impulse buying," one she almost never used. She planned to go home and get online to research support groups she might join in the area, such as step or adoptive family groups for people who suddenly find themselves in a family unit with children who have grown up somewhere else or with other caregivers. She hoped she could persuade Alex to join her in these groups, but even if he didn't, Joan felt confident that Alex would become a great dad.

Joan understood her brother in some ways better than he did. It might seem to those who knew the two of them that Joan served as Alex's conscience. It even seemed that way to Alex himself. But Joan knew that, although he certainly had a naughty side, Alex's main concern in life was to provide for his loved ones, and to that end he had been working since he was sixteen, putting himself through college and then business school at UCLA and getting go-fer jobs in the film industry for years. His goal from the time he started working was to buy a beautiful house for their mother in which she could retire. She died as he was on his way up, just three years shy of his first big check. He used that check instead to purchase Joan's house in Topanga, the ramshackle old place she had rented for the previous decade, which they had informally made their family home. She had come into the kitchen after work one night and found the deed, exclusively in her name, lying on the table next to a single white lily and a note with the words of the old cliché: "Who loves ya?" God knows what he paid to pry the property from her landlord, the old codger whose family had owned the place for a hundred years. Soon after the purchase, workmen started showing up at regular intervals to repair the roof and plumbing or paint the exterior of the house or re-gravel the driveway after a heavy rain. One day a truck full of Guatemalan laborers arrived and put in an entire flower and vegetable garden. Knowing that Joan took pride in her own style and in her independence as well, Alex was careful not to assume improvements to the interior of the house but wanted to, as he put it, "make sure that the maintenance stuff was handled."

His caring was not limited to generous material gifts. Whenever she was sick, he was there. When she needed just to talk to someone in the middle of the night, Joan knew she could call her brother. In the last weeks of their mother's life, when she herself had fallen apart and become virtually useless, he handled everything; arranging hospice care, making sure the pain medications were exact, and monitoring the flow of visitors into their mother's room. On the day before their mother died, she had seen him in the kitchen pantry, his head hung low, tears flowing down his cheeks, but as soon as he saw his sister, he wiped his face and carried on with what he was doing. He had been the man of the house for nearly his entire life, and he wasn't going to let them down in the time of the crunch.

Yes, Alex would be a great dad once he got the hang of it. Joan was more concerned about Fiona. Her talk with Aine on the porch Sunday morning revealed just how sensitive a creature was Fiona, like a high strung thoroughbred about to be shipped to a foreign land.

10

In the weeks following their return to Ireland, Aine and Fiona's formerly peaceful home became a battleground. Despite her grief over her mother's illness, Fiona fought for her own fate, screaming and begging to be allowed to stay in County Galway with either the Keatons or Maria Girardi. She even enlisted the help of those two households, both of whom made calls to Aine on Fiona's behalf and offered to take over her care. But, although Fiona's pleas and the offers from their friends gave Aine pause, her decision in the end remained the same. It would be better if Fiona went to America and was cared and provided for by family. She couldn't rationalize this to anyone since she had so little connection to her own family, but she knew it in her bones. Of all the possibilities at hand, this was the best. So Aine quietly proceeded with the plans.

Alex's lawyers in the U.S. and Europe had been working on expediting the legal papers for Fiona's entry into the U.S. as the child of a citizen. Alex also sent a check to Aine in the amount of €100,000 to cover her coming expenses should she wish to quit work. He had thoughtfully included a note saying that, should she feel any reluctance to accept the money, she must consider it partial back payment for child support. His generosity was timely as she had twice collapsed at work in the week after her arrival from the States and had been forced to tell her boss that she would likely need to quit soon. He immediately placed a Help Wanted sign on the bookshop door and assured her that she could have as much time off as she needed until they found someone to take her place. Fortuitously, Alex's check arrived in the same week that a new helper turned up at the bookshop, and Aine stopped going into work.

Fiona withdrew from her mother. It had become unbearable to look at her without feeling rage, despair, or worst of all, fear. She would leave for school in the mornings, slamming the door, and upon returning head directly to her room to practice the violin until supper. She would then sit sullenly at the table picking at the ready-made food that was their fare now that her mother could no longer cook and then return to her room to do homework and read until she fell asleep. On Saturdays someone from school would drive her to Maria Girardi's for her lessons.

But for several Saturdays there had not been any violin lessons when she arrived at Maria Girardi's house because Fiona would break down in violent sobs of fury and despair upon entering. Maria would explain that Fiona's mother was doing what she thought best for her and would never want to hurt a single hair on her head and that perhaps her mother had the wisdom of age to judge these matters. "She's not a better judge than me for what happens to *my* life," Fiona screamed. "She's sick and stupid, and I don't care if she dies." Fiona buried her head into the couch, sickened and ashamed of her words, but having no way to take them back, she cried into a velvet pillow instead.

Maria Girardi said softly, "Fiona, you have heard that I was married and that my husband died, yes?"

Fiona nodded without lifting her head. This was the first

time that Maria Girardi had mentioned the death of her husband.

"I would like to tell you something, something that I have never spoken of with anyone," Maria continued. "Would you mind sitting up?"

Fiona immediately sat upright and, forgetting her own plight for the moment, stopped crying.

"On the day that my husband died, we were supposed to have planted our summer garden," began Maria Girardi. "We woke up early to a dew-covered morning and a clear blue sky on a beautiful spring day. It was the season in which we met in London, and we always celebrated spring as our anniversary time. For me, it was the season of love. I was very much looking forward to spending the weekend with my husband. I made coffee and polenta with grilled tomatoes, and we were having breakfast when he said, 'Maria, this is a fine day for fishing.'"

"Yes, it is a fine day for fishing," I said. "But it is an even better day for planting the garden."

My husband laughed and said that we would plant the garden the next day. "Oh no, you don't," I said to him. "You're not going off fishing today."

"But he could sometimes be stubborn, and when his mind was made up about something…well, let's say that he usually did exactly what he wanted. Now, most of the time what he wanted was to make me happy but sometimes he went his own way. 'Maria Girardi O'Shaunessy,' he said, 'I'm going fishing today and tonight I will bring home some beautiful fresh cod and maybe you'll fry it Roman style with olive oil and lemons and parsley, and we'll open one of our best bottles of wine to celebrate.'"

"I became angry. I told him that I had no intention of preparing his dinner or cooking any fish he brought home and that, in fact, I would have dinner in town and not be home when he returned. I left the room without saying good-bye, and he went off to his day of fishing. That was the last time I saw him alive."

Maria Girardi paused at this point in her story and looked at the sea through the large window of the music room. Fiona sat completely still.

"Now the thing is, Fiona, my husband and I had a very happy marriage. We rarely had an unpleasant word between us. What happened that morning was unusual. But because it was the last conversation, it is the one that plays over and over in my mind. I would have endured a thousand other times of fighting to have that last conversation be a happy one. I would give anything I have, even my life, to replay that last morning and to say to my husband, 'Yes, dear. We can plant the garden tomorrow. Have a wonderful day."

"I know it is irrational to put so much on one conversation, one out of thousands, especially when it was not typical of how we were with each other. He would never have wanted me to spend a moment of worry on it, and if he could communicate with me now he would surely say that he knew I loved him and that my behavior that morning was of no consequence. But because it was the last…" and here Maria Girardi stopped her story because no more words would easily come and because she could see that Fiona understood the words she couldn't say.

When Fiona returned home that day, she found her mother asleep on the living room couch. Fiona went directly to the kitchen to prepare a meal with what she could find there, mostly breakfast food. She tried to remember some of the things that Joan had taught her to make the food look festive. She scrambled eggs with cheese and sprinkled paprika on the finished product. She would have liked to put parsley sprigs on top as she had seen Joan do, but since they didn't have any parsley or other fresh herbs, she went outside and picked a few tiny wildflowers from their yard and put them around the edges of the plate, inspired by the marigolds Joan had placed around the brownies that were waiting for them when they first arrived at her house. She then made tea in a large pot and covered the pot with a tea cozy.

Aine was so soundly asleep that she didn't hear any of her daughter's activities in the room adjacent to her. Her sleep in the previous weeks had become a kind of death in itself. She seemed to no longer even have dreams. It was as if she were deeply anesthetized, body and mind, as though her body required a full shutting down in order to function at even the limited level she could manage in waking consciousness. In her more metaphysical moments, Aine felt it also as her psyche's preparation for the nothingness to come. For, try as she might, she sensed nothing on the other side of death.

Having let go of most of what comprised her life—the expectations and plans that are the domain of the living—Aine had, in a conflict with her own will, begun to detach from Fiona. Just as she had always experienced her own biological functioning as naturally bound to Fiona, this same biology, in its disintegration, began to release its bond to that young life. It was not because Fiona had been so difficult of late; her mother understood her daughter's fear and anger. It was simply that the threads that had held Aine together as a living organism were growing bare, and she began to feel like a balloon about to be untethered, while the concerns of those around her slipped far away into a significance she no longer shared.

However, Aine was determined to finish the one last thing she needed to do. How interesting to come to a point when there was only one thing left to do. After a lifetime of things to do, lists and lists of activities—first the efforts required to care for herself when she was young; her schooling, work, friendships, relationships, and then later, with the birth of her daughter, the caring that was required as a parent—all of it had come in the end to a single point.

Upon returning from America, she had purchased a leather-bound writing journal from the bookstore where she worked. She brought it home and opened to its first page of fine blank parchment on which she wrote: "To Alex and Joan, In gratitude, Aine." Over the next few weeks, Aine wrote in the journal the story of Fiona—whatever memories she could snatch from her mind while Fiona was at school or her music lessons— from the time she touched her daughter's tiny fingers in the hospital to the past weeks of discord, and as she wrote she pasted in photographs from a shoebox. Aine did not require her memories to be chronologically correct or censored in any way. She had no time for that kind of effort. She simply gave herself the freedom to write whatever came to her about her daughter, and through this exercise she relived the wonder of their lives together and forgave herself for not taking Fiona to Italy and not allowing her father into her life until then. She forgave herself for dying.

Aine trusted that she would know when the book was complete enough to stop. It would not be because she had conveyed every important detail there was to know about Fiona; there was no way to accomplish that in a hundred years, let alone a few weeks. But Aine knew the book would be thorough enough when the words on the pages allowed Fiona to come alive in the mind of the reader, when they gave a clear enough sense of who she was—her talents, struggles, dreams, and fears. Thus, the story of young Fiona, as written by her dying mother, contained a clear-eyed objectivity that was not possible at any previous or future time, and years later, whenever Fiona needed to remember from where she had come, she would consult her mother's book.

Fiona went to her mother on the couch and kissed her on the cheek. Aine woke with a start and momentarily did not know where she was or who had kissed her. Surprised to find Fiona there and to realize that the icy past few weeks might now be behind them, Aine asked in an attempt at normalcy, "What time is it?"

"Time for dinner!" Fiona said sweetly and took her mother's hands to help her from the couch.

11

In the weeks following Aine's and Fiona's visit, Alex's home had become a battleground as well. Mandy could not be mollified and had been in one long temper tantrum that involved fits of crying, screaming, and threats of leaving. She finally issued an ultimatum as she slammed a hairbrush onto the bed: "If you think I'm going to hang around here with another female in the house, you'd better marry me!"

He thought about it. Should he just do it? Maybe it would calm her enough to restore peace in his home. Maybe she and Fiona would sort of become friends and Mandy could help with Fiona's care and the three of them could do things together, like....well, they'd figure out what to do when the time came.

"Are you out of your mind?" Joan roared when Alex shared his thoughts with her. And that was that. He knew Joan was right. Mandy wasn't the one, but she was the one for now, and he needed an olive branch for her. He was about to begin production on a movie to be shot in Australia. There was a part for a young actress that had not yet been cast, a relatively small role with just a few lines but an intriguing character nonetheless: a young woman who had left everything behind in England and moved to Australia to run an inn in the bush, where much of the movie takes place. Mandy would need a dialect coach and maybe, yes, maybe she should make a trip to London and study with a dialect coach there so as to be immersed in the accent until shooting began. He would pay for everything and put her up at the Ritz. He needed a break from her, and although he shuddered to think of what the tab would be, it would be cheaper than getting married. Buying a football team would be cheaper than that.

Mandy was thrilled with the offer of an acting role, throwing him onto the bed and practically ripping off his shirt and pants. They hadn't had sex for weeks, not since the day she had returned from Santa Barbara, and he was now ready for it. Not sure if his last batch of Chinese herbs was particularly strong or if his virility was merely the effect of deprivation, Alex couldn't seem to get enough of her, and they spent several nights until nearly dawn in adventurous passion. When it came time for her to leave for London, he even drove her to the airport. She was sure he was softening to the idea of marriage. He had been so amorous lately.

Flying first class on Virgin Atlantic to Heathrow, Mandy began planning a wedding. She wondered if they should consider getting married in Australia after the movie was done. She had been to Sydney once on a modeling shoot. What a beautiful city. They could rent a large yacht and have the ceremony on the boat right in Sydney Harbor with the lights of the buildings twinkling in the hills around the water and the Opera House shining like a series of enormous white fans thrown into the sea. She could see the DVD of it all in her mind. Of course, they would have to do the legal part in California where there is community property law. And she wasn't going to sign any damn pre-nup! As for the girl (if she really was his daughter) she would try to be open to her, keep her heart open as she had learned through her spiritual training. Who knows, maybe they could find a school the girl liked somewhere, like somewhere *else*. On the other hand, maybe this girl was some sort of lucky Irish charm. After all, because of this kid, her own life had taken a sudden upward turn. Her rich and handsome boyfriend was on the verge of a marriage proposal (she was sure of it) and on top of that, she was about to become a movie star!

Back in L.A., Alex was having problems on his current project. Movie making was all about solving problems. Shit wrangling, as one famous producer called it. Alex had been wrangling for weeks in preparation for his upcoming film shoot. The studio that was bankrolling most of the project (Alex was putting in some of his company's money and keeping a tidy piece of the business) was already balking at the budget and the number of days on location in Australia. To bring costs down, Alex had decided to do some of the postproduction in Australia since it was cheaper there (no unions), but it meant that he would be away a lot in the coming months. With several other projects in the works, each day of his absence would result in trunk loads of mistakes and problems that would await his return. In addition to all this, Joan wanted him to start attending support groups to learn about parenting. He had begged off. He couldn't be everywhere at once. He barely had time to read the paper anymore. He would have to learn about parenting on the job. Isn't that how most parents in the world do it? But when in hell would he have time to fit a kid into his life? Do they take up much time? he wondered. Aren't they at school or at their friends' houses or at sleepovers and movies a lot? God, my life is going to be unlivable, he concluded. At least Mandy was out of his hair for the moment.

Joan was always on him to cut back on work. "Why are

you under so much pressure? You have enough money to never work again," she would say. He supposed it was true. His last five films had grossed a combined total of $420 million, netting his company $75 million. He had a smart investment advisor who put most of his dollars into euros and gold just before the dollar started to sink and metals started to climb. In that one move alone he had increased his wealth by thirty-five percent and counting. And the ancillary revenues from his films just kept rolling in. Foreign theatrical rights, U.S. and foreign television, pay TV, and worldwide DVD. His company was a goddamn goldmine. He had no intention of quitting any time soon. It wasn't about the money anymore. Sure, the first few millions were a thrill. Buying whatever he wanted, buying the best. But now it was more about the game. He was in the game and he was good at it. He could go thirty more years doing this. Make hay while the sun shines and all that.

Joan was a different animal. She loved routine and long stretches of quiet and walks in nature. She was always trying to get him to go with her on hikes, which were more like strolls, in the hills around her house. He would show up with his mountain bike, ready to conquer the trails, and she would put her hands on her hips and shake her head, saying, "You're hopeless." She had given him a T-shirt one Christmas that read, "Don't wait till you're dead to rest in peace." He thought it was hilarious although, annoyingly, the phrase often popped into his mind at stressful moments.

Thank god Joan was on this Fiona project. He probably shouldn't think of his daughter that way—as a project—but hell, that was the truth of it. Joan had already visited every private school in west Los Angeles and had what amounted to a closet full of packets and materials from each. His assistant had, meanwhile, been interviewing childcare applicants to narrow the candidates down to a few for them to consider. He had carpenters and interior designers in and out of his house every day for three weeks creating a bedroom suite and music room for Fiona, and he had personally shopped for an entertainment center for her that consisted of a high resolution flat screen television, state-of-the-art CD and DVD players, and the newest Apple computers, both desktop and laptop, complete with iPod Nano. He had the idea that Mandy could take her shopping for clothes when they were all back in L.A. together. Mandy knew everything there was to know about clothes shopping for girls and women under the age of forty, and it would be a good way for the two of them to get to know each other.

Although he had phoned twice, he had been keeping up with the situation in Ireland mostly through Joan, who phoned Aine and Fiona every week. He was aware that Fiona was not looking forward to her new life in Los Angeles and that she wanted to stay in Ireland. According to Joan, Fiona and her mother had hardly spoken for weeks over it, and although the latest report had them reconciled, Fiona was still hoping not to leave Ireland. He didn't like the sound of this. "Don't worry," Joan said. "What would you expect? Any child would feel that way. Any person of any age would feel that way, losing her mother, uprooted from her home, her friends, her country, everything that is familiar." Joan was right, but having a child was already enough of a stretch for him. Having a disgruntled child might be too much. "As I've told you," Joan reminded him, "I will take her if you can't handle it, but at least give it a try."

They planned to go to Ireland when Aine's time was near. Aine felt sure that she would know when that time came. They would all be together for a few days in Ireland before the end, and then Alex and Joan would take Fiona home to America.

12

Fiona's thirteenth birthday loomed near. For most of her friends, that milestone provoked happy excitement, a rite of passage into new independence. To have the word "teen" attached to the number of your age meant that you were no longer a child. Teenagers were their own breed and were allowed all kinds of indulgences and understandings by virtue of being a teen. But turning thirteen provoked only dread in Fiona. She believed that it would be sometime in that year of her life that her mother would die and that she would leave the home and homeland she loved. Thirteen. An unlucky number, thought Fiona, though she was not usually prone to superstition.

Her mother faded out of consciousness more often in those days. In fact, she spent most of the time sleeping, heavily medicated due to the pain. She and Fiona would be talking one moment and the next Aine would be slumped in her chair, sound asleep. Fiona would boost her mother's feet and legs onto a footstool and prop her head onto a pillow so that she didn't wake with a neck ache, and Aine would sometimes sleep this way for five hours at a stretch. She was no longer the attentive and interested mother who had cared for Fiona all the previous years. She was barely there at all. Thin and ashen in color, unable to eat, she sometimes seemed transparent to Fiona's young eyes. But, still, there were times when mother and daughter reminisced about little things or sat together in the garden, and Fiona clung to those moments and never wanted them to end. And so the days passed, with Aine drifting in and out of this world and Fiona in a state of quiet dread.

On the morning of Fiona's thirteenth birthday her mother got up early and baked a cake! School had let out for summer the week before so Fiona had the whole day to celebrate her birthday. She had invited a couple girlfriends from school to come by and climb down to the beach from the cliffs along the rocky trails that wiggled down the hillsides. She didn't expect her mother to bake a cake or even to be up and around. But there on the table when Fiona awoke was her favorite, lemon butter cake with white icing, and thirteen candles on top.

A few hours later, Fiona and her friends made lunch together as Aine looked on, face radiant, eyes gleaming, and feeling ten years younger than she had the day before. It was the best birthday present Fiona could have imagined, seeing her mother like that. After Fiona had blown out the candles and the girls had eaten the cake, Aine handed Fiona a long narrow package, beautifully wrapped in gold paper. Inside was a violin bow made in 1920 with the stamp of W.E. Hill & Sons, the famous British violin company whose craftsmen made some of the most beautiful bows of the twentieth century. Its stick of dark red pernambuco, the now endangered Brazilian wood, gave the bow a weight and density difficult to achieve with other kinds of woods. The frog, or base, was of rich ebony mounted in plain silver with a silver cap, the use of silver instead of ivory being distinctive to British bow makers. The bow was in excellent condition and had never been repaired as it had likely been in a private collection for much of its existence. Fiona had only seen this quality of bow used by great violinists on stage or on television. Awed with gratitude and deeply relieved to see her mother feeling so well and looking so happy, Fiona wept with joy, which was in its own way more tenderly excruciating than all the sorrow she had experienced in the past months.

The girls went off to the beach, wearing sun hats and looking for all the world like large versions of the wildflowers through which they walked in the fields leading to the cliffs. Aine watched them from the window for as long as they were in view. She felt surprisingly well, better than in a long time. She would take care of a few things while Fiona was out.

Just then the phone rang. It was Alex calling from Sydney where he was working on his new film, *Entropy*.

"How are you, Aine?"

"Oh Alex, I'm doing quite well. I actually feel good today. Did you know this is Fiona's birthday?"

"Yes, that's why I called…and to see how you are."

Aine explained that Fiona was out and that she was sure she would have liked to say hello.

"She's having a good day today, Alex. You know, it's been kind of rough here."

"Yes, I know." Alex replied.

"But things have calmed down and I think it will all work out."

"Yes, I imagine so," Alex said encouragingly. "Well, I just wanted to touch base before I go into the bush tomorrow. We'll be shooting for six weeks in a remote place, but I'll get phone numbers to you as soon as we're settled in there."

"No worry, Alex." All is well here. I don't think I'll be leaving just yet. I seem to have a second wind."

"That is wonderful news, Aine. Truly wonderful news. All the best to you. Good-bye."

Aine went to the desk in the living room, paid some bills, and sorted through the mail that had been collecting there. She spent a little while writing in the journal about the morning they had just spent and about Fiona's birthday surprise. She still had energy when the girls returned from the beach, and they played a game of Scrabble, which Aine narrowly won. In the late afternoon, Joan called from America and had a good long chat with both Aine and Fiona. That evening, Fiona dared to ignite a hope that had glowed in her thoughts all day: "Mother, you seem to be feeling so well suddenly. Do you think you could be getting better, that you could….be okay?"

"Well, I don't know, Fi," replied Aine. "I certainly feel well today. If this is some kind of turnaround, it couldn't have begun on a more perfect day than on the celebration of the day of your birth, which was the happiest day of my life."

They held hands on the couch and talked about possibly going to see a film in Galway in the coming week. Then they kissed each other and said goodnight. Fiona laid in the darkness of her room and, for the first time in many months, drifted to sleep without a quiver in her chest. So far, turning thirteen wasn't so bad. Not bad at all.

When Fiona went into her mother's room the next morning, Aine was dead.

Over the next days, Moira Keaton took charge of the service and funeral arrangements according to the instructions Aine had given her over the previous months. In deference to their rural Irish community and to Aine's family, they were to hold an approximation of an Irish wake, although Aine was adamant that she didn't want a fully traditional one. They borrowed from the tradition "only the best bits" as Aine had put it. Women friends washed Aine's body and laid it out in her finest clothing in a coffin in the living room. Candles were lit near the coffin, and plenty of food and drink were brought in for the mourners. Someone would stay with the body at all times during the period of the wake, and the friends and family would share stories and memories of the loved one.

Moira brought Fiona to her own home as she and Aine had planned in order to let Aine's family, who had traveled from inland, stay in the house for the time of the Wake and also because Aine had known that it would be better for Fiona to be away from the house for at least some of the time in the days following her death. She had hoped that Joan and Alex would have been there to help care for Fiona but had made contingency plans with Moira in case they weren't. Joan booked a seat on the next flight to Shannon Airport as soon as she received the call though it would be a couple days by the time she could get there. Alex was unreachable in the outback of Australia as he was in the middle of moving the film's location.

Throughout this period, Fiona didn't speak, eat, or cry. The Keatons were so concerned for her that they phoned Maria Girardi in the hope that she would talk with Fiona on the phone. To their great surprise, Maria Girardi said, "I will be there in an hour." It would be the first time Maria Girardi had ventured out to such a gathering in years. Most people had never even seen her. Fiona was sitting in the room with her mother's body and numerous mourners when her teacher arrived. Maria Girardi took a seat next to her on the couch as the murmurs of the others continued around them. Fiona's grandmother crossed the room to them, her tight lips and stocky frame looming over Fiona and Maria where they sat.

"So you're the violin teacher we been hearin' about," she said to Maria.

"Yes, I am Fiona's teacher. And you are Fiona's grandmother, yes?" Maria replied politely, quickly assessing the role of the odious woman standing before her and covering an immediate dislike. How on earth was she going to get through this?

"Ay, I'm her grandmother alright, but we hardly see the girl. Her mother never brought her 'round much, and now she's sending her off to America, god rest her soul. We hear the girl's pretty fancy with the violin these days," she continued as if Fiona were not there. "We're hoping she'll play at her mother's service." Finally acknowledging Fiona, her grandmother turned to her and asked, "What do you say, girl? Wouldn't it be nice if you played something sad at your mother's service tomorrow?"

Fiona nodded, hoping that her grandmother would be satisfied with the conversation and leave her alone. Moira Keaton had already talked with her about playing at the service. She told Fiona that morning about the memorial that Aine and she had planned. It was to be simple and non-religious. Aine had wanted Fiona to participate in some way in order to give her daughter a ceremonial moment of saying good-bye to remember in years to come. She knew that having Fiona say anything at the memorial would be too hard for the girl but that playing the violin would come more easily. So she had requested that Fiona, if she wanted, play something at the service.

Fiona had not practiced in some days and with the house full of guests and the Keatons' house full of rowdy boys, she had no place to do so now. She turned to her teacher and speaking for nearly the first time in two days, said in a tone of desperation: "I have no place to practice, and I don't know what I should play."

"We'll figure it out. Why don't we go for a walk along the cliffs?" Maria Girardi suggested. "Get your violin and bow."

Fiona shuffled lethargically to her room and brought out her violin along with her new bow. As Maria Girardi had not seen it before, she was taken aback by its perfection. "*Mio dio*! Fiona, this bow is exquisite. Where did you get it?" she asked as they left the house.

"My mother gave it to me for my birthday," said Fiona, holding back tears and shaking her head in near disbelief that it had been just a couple days since her mother had baked a cake and presented her with the object she now held in her hand. So near in time and now gone forever. For it was clear to Fiona that the body laying in the living room was no longer her mother.

Maria took the bow from Fiona to admire it. Running her hand along its clean wooden lines and ebony tip, she whispered, "*Che meraviglia*." But mindful that this was not the time for gushing over a violin bow, she led Fiona onward across the fields to the cliffs. Though it was summer, the day was overcast and chilly and the sky threatened rain. They should not dally any longer than necessary, thought Maria.

As they walked, the wildflowers and grasses of the fields undulated in haphazard rows, bowed by an invisible wind that picked up speed and contained moisture from clouds. Maria thought it wise to turn back and called out, but Fiona, far ahead of her and walking too fast, seemed not to hear and didn't respond. Fiona reached the cliffs and stood at the edge for a moment. Maria Girardi, approaching from behind, suddenly had a fleeting foreboding, a shiver that went through her body as if her brain recorded something that had not yet happened in the split second before she saw Fiona fling her prized violin into the rocks and sea some two hundred yards below.

Frightened now, Maria ran the last distance to Fiona, dropped the new bow she carried, and threw her arms around the young girl, holding her tightly, not knowing if the child intended to fling herself over next. Fiona stood still, satisfied that she would now have nothing to remind her of her life in Ireland.

"Fiona, what have you done?" Maria Girardi said, more as a statement of shock than a question.

"I will never play again," said Fiona. "You can have the bow."

"No, Fiona, I cannot accept the bow. It is your mother's gift to you."

"Then I'll throw it into the sea," said Fiona, bending to retrieve it from where it lay on the grass.

"No, Fiona!" screamed Maria Girardi. "Enough of this! I will take the bow."

And so, in single file they walked back to the house where Aine's body lay and where Fiona's aunt Joan had arrived to attend the memorial services with Fiona the following day and to take her to America a week later.

On the day that Fiona threw her violin into the sea, Maria Girardi understood the meaning of redemption. In the young girl's rage and despair she saw her own life of the past years, and she realized the futility of that despair. There would be no merit from on high to reward her martyrdom of isolation. It wouldn't matter to anyone living or dead that she sacrificed her pleasures in life. And no amount of fervent thoughts and replayed memories would bring her Patrick back to her. Maria Girardi decided on that day to sell her place in Galway and return home to her family and country.

13

Alex received news of Aine's death the day after her memorial. The timing was terrible and he simply couldn't leave the set in Australia. He would have to let Joan take care of getting Fiona to Los Angeles and he'd get back as soon as he could, at least for a visit. He was under an avalanche of problems on the film. His pre-production team had obtained permission months before shooting began to film in the Uluru National Park near Ayers Rock. They had installed themselves in the nearby resort town of Yulara and were just setting up on location when two Australian National Park Service rangers arrived by jeep to tell them that permission to film there had been rescinded due to recent environmental findings that the area was "overexposed." They had to immediately find another place to shoot, one that would not require permission from the government but would still be a spectacular natural setting. Doing this at the last minute and forced to choose a place the trucks and trailers could reach in a day restricted them to few alternatives. Alex had prepaid six weeks' lease of the resort at Yulara for which they now would have no use. He scrambled to relocate everyone to Tennant Creek, a former mining town and notorious hellhole in the outback, but not far from a little known geologic wonder called Devil's

Marbles, which consisted of enormous smooth granite boulders spread across 4,500 acres of desert flatland that looked to have been dropped from a galactic crane and were now, many of them, balancing on points and edges that seemed to defy the laws of physics. It wasn't Ayers Rock, but it would do for a dramatic backdrop.

The move cost them nearly a week of shooting and they would now come in way over budget even if nothing else went wrong. In addition, the young director Alex had hired was at war with the seasoned and legendary cinematographer, hired by the studio, over the minutia of every single scene, the director wanting to move the picture along and the cinematographer wanting to make sure the scenes looked perfect. They would argue on set all day and again at night while watching the dailies in the tech trailer, the cinematographer certain that the lighting or makeup in a particular shot didn't work and needed to be redone, and the director insisting he wanted the look of the film to be natural and raw. Alex was working overtime as referee and therapist for the two of them as well as keeping an eye on everything and everyone else. One situation he had to watch with eyes in the back of his head was the budding friendship between Rick Sole, the male lead, and Mandy. Sole had developed a sudden interest in yoga and was taking lessons from Mandy under the food canopy in the early mornings. Alex also noticed the two of them talking together during breaks in filming throughout the day. Mandy told Alex that Rick thought she had exciting potential as an actress and that his film character, who was supposed to be part aboriginal, was enriched by their conversations about spirituality. Yeah, right, thought Alex. For Mandy, it's spiritual conversation. For Sole, it's foreplay.

Prior to her departure for Ireland, Joan asked her boss for a couple months' leave of absence in order to get Fiona settled when they returned to Los Angeles. Having taken almost no vacation days in a decade and having run the restaurant with efficiency and friendliness such that the business was consistently flush, the owner had no choice but to acquiesce to Joan's request and find a temporary replacement for her. She would have the entire summer free to spend with Fiona.

On the day of the memorial and the week afterward, Fiona kept mostly to herself, exhibiting no emotions, as though her senses were not quite working. Though the people in her community didn't know exactly what had happened to her violin on the cliffs that day, many of them speculated fairly accurately, and it would be a subject of distain and gossip for a long time to come. Joan let Fiona be. She focused instead on getting to know the people of Fiona's world as they cleared out the house and closed Aine's accounts. She spent time with the Keatons and with Fiona's grandmother, who, though initially resentful of the American stranger about to abscond with one of her kin, grudgingly warmed to Joan during their days together as Joan plied the family with delicious foods and beverages from Galway and stories of her animals back in Los Angeles. She was determined to keep the roots of Fiona's life in Ireland as intact as possible and promised everyone that Fiona could frequently come back to visit and that they all had a place to stay in the U.S. None of them had plans to go to America, but it was nice to have the offer.

Joan also visited Maria Girardi, who had not attended the

memorial. Maria told Joan that Fiona threw her violin over the cliffs and had then announced that she would never play again. Joan thought it to be the impulsive act of a highly distraught child and speculated that Fiona would probably return to her music after a time of mourning. But Maria, knowing that the seasons of mourning were unpredictable in length and could last for years or even a lifetime, had no sense of when or if Fiona might again pick up a violin. For Fiona to abandon music would be a tragedy, thought Joan. Having read most of the journal that Aine left, Joan was beginning to understand what the violin meant to Fiona.

Moira Keaton had procured Aine's leather journal several hours after Fiona had rushed into her kitchen, face flushed and eyes like those of a cornered animal, to say in a voice as flat as her eyes were wild, that her mother was dead. Moira had known to look for the journal and found it exactly where she expected, in Aine's desk. She presented it to Joan the first time they were alone together. As Joan held the precious book in her hands, thumbing through its pages and photographs, she thought, "So this is where Aine kept her treasure." With Fiona's violin gone, there had been nothing of any great material value in the house. As had happened at the time of her own mother's death, Joan had been inwardly fascinated by the closing of a life, how easily the things one relied on in existence became irrelevant objects of disposal. The carefully chosen bowls and plates, the winter coat, the saved magazines and books for later reading. Others carted away these and everything else of Aine's, and in the space of a few days the house was emptied of its things and of any trace that they had lived there.

On the plane bound for Los Angeles, Joan said to Fiona, "Although I also lost my mother, I was not nearly as young as you, and it was the most devastating thing that ever happened to me. No one can know your feelings and you don't have to express them if you don't want. We'll just take everything as it comes when we get home."

"It doesn't matter," Fiona said, staring at the clouds from her window seat. "None of it matters. Everyone just dies in the end."

14

During their first week back in Topanga, Joan took
Fiona on various outings. They went to Disney World and to the
Getty Museum. They hiked into Solstice Canyon through
marvelous rock formations and then had fish burgers and fries
near the ocean. They saw a double feature at the American
Cinematheque in Santa Monica one afternoon and then watched
various street performers that night on the Third Street
Promenade singing reggae, juggling, and dancing the tango. Any
one of these activities would have qualified as among the most
unusual experiences of Fiona's life, but none of them lifted her
spirits. Although she offered an occasional observation or opinion,
she never smiled.

On the second week, they visited the private schools of
west Los Angeles. Some were co-ed and some were all girls', but
they shared one thing in common. They granted admission to only
a tiny percentage of applicants. Joan had hoped that Fiona's
musical gifts in combination with her Irish background would
give her an edge in getting accepted since the schools favored
diversity and unusual talent. But with Fiona's recent refusal to
play the violin and her less than enthusiastic attitude about school
and everything else, Joan doubted she would get past the first

admissions interview. It was time to get in touch with Alex and see if he could help. Alex always had connections.

His office tracked him down and he phoned Joan that night as she was getting ready for bed. She explained the problem to her brother who responded with a disturbing impatience in his voice. "Christ, Joan, you have no idea what is going on here."

Alex often seemed stressed when in production on a film, but there was something else in his tone, something more than the usual exhaustion and frustration. Nevertheless, Joan had her own frustrations and, unwilling to focus exclusively on her brother's, she unleashed the pent-up feelings of the past few weeks: "And you, dear brother, have no idea what is going on *here* since you seem to think that burying a close friend, packing up her house, and then bringing her depressed daughter—your daughter, let's not forget—to a foreign land is a day at the beach. But maybe you don't think it's a day at the beach because maybe you don't give us any thought at all. You have more important things to think about than your daughter and the death of her mother and the fact that I don't know what the hell I'm doing in taking care of a kid who doesn't want to be here."

That should shut him up, thought Joan, though she immediately felt guilty. It was true that she had no idea what difficulties were going on at his end, and he would probably not give her the gory details at this point. Alex sighed and said, "Okay, I'll make some calls tomorrow, Sis." He called her *sis*. A concession. She felt even guiltier.

Though it was late and she should have been asleep, Fiona heard every word of Joan's end of the conversation and could easily fill in Alex's side. She closed her eyes, but neither sleep nor tears would come. After a short while, she got up to get some water and found Joan in the kitchen. Joan immediately guessed that Fiona had overheard her end of the call as it was clear that the girl was wide awake.

"Fiona, I am so sorry." Joan said, suddenly worried that the little progress they had made in the previous two weeks, the small amount of trust that had allowed Fiona to even begin speaking again, was now shattered.

"It doesn't matter," Fiona shrugged, as she poured a glass of water.

"No, it does matter, dear girl," said Joan. "It matters that while we're here, we have to live with whatever is offered us by fate or by the gods or by whatever. We let it break our hearts and then we keep going. Maybe it is too soon for us to have this conversation, Fiona, but since you overheard me on the phone, I have to tell you that it's been very hard for me to see you like this."

"I can't help how I am," Fiona said and added, "I have no place to go where people wouldn't mind. I have nowhere else to go." With this, the tears that Fiona had held back since the day she found her mother cold in the bed flowed out in rivulets down her cheeks. Joan cried with her and soon even Hamlet began whimpering. His whimpering became louder and louder until it turned to barking in thunderous bugle-like shouts spaced evenly apart. The barks eventually became so predominant in the room that the aunt and niece started to alternately giggle amidst their crying. After awhile the giggling won out, and they found themselves dropping to the floor in hysterics. The very picture of themselves prolonged the situation by infecting their imagination with how funny it must have looked: two people in fits of laugher sitting on a tile floor, faces dripping with tears, and a large dog standing over them, barking in rhythmic intervals.

They finally got to their feet and took several deep breaths, a few last chuckles escaping their newly established decorum.

Fiona wanted to take back the mirth, return to being serious and sad. She hadn't meant to laugh out loud—ever again—and managed after a few moments to retrieve her solemnity. Joan put her arms around her and said, "Fiona, I've just had an idea. Tomorrow we're going to do something different."

"Like what?" Fiona asked.

"It's going to be a surprise."

Alex woke early the day after talking with his sister to face another round of shit wrangling. This film had already won top prize for being the biggest pain-in-the-ass production he had ever experienced and they were only half done. The wretched little town of their after-work encampment had only the seedy motel where they were staying and a dusty decrepit pub which served as the hang-out place for the cast and crew and was also filled with locals who made the hicks of America seem like Parisian sophisticates. Unfortunately for all the "essential elements" of the film—the main actors, director, and cameraman—they were enjoined by the insurance bond not to get intoxicated or use drugs during the six weeks of filming, a rule that forced Alex into the role of policeman at night after his long days on the set. He would drop in at the pub at odd hours and invariably catch one of them falling-down drunk. The director and cinematographer had almost come to blows there one night after the cameraman made a comment about "directors who should have stayed in MTV."

Life on the set was another kind of nightmare. Although it was Australia's winter, the days were scorching hot in the outback. Why hadn't he picked a script that was set on a coast? Alex ordered truckloads of bottled water brought in from great distances each day. The makeup people repaired dripping foundation and mascara several times in each scene. The actors and crew complained constantly and seemed to be moving in slow motion. Tempers were short. And the female lead fainted in the middle of one of her scenes due to heat stroke, which the director blamed on the cinematographer who had insisted on using extra lighting for the shot. The next day, the actress developed a rash, and shooting stopped for two days until the rash faded enough to be covered with makeup.

Mandy was driving him crazy. For reasons he couldn't fathom, her flirtation with Rick Sole had made Alex more sexually aroused by her while at the same time hating her guts. He figured it must be an evolutionarily programmed response, an alpha male reaction designed to protect one's potential genetic vehicle, and he was unable to resist it. Mandy, being the calculating creature she was, of course reveled in how her dynamic with Rick was affecting Alex and laid it on thick, always touching Sole in conversation, laughing at his dumb jokes, and advancing him to what she called "partners yoga," which involved the two of them being intimately conjoined into yogic pretzels.

In addition to all this fun, Alex now had to get Fiona into a private school in L.A.—an almost impossible task from what he had heard from his parent-friends—and he had to accomplish this from the outback of Australia. He could see a big donation to an educational institution in his future.

Of the schools they had seen, Fiona had shown a small flicker of interest in only one, The Santa Monica Academy. Not surprisingly, it was the most artsy of the schools and had a progressive academic program, which approximated that of the school Fiona attended in Ireland. It was also one of the most desirable and expensive. Alex called Linda, his PA in Santa Monica. "Find out who we know at The Santa Monica Academy, anybody whose kid goes there, anybody who is involved with the place in any capacity."

The next day Linda called back. "Good news," she said. "John Kramer's kids all go there, and he's on the board of the school. I already talked with him. He said he'll work on it but that you should also make some kind of gift to the school, like a new technology lab or something."

John Kramer was one of his poker buddies and they had also taken fencing lessons together a few years back. A good guy and someone who gets the job done. As usual, it's all connections and money. Wonder what a new technology lab costs, Alex mused. Sounds expensive. Anyway, at least the thing was handled. He told Linda to get back to Joan and let her know they had a lead on the school and were working on it. He didn't feel like talking to his sister just then, especially if he had to hear any more of her grief about Fiona. After all, it was Joan who told Aine that they would take the girl without even talking it over with him.

He had been getting headaches for the first time in his life and suspected they were due to the heat. Mandy diagnosed him as being dehydrated. "Most diseases can be cured simply by drinking water, you know." It was simplistic enough to possibly be true, but no matter how much water he drank, the headaches persisted. He turned to drugs and depleted the crew of their stashes of Advil, Excedrin, and Tylenol with promises that he would have a box FedExed to Sydney and trucked out to them within a few days.

Mandy, on the other hand, had never felt better and was having the time of her life. Her day began at five a.m. when she would get up, shower, have some fresh juice from the crates of fruit that Alex arranged to be brought in for her, and then dash off to meet Rick Sole for his yoga lesson. Alex would usually come as well as he had to get to the set early and stay on top of things there.

Mandy was delighted with Rick's progress in yoga and decided that she should go through the instructor's training program at her yoga studio when she got home as it was clear she had a gift for teaching. She wouldn't need to support herself by being a yoga teacher (god forbid!) but she would at least have the official training so that she could teach whenever she felt like it. She noted the idea in her journal.

She and Rick Sole had become true friends. She could hardly believe it. She had been a fan of his forever. He was one of the biggest celebs in the business, and almost every schoolgirl in the country had a crush on him. Even some of her supermodel friends would kill to spend a night with him. And she was his teacher! Well, his yoga teacher anyway. But she was also sort of his spiritual teacher, which was more important, of course. Yoga was just about the body. Spiritual training was about the mind and the *soul*. They had the best conversations about spirituality, and she often saw him watching her when he didn't think she noticed, and she just knew that he was thinking about something she had said that might have changed his life. He was really very sweet but kind of naïve about things. Like, he had suggested that they go to Bali after they wrapped the film to study yoga with Balinese teachers. Who ever heard of Balinese yoga teachers? There were probably more yoga teachers in each square mile of west Los Angeles than on the entire island of Bali. Besides, she couldn't exactly run off to Bali with Rick Sole and leave Alex behind. Rick completely understood when she pointed out these problems. He was so dear. Like a big beautiful child.

And this connection with Rick had done wonders for her love life with Alex. He was jealous, which must mean that he was crazy about her. It had really turned a corner in those last days at his house before she went to study dialect in London. And now, since being in Australia, he was all hers. She had fixed up their dumpy little motel room with Thai silk pillows and sheer squares of colorful fabrics thrown over the lamps. In addition to a copious supply of essential oils and soaps, she imported sheets, towels, and a bed cover and hung a large Sri Lankan batik on the wall behind the bed. She kept candles and incense going whenever they were hanging out in the room and even a white noise machine that simulated the sound of the ocean in order to drown out the noisy AC window unit. She played Alex's favorite jazz CDs on the portable sound system they bought in Sydney and always had lots of fresh fruit washed and waiting in a ceramic bowl on the rickety dresser in their room. When in London, she had also splurged on a few rare books of erotic drawings from the eighteenth and nineteenth centuries, which she and Alex would sometimes examine by candlelight while enjoying a glass of wine. She had turned this depressing hovel into a palace of love!

15

Joan made a Mexican-style breakfast of *huevos rancheros* for the two of them and told Fiona to get dressed "and wear something that you don't mind getting grungy." In Fiona's mind, that would cover almost everything she had, so she put on her usual cotton pants and T-shirt and they drove off in Joan's car to the San Fernando Valley where, unbeknownst to Fiona, they were headed to the animal shelter. The previous night Joan realized that she had handled the situation with Fiona all wrong. It had been too soon to expose Fiona to Disney World and movies and the other normally fun events while she was in a state of mourning. Joan remembered a time years ago when a boyfriend had left her for someone else and she had gone to Hawaii with some friends to heal her broken heart. But every rainbow and every plumeria-scented breeze reminded her of her loss, and as a result her memories of Hawaii were so sad that she hadn't been back since.

They pulled into the animal shelter, an unassuming concrete rectangle with a large open field behind it containing numerous animals in various forms of restraint on tie lines and in pens. Joan turned to Fiona and asked, "How would you like to walk some dogs?"

Fiona nodded cautiously, not sure what this would entail.

"It's very safe. We'll go in and check on the animals, find out which ones need a walk, and then we'll put them on leashes. And if we feel that one of them might be too frisky or dangerous, we can use a muzzle as well, although I've never had to," Joan explained.

"Okay," said Fiona. And for a split second, Joan thought she saw excitement in the girl.

As they neared the entrance, a man flung open the door and greeted Joan like the old friend she was. "Mike, we've come to walk a few dogs," Joan announced, stepping inside. "Got some leashes for us?"

Inside the shelter the decibel level approached that of a kindergarten at recess. The dogs went wild any time someone new arrived because it meant they might get taken out of their cages. Mike led Fiona and Joan down the aisles and pointed out which dogs had been walked in the last day and which had not. Fiona stopped in front of one of the cages, which contained a gorgeous Labrador mix, black as night, and practically still a puppy.

"That little fellow arrived just two days ago," Mike said. "A motorist found him on the side of the freeway. No tags on him."

"May I walk him?" Fiona asked.

"Sure," Mike replied, opening and holding the cage as the young dog leapt out, tail wagging, and wriggling his body, crablike, all around Fiona's legs.

Joan picked a couple older dogs who she felt were not likely to get adopted and would probably be put down soon. She would give them a good walk and some of the dog treats she always had on hand on what would likely be one of their last days of life. She often wished that she could just take the whole lot of them home, but there were more arriving every day and over the years she had learned to restrain these impulses. "Unwanted pets are a fact of life, Joan," Alex always said. "You can't rescue them all. Just be happy that you find homes for as many as you do."

They walked the dogs for almost an hour through the nearby neighborhoods and along a creek. Fiona seemed to be genuinely enjoying herself and laughed once when the big puppy tumbled while attempting to climb down the bank of the creek at the end of his leash.

"Can we take him out next week?" Fiona asked as they headed back.

Joan was silent. About the last thing Fiona needed to hear was that it was likely this beautiful puppy would be dead by then. At the same time, she didn't want to lie to the girl. Maybe bringing Fiona here had not been such a good idea after all. Nevertheless, Joan decided to tell Fiona the truth of what happens to unclaimed animals that don't get adopted.

"But we can't let that happen," Fiona said, tears immediately filling her eyes.

Joan found herself at a familiar crossroads, considering what to do. As always for Joan, love was simple.

"Of course we can't let that happen," she agreed. It was obvious. Fiona should have a dog. This dog.

They went back to the shelter. Joan made arrangements with Mike for them to take the little dog for the time being. If anyone came to claim him in the next few days, they would bring him back. Mike bent the rules, trusting Joan and betting that no one would be coming to claim the little guy anyway. And off they went, the new puppy squiggling in Fiona's lap in the back seat and Fiona smiling more than she had in months.

"I'm going to call him Blue," she said to Joan, "because he's so black, he's almost blue."

On the drive home, certain disturbing images entered Joan's awareness; images of Alex's pristine white house of minimalist design, his white couches and oat Berber carpets and light maple wood floors, the Edward Hopper and Lucien Freud paintings on the walls, the ceramic sculpture by Noguchi standing in a special nook designed for it in the living room corner. She was trying to insert into these mental pictures a little black mutt running through the house, but it wasn't an easy fit. Her brother was not going to be happy about this. She'd have to at least make sure the dog was house trained before he went to live at Alex's.

Fiona was on pins and needles for the coming week in hopes that no one came to claim Blue, and when the week ended they celebrated by declaring it Blue's official birthday. They took Blue and Hamlet and the other dogs for a long walk in the hills after which they came home and cooked hamburgers for all of them. Joan had never subscribed to the lore of most dog "experts" that one should not feed dogs from the table or give them meat. What the hell did dogs, which were genetically wolves, eat in the wild? Joan always suspected that the science around those myths was propagated by dog food companies, owned, of course, by the multi-national corporations. She dismissed any "science" that she suspected originated from a multi-national corporation, whether about pharmaceuticals for humans or food for animals.

Blue stayed by Fiona's side during the day and slept in her bed at night, often licking her face and waking her during one of her sad dreams when she had been rolling about in apparent distress. Joan taught Fiona how to care for her dog: about feeding and making sure he had water at all times, about bathing him and using medicinal oils on his coat to inhibit fleas. They were happily surprised to discover that Blue was already house trained so they concentrated on teaching him other commands such as "stay down," meaning not to jump on people, and "outside," meaning he was too dusty or wet or muddy to come into the house until he had been hosed down and dried outside. Because Blue was young enough to qualify as a puppy and because Joan instinctively knew not to show him too much affection, Hamlet accepted him with only a few snarls to make sure the puppy knew who was boss. Blue caught on quickly enough and behaved in an appropriately subordinate fashion when Hamlet was around. And so a month passed in what Joan and Fiona began to refer to as *dogworld*. They took the dogs to the beach and for walks in the hills. They made fires and hung out for hours watching movies on DVDs or just talking while the animals slept by their sides. The dogs were a constant source of entertainment as they were always up to something, especially the new puppy who on one day chewed every loose piece of plastic in the house (Joan had laughed and said, "I always hated plastic anyway") and on another came prancing into the kitchen proudly dragging a large branch, leaves and all, to which Joan had joked, "We can always use more firewood."

For Fiona, life in *dogworld* required a precarious balance of staying poised in the present. A mental toe step into the past led to feelings of ruinous loss; images about the future led to the uncertain life that she faced when she would no longer be living with Joan. Fiona's mind had nowhere to rest except the present moment, and she filled it with Blue and with their life in Topanga Canyon in the immediate here and now.

16

Alex returned to Los Angeles for a week during that summer, Mandy in tow. They had wrapped the film and were now in postproduction in Sydney. Rick Sole was hanging around Sydney as well, "decompressing" after the film by surfing and continuing his yoga lessons with Mandy. Alex knew better than to leave the two of them there alone while he was in the States and asked Mandy to come home with him for the week. Mandy had balked: "We'll barely be over jet lag by the time we have to come back." Alex convinced her that he needed her to be with him and that he wanted her to meet Fiona as well. Although Fiona was a sore subject, Mandy liked the idea of Alex wanting the two of them to meet. It was one more sign in her growing armory of evidence that Alex was getting ready to pop the question. Why else would he want her to meet his daughter?

Actually, Alex was very nervous about the two of them being in the same room together. The more he thought about it, the less compatible they seemed. He decided that Fiona should stay put at Joan's house while he and Mandy were in town for the week, and they would just have a few visits or outings with Fiona during that time.

On the first of these outings, Alex drove to Topanga to

spend some time with Joan and Fiona before they got on their way. They were to meet Mandy for lunch at The Ivy in Santa Monica and then take a walk along the boardwalk by the ocean. When Blue greeted him at his car door, Alex called out affectionately to Joan, who was standing on the front porch, "Don't tell me you've adopted another puppy."

"Well, no….um, actually, that's Fiona's dog. His name's Blue."

Alex's face darkened. Goddamnit, he thought, but managed not to say out loud. He hadn't seen his sister in a long time and didn't want any rancor between them, but when was this going to end? She had to stop filling his house with creatures, be they humans or dogs. "Is he house-trained?" Alex asked feebly, walking up the porch steps.

"Yes, he's completely house trained and he's a wonderful little fellow; very smart," Joan said, relieved that Alex had not exploded. "It's been really good for Fiona. I've wanted to tell you about this on the phone but I thought that once you saw him, you might warm to him. The puppy was rubbing his wet nose on the left leg of Alex's beige khakis, leaving a large damp stain.

"Sis, you know I'm not exactly an animal person and my house is not particularly dog-friendly," Alex said, moving away from the puppy. "Plus, Mandy is allergic to animal hair," he added, hoping that Joan would volunteer to keep the dog at her house.

"Alex, the dog goes with Fiona. There is no way we could or should separate them."

Just then Fiona came out of the house, dressed in her best for lunch with Alex. She had grown in the months since Alex had last seen her. God, she is beautiful, he thought. Not only did she look more like a young woman but there was something mysteriously haunting in her eyes. It reminded him of the same something in Aine, a melancholy that opened a portal to tender feelings in himself. He was both fascinated and repelled by these feelings and chose to ignore them instead. Nevertheless, he was overcome by the familiar awkwardness he experienced on the first day he met Fiona. The girl had a positively bizarre effect on him and he wasn't sure it was one he could live with.

"Hello there, Fiona. How are things going?" he blabbered. What the hell was he saying? The girl had just lost her mother and he's asking how things are going. He just couldn't get a grip on being regular around her. "What I mean is... how do you like your new dog?" he managed to ask.

"I like him very much," Fiona replied.

"Well, let's get going. Mandy will be waiting for us at the restaurant, and I'm sure you're hungry." Alex said, clapping his hands together like people did in old movies to signify it was time to get a move on. Next he would be starting his sentences with the word *why*. *Why, isn't it a fine day, Fiona?* What the hell was wrong with him?

Fiona seemed a little apprehensive about even getting in the car with him. He sure was acting weird. Joan, fully aware of her brother's odd behavior and understanding the reasons for it, jumped in to change the mood with a little reassuring levity. "The dogs and I will hold down the fort, Fiona. Don't worry. Alex will get you back here safe and sound. He's kind of a local, you know."

A few nights before Alex's arrival, Joan and Fiona had had a conversation about the upcoming visit. "Do I have to call him *father*," Fiona had asked.

"No, Fiona. You don't have to call him *father* or *papa* or *dad* if you don't feel like it. *Alex* will do just fine."

They drove off to meet Mandy for lunch, Alex at first

trying to make small talk that somehow ended up in telling Fiona about his problems on the set in Australia and finally giving up on conversation and putting on a CD of Getz and Gilberto.

Mandy was waiting at their table when Alex and Fiona arrived. She took one look at Fiona and felt a panic attack coming on. There was no need for the paternity test she had been urging on Alex. Damn. The girl looked just like him. And worse still, she was exceptionally beautiful. The kind of beauty that Mandy knew you couldn't buy. That rare natural beauty that would not have to rely on daily workouts and skilled hair colorists and makeup artists and clothing stylists and expensive facial products. With Mandy's trained eye, she knew in a glance that her own formidable beauty would pale in the presence of this girl's and not just because the girl was so much younger since Mandy looked like a teenager herself in many ways. No, Fiona was one of the great beauties, like a young Elizabeth Taylor. Her coloring, the dark hair and green eyes, was exactly that of Alex's but squared to a hundred. Her black hair shone like wet granite, her skin was flawless and the color of light mocha with a pink flush in her cheeks; features perfect—lips, cheekbones, nose. And those eyes. Could she be wearing contacts to produce that color? Somehow Mandy knew with a sinking feeling that she wasn't. They were the pale green of the Caribbean and seemed to catch light. She was tall and slim and walked like an unsteady gazelle, entirely unselfconscious of her beauty. Mandy was accustomed to being the most beautiful woman in the room in most rooms. True, when on modeling shoots or runway gigs, she had some stiff competition around, but in her own life circumstances she was almost always "the fairest of them all." Once she officially moved in with Alex, she was going to have this gorgeous girl/woman in her own home, every minute. Mandy didn't know how she would get through lunch, let alone the next five years until Fiona went away to college.

She tried to calm herself. Obviously Alex wasn't going to be attracted to his own daughter. She knew him inside and out, and though he sometimes agreed to a little kinkiness (they had once tried a threesome with one of her model friends), he had a noble streak when it came to family. It wasn't about Alex being attracted to Fiona. It was the vision of the two of them, herself and Fiona, sitting side by side that bothered Mandy. It was simply the picture that would imprint on Alex's and anyone else's mind. She would have to make sure never to be in the same shot, as it were, with Fiona. Position herself at the other end of the table so that one would at least have to turn one's head to look at her. Leave the room when she entered. Sit on a faraway couch or chair, and so on. This was going to require constant vigilance. What a disaster. Damn that Irish woman for not taking better care of herself, dying young and leaving us to deal with this, this...

"Mandy, I'd like you to meet Fiona," Alex said, strangely formal, as though he were introducing two people at a charity function.

Throughout the lunch, Mandy pasted a smile on her face, but her eyes felt like ice cubes staring out of her head, and she wondered if anyone noticed. She had no way to soften them because things kept getting worse. The girl didn't speak much, but when she did her words seemed wise beyond her years. She had Alex's intelligence combined with an almost old world European conditioning. She'd had a rigorous academic education but one that was also liberal and pretty hip for a country girl. She was apparently a virtuoso at violin and half fluent in Italian. And that charming Irish accent and way of putting things. Mandy began to feel like an uneducated wallflower.

She had grown up in Tennessee and gone to New York when she was nineteen to try the modeling business since everyone back home thought she was the prettiest girl in the state. Of course, being the prettiest girl in Tennessee was not the same as being the prettiest girl in New York City, but she had done well and eventually moved to Los Angeles, preferring the climate and wanting to break into film. She had come a long way and rarely felt insecure about her roots or her looks. Yet everything about the girl sitting before her caused an internal deflation, and she began to feel sorry for herself. She tried to conjure Ramu in her mind, imagining him quoting some Indian text or other in yoga class: "One to me is praise and blame, one to me is fame and shame, one to me is loss and gain." But no matter how fervently she concentrated, she couldn't overcome her insecurity. Her remarks and responses in the conversation ranged from strained to downright ludicrous. Alex didn't seem to notice since his end of the conversation was just as odd. They got through lunch, foregoing coffee and dessert, and were all three relieved when it was time to walk along the boardwalk so that at least they were not obliged to speak face to face. Fiona didn't know what to make of either of these adults. She had never met grown-ups who were so like children, and difficult children at that.

The next two times Fiona saw Alex that week, he came alone. They had dinner at Joan's one night, letting Joan carry the conversation, and went to Malibu on another to see a movie. Alex then flew with Mandy to Sydney for the final month of postproduction on the film.

17

Mandy couldn't shake her gloom at the prospect of living with Fiona, nor could she talk with Alex about it because it would break all the rules she had learned in her marriage books. If you wanted a man to marry you, you didn't hassle him about his kid. But did this rule apply if the man barely even knew the kid? She felt somehow that it did, at least in this case. There was already a bond between Alex and Fiona even though they seemed to have nothing in common but their genes. She thought about that annoying remark Alex had made on the flight back to Sydney, about how Fiona seemed so mature for her age—so smart—and how he wanted her to take Fiona shopping for some cool clothes and that they should splurge on a whole new wardrobe and get her out of the quaint and dreary attire that was her current style. Mandy cringed at the idea. The last thing she needed was to participate in making Fiona look *better*.

The only time she felt free these days was with Rick Sole, who seemed to think she was the most beautiful and inspiring woman on earth. He would practically leap from his seat when she entered the beach café where they would sometimes meet for LSDs, (which in Australian cafes stands for latte-soy-dandelion smoothies) before their morning yoga sessions. And though she was sometimes tempted to pour out her heart to Rick, she restrained herself knowing that it would destroy his respect for her wisdom to see how petty she could be about a thirteen-year-old girl.

Alex had his own problems. The sound in some of the scenes they had shot on location had been compromised by wind whistling, and they now had to loop in voiceovers to fix it. Most of the actors had scattered after the film wrapped, and Alex had to track several of them around the globe and appeal to them to come back to Sydney for the looping process. Several of them had scheduling conflicts as they were about to begin other films, and Alex was forced to engage in delicate and expensive negotiations for their return.

Throughout the previous couple months, Alex had grown more concerned about the headaches he was experiencing. They had become so severe that he started taking Viocodin, a prescription pain killer that he knew was highly addictive. Mandy was horrified that he was putting a powerful chemical into his blood stream every day and continually came up with alternative treatments, which, other than the cranial sacral adjustments and massages she arranged for him, usually involved some unpleasant form of renunciation of things such as coffee and wine, or being stuck with numerous acupuncture needles in places that needles hardly seemed welcome, such as his ear ridges. But none of the alternative treatments had helped. In order to function at the level required to finish the film, he would need drugs, the real deal, the legal kind that curl your toes. He also made an appointment for an MRI when he got back to the States even though he suspected the problem was stress and would subside when he got back to his routine at home. He was tired of living in hotels and, god knows, he was exhausted from months of nonstop work. Plus, Mandy's thing with Rick Sole was getting under his skin. He would be glad to return to Los Angeles.

But he also worried about what faced him there. A daughter—and a dog. And he wasn't sure about the chemistry between Mandy and Fiona. He certainly didn't sense the beginnings of a close bond on their lunch visit. He hadn't even mentioned the dog to Mandy. His life at home might be even more stressful than this trip had been. Being with Fiona those few times was stupefying for him. On the one hand, he was painfully self-conscious and uncomfortable around her, but on the other, he experienced feelings of familiarity such as he had never known.

He resolved to deal with each situation as it arose during the next phase of his life. He was, after all, a problem-solver.

Alex's friend on the board had prevailed with the admissions committee of The Santa Monica Academy, aided by the handsome donation Alex gave to the school. Fiona and Joan spent their last month together preparing for Fiona's entry into her new school. Fiona needed books, pens, pencils, notebooks, calculator, a USB drive for storing any work done on the school computer, gym wear and a backpack. On their last Saturday before Alex's arrival back home, she and Joan carted her personal belongings and school supplies over to Alex's house to move them into what would be her new room. It was Fiona's first glimpse of her father's estate, and she could hardly believe her eyes. It reminded her of the resorts she had seen pictured in travel books. Situated on three acres in Santa Monica canyon with gardens, pool, and guesthouse, it was designed by Yoshio Tamiguchi, known for her stark contemporary style. The interior of the house seemed more like the modern museum Fiona had once visited in Dublin, with art pieces in the corners and paintings on the walls. So much open space and almost no furniture. Fiona wondered where someone actually lived in a house like this. Joan showed Fiona the suite that would be hers, which was all white like the rest of the house, white walls and bleached maple wood floors. One room contained a desk and wall unit filled with high tech equipment; the other, a bed and dresser. All of it ultra modern, consisting of burnished metal and clean minimalist lines.

As Fiona stood in the starkness of the space, a picture of the hundred-year-old rented house she had lived in with her mother flitted across her awareness: her room with its pale green walls and the bed with the patchwork quilt they got at a county fair where Fiona had played the fiddle, the rocking chair in the corner on which sat the stuffed bear she had since she was three, her violin in its case on the dresser. Fiona's throat began to tighten; she released these memories and concentrated on the situation at hand. At least the suite overlooked a garden.

"Where will Blue stay?' she asked Joan, afraid that this room and even this whole house had no place for a dog.

"Blue will stay right here with you," answered Joan. "In fact, we need to make this room a bit cozier for him, don't you think?"

Fiona couldn't have agreed more.

They put Fiona's belongings in the closet and drove to Bed Bath and Beyond to load up on things for Fiona's room. Since Fiona's arrival, Joan had been making good use of the "impulse buying" credit card Alex had given her and decided to have one last spending spree before Fiona moved to his house. They bought sheets and towels in bright colors and a yellow cotton embroidered bedspread and loads of scented candles with tall candelabras to put in the corners of the room. They found a large fluffy mat for Blue, yellow and white striped silk pillows for the bed, and colored soaps and lotion jars for the bathroom. They then went to a rug store on Montana Avenue in Santa Monica and bought a Persian area rug in colors that were as close as they could get to being acceptable in the house; creams and tans, with little sprays of yellow and orange flowers on the borders.

"Now, the walls," Joan said. "What would you like on the walls in your room, Fiona?"

Fiona's mind went to her bedroom in Ireland and the large poster of Nigel Kennedy playing violin with his purple-streaked hair flying wildly about his face and his bow arm so charged that it looked as if it might lift off into space. She shook off this image and said to Joan, "I can't think of anything to put on the walls right now. We probably have enough for the room. I guess we should go back and see how it looks."

When they were done, they admired their work. The room certainly seemed a lot more inviting. "We can get more things whenever we see something we like," Joan said, plunking herself down on the big yellow bed. "But for now, it looks pretty good, don't you think?"

Fiona nodded and then sat on the bed next to her aunt. She had been waiting for the courage to speak about something that had been on her mind, and at last her courage had come.

"Couldn't Blue and I just stay with you, Joan?" Fiona asked, holding back her tears once again.

Joan, too, fought off the tears that would have liked to come and sat in silence for what seemed to Fiona a long time.

"Tell you what, Fiona," Joan at last replied. "You can spend every weekend at my place. That will be practically all of your free time since you'll be in school during the weekdays. And you can spend any vacations or school breaks that you want with me. What do you say?"

Fiona threw her arms around her aunt and buried her face into Joan's ample breast.

18

By some unspoken agreement, Mandy and Alex went to their respective homes upon arrival into Los Angeles from Sydney. They had been living in hotels together for nearly three months and Alex was ready for a break. Mandy assumed that he needed a little time to get Fiona settled and perhaps used to the idea that she might soon have a stepmother. After their exciting sojourn in Australia and having Alex more or less to herself, Mandy was sad to return to her empty apartment but confident that things were about to change. Alex wanted to have a welcoming dinner party for Fiona the following weekend, which Mandy knew was actually Joan's idea, and he had asked her to help him organize it. She would simply hire Alex's favorite caterer and buy a few flowers for the place. She resented having to make a fuss over the girl, but she was also flattered that Alex wanted it handled by her instead of Joan. She was so tired of his undying admiration for his sister, who, as far as Mandy could tell was just an aging hippie whose life consisted of hanging out with animals. To Mandy, Joan was a frumpy bore, but to Alex she was Saint Joan. Well, she knew better than to let on for a second what she really thought, at least not until they were married.

Fiona moved with Blue over to her father's house on the

Friday after Alex returned from Australia. Joan came and stayed until it was time for bed. They ordered pizzas and watched a movie in Alex's media room, which resembled a small movie theater, only with couches and a bar. Although their bedrooms were on the same floor, they were at opposite ends, a distance that would prohibit them hearing each other even if one of them screamed. Fiona had never slept in such isolation and was grateful to have Blue to curl up with in her big new bed. What a strange house this was. And Alex seemed sort of distracted or nervous or something. Fiona wondered if his behavior was because of her. She felt sad and alone and tried to concentrate on Blue's gentle snores as she drifted into a light sleep.

Mandy arrived the next morning after her yoga class wearing sweats and a T-shirt but bringing with her the clothes she intended to wear that night. She had left a number of things in Alex's spare closet over time and little by little hoped to leave more. She loved the idea of sharing a closet with Alex, even though the spare closet she was using contained only a few of his tennis rackets and some extra blankets for the bed. As she entered the house, she was shocked to see a small black dog run toward her through the hall entryway, bark once at her, and then tear off into the front garden through the open door. At first she was annoyed, thinking that one of the Mexican groundskeepers must have brought his dog to work, but then she remembered that the grounds people didn't work on Saturdays, and a more sinister thought occurred to her. Oh my god, don't tell me that damn kid of his has brought a dog with her!

Mandy rushed through the house and out the back to find Alex who was sitting by the pool. Fiona was nowhere to be seen. Trying her best to remain calm and cheerful, especially since they hadn't seen each other for three whole days, which had been a little disconcerting, Mandy came up behind him and, putting her arms around his neck, gave him a big kiss on the cheek. Alex put down the paper he had been reading and patted the chair next to him to indicate that she should take a seat.

"Amanda-panda," he said. "I didn't know you were coming over so early. Have you had breakfast?"

She usually liked his affectionate derivation of her name, but for some reason, this time it annoyed her. "I had a veggie shake at Whole Foods," Mandy replied. "Thought I'd come early to get a start on tonight."

"What's there to do?" Alex asked quizzically. "The caterers don't arrive until four."

Mandy didn't like the implication. It made her feel that Alex didn't think she should have come so soon, that he wasn't even that happy to see her. She tried to stay upbeat. "Well, I just wanted to make sure the house looked nice and that we had thought of everything. By the way, I just saw a little black dog running around. What's it doing here?"

She hadn't meant to say it that way, but it just came out.

"That's Fiona's puppy. Looks like he lives here now," Alex shrugged in a kind of neutral resignation.

Rage and fear engulfed Mandy's mind. How dare he let a dog live in his house when he knew she was allergic to animal hair. Plus, she particularly didn't like dogs, and they didn't seem to like her either. But she had to stay calm. Remember what the books say.

"But Honey, you know I'm allergic to animals. We'll have to find another home for the puppy. I know lots of people who..."

Alex looked at her with an expression she had never seen before, and the rest of her sentence died a sudden death.

"It's Fiona's dog and he lives here now. I'm not going to

tell a girl who has just lost her mother that she can't have her dog. Case closed."

As if he knew he was being discussed, Blue came tearing around to the back lawn from the front and made a beeline for Mandy and Alex by the pool. Mandy began to scream, which forced Blue to reply in five minutes of sustained barking and even a few growls as Mandy continued to scream, knocking over a lawn chair in an attempt to put a barrier between them. Fiona, who had slept in after a fitful night's rest, got out of bed when she heard the commotion and, seeing the scene in the back garden from her window, ran out as fast as she could. Alex was holding Blue's collar so that he couldn't actually get to Mandy as she ran into the house, passing Fiona on the way out.

"I'm so sorry," Fiona said to Alex as she arrived poolside, breathless and scared. "He's never done that before."

"Maybe we should keep Blue in your suite when Mandy is here. She's very afraid of dogs," Alex said. "We can let him have run of the place when she's not around," he added.

Fiona nodded, grateful that he hadn't said that Blue would have to leave. "Thank you, Alex," she said. "I'll take him upstairs." Alex watched as she walked to the house, bending on one side to hold Blue by the collar and wearing worn flannel pajamas that were a bit too small, imprinted with dozens of little banjos, an import, no doubt, from her Irish wardrobe. That strange feeling of familiarity came over him again. God, she is rather a reasonable person, he thought. He had explained the situation, and she had taken care of her end, immediately removing the dog. No whining or attitude of any sort. What more could he ask?

Mandy was another matter. He found her sulking in the kitchen and near to tears.

"Alex, I can't be in the house with that dog," she blurted

out, unable to control herself.

"Don't worry, Mandy," he said, putting his arm around her in a more paternal fashion than she liked. "It's handled. The dog will stay in Fiona's suite whenever you're here."

Mandy was taken aback. Did he say, *whenever you're here,* she asked herself. *Whenever you're here!* Oh my god. He doesn't mean for me to be here full time. He doesn't mean for me to be here much at all. Her heart, already racing from the incident with the dog, pounded in her chest so forcefully that she couldn't stand still any longer. As the tears came gushing, she ran out of the kitchen and out of the house to her car, hopping in and slamming the door as Alex jogged across the lawn toward her, saying, "Mandy, what the hell are you doing? What's wrong?"

"Nothing, just never mind," she yelled through her tears and roared out of the driveway.

Alex stood helplessly watching the car disappear out of sight. Women! he thought, shaking his head. Understanding them was an exercise in cross-species communication.

By the end of the day he had managed to talk Mandy into coming back for the dinner party. Of course, it had cost him. He calmed her with the fact that Fiona and the dog would be at Joan's every weekend anyway, and he had only meant that whenever Mandy was there during the week they would keep the dog out of sight. He further promised that he would take her anywhere she would like to go in the world as soon as *Entropy* premiered.

He now had a splitting headache. The headaches were not subsiding as he had hoped they would upon returning home. Nothing had shown up on the MRI and he would next be checked for food allergies. He'd have to take a Vicodin. He hated having to rely on drugs all day, but he would be dysfunctional if he didn't. And being dysfunctional was not in his nature.

Fiona stayed in her room most of the day, only once venturing out to see if it was okay to take Blue for a walk.

"Of course," Alex said. "He only needs to be in your room when Mandy is around. Otherwise, yes, you can have him around the house or in the gardens or wherever you want."

He could scarcely believe these words had escaped his mouth. He'd never imagined having a dog around his house. Mandy aside, he didn't really have much affinity for animals. His mother had discouraged pets when they were growing up as she was so hard pressed to feed her family, and caring for two children on the little time she had free was more than enough. He had no idea how Joan had become such an animal lover, but he had never really taken to the concept of living with animals in one's house. Yet, because it meant so much to Fiona, he found himself helplessly softening to the notion. Hell, other than the art, which he would have to find some way to protect, everything else could be replaced. If the dog ruined a floor or a couch, he'd get a new one. And he'd make sure the dog was bathed at least once a week.

Dinner was served on the back patio. In the late summer, the sun set around eight p.m. and it was warm enough to sit outside until much later. The caterers spread a feast of Italian delicacies—roasted peppers with anchovies and olives, arugula salad, penne arrabbiata made with porcini mushrooms in a hot tomato sauce, and braised beef in a marinade of parsley, tomatoes, garlic, red wine, and nutmeg. Joan had baked a cake for Fiona and decorated it with an enormous heart containing a stick figure approximation of a girl, a dog, and the words, "Welcome Fiona and Blue."

Mandy was silent through most of the dinner. Joan kept

the conversation on neutral subjects, intuitively sensing that too much focus on Fiona would inflame Mandy, but Joan resented this constraint. After all, the purpose of this dinner was to welcome Fiona to her father's home. Nevertheless, she knew that Mandy would somehow make life harder for the girl if they were not careful. The incident with the dog, which Alex had reported to Joan on the phone earlier that day, portended badly. And the way Mandy looked at Fiona gave Joan a chill. She would have to closely monitor the situation since Alex seemed oblivious to the dynamic between the two females who would now be part time under his roof.

19

Fiona's weekend at her father's was the last of the summer break from school. On Monday, the newly employed Gwenneth Hanford, a young Welsh woman who was to be Fiona's minder during the week, took the girl to The Santa Monica Academy and deposited her at the front door. "I'll be back to pick you up at four, Fiona—your freedom chariot at your service," she said with a wink. Fiona had taken an immediate liking to Gwen that morning when they met. She tried to overlook the fact that Gwen was from a Gaelic culture because it would remind her of too many sad things, but she couldn't help feeling comfortable with someone who sounded and seemed so much like someone from home. And Gwen had laughed and clapped her hands when she met Blue, happily bending down to let him lick her face as she rubbed his soft furry sides with both hands. She promised to take him to the park every day and make sure that he was properly spoiled with treats and fun in Fiona's absence. Fiona's relief shone on her face. Joan and Alex had chosen well in hiring Gwen.

But these were the last happy moments Fiona would experience until school let out later that day. With the speed that is the province of teenagers, the kids at The Santa Monica Academy saw in Fiona an outsider. Not only was she dressed in fashion that looked like it was from an old movie about poor people but she had an aura about her that was completely uncool, like an innocence more suited to a seven-year-old. The girls saw at a glance that Fiona was a naturally gorgeous farm-girl type, but they didn't feel in the least threatened since she was so dorky, and they had no interest in including her in anything.

Fiona looked around the homeroom class and felt disoriented. She had never seen girls her age dressed the way these girls were and certainly not in school. Some were wearing skirts so short that their thong underwear could be easily seen when they bent over. Some wore torn jeans that also revealed areas that Fiona thought were meant to be covered. Some were wearing low cut tops without bras and one girl had on a T-shirt with an arrow pointing to her left nipple. Almost all wore heavy makeup and dangly earrings and big jewelry. To Fiona, it looked like a costume party for ladies of the night.

They carried cell phones with customized ring tones and iPods and MP3s that they furtively listened to in the hallways between classes. On the lunch break the music blared out loud and the conversation at the tables all around her instructed Fiona as to the prevailing interests of her fellow classmates. By the end of the week, Fiona understood what it meant to hook up, which referred to a no-strings sexual encounter. She figured out the meanings of the terms "friends with benefits" and "crazy cool," both of which had to do with loose sex among acquaintances. She heard about the websites facethejury.com and hotornot.com on which kids posted their photos and were rated by their peers but were also able to hook up with kids from other schools in the greater region. She even heard of girls hooking up with older guys they met on those kinds of websites. She learned of the astonishing variety of eating disorders and all types of diets and "script" drugs and street drugs and with each new piece of information, she felt more alienated. She found their hip hop and rap music barbaric and simplistic, stupid lyrics and horrible noise devoid of the slightest musical value and requiring no skill. The girls of her new school were obsessed with shopping, celebrity gossip, and sex; the boys, with sex, drugs, and violence, usually in the form of cyber games. She hated that school from the first day she walked into the place.

How prophetic were Gwen's words, *your freedom chariot at your service*. The sight of Gwen and Blue at the end of the day enabled Fiona to get through the first week. She would come home with Gwen or they would attend to a few errands. Fiona would then play with Blue outside for a while, have dinner, do her homework, bathe, and go to bed. Gwen would stay until Alex arrived, usually long after Fiona was asleep, as he was typically out late, either at his office or with Mandy at an event. Mandy spent the night with Alex on Tuesday, but Fiona hardly saw them and dutifully kept Blue in her room. She couldn't wait to move to Joan's for the weekend.

"I hate that school," she blurted to Joan only moments after Gwen had dropped her off. "I don't want to go back there. Can't I just go to a public school?"

Joan looked at Fiona for a few moments before speaking. She faced the disgraceful truth that could not be avoided in her own country. There was almost no possibility of getting a decent education in a public school. "Fiona, all the things you hate about that school are far worse in public schools. They are more violent, there is no real education, and the kids are more out of control. The public schools of America are becoming nothing more than dangerous warehouses for poor people's children."

"Then what about another private school?" Fiona asked dejectedly.

"You know how hard it was to get into The Santa Monica Academy, Fiona. Alex had to pull some strings and whatnot. At this late date, I don't think it would be likely for you to transfer to another private school. If you really hate it we can try for another school next year, but I'm not sure any of the others will be much different. I am so sorry."

Fiona hung her head. She felt trapped in all directions. She was forced to live in the care of a man she scarcely knew and barely saw in a large house that was virtually lifeless. And she had to spend her days in a place as alien as any she had known in a country that seemed ruthless and cruel and didn't even provide public education for its young people.

Joan, sensing it was time for a mood change, said, "I have a surprise for this weekend. We're driving up the coast to Big Sur tomorrow morning and staying in an inn that allows pets, high on a cliff overlooking the ocean. Wait till you see this, Fiona. It's magnificent up there and a beautiful drive getting there. We'll be back Sunday night and I'll drive you to school on Monday morning. What do you say?"

Fiona brightened a little. She was ready to see the ocean from high on a cliff once again.

On their return Sunday night, Joan phoned her brother. After a few words of small talk about their weekend, she broached a difficult subject. "You know, Alex, having Fiona live with you is more than just allowing a boarder to stay in your house. It seems that you haven't spent a single night at home with her or taken her anywhere since she moved in. She must be very lonely there."

"She has Gwen to have dinner with and to drive her around," Alex protested. "I can't be everywhere at once."

"But you can be at home a bit more than you have been. There's no point in farming out the raising of your daughter to a stranger. We'd just as well have her come back and live with me."

"Is that what you think is best?" asked Alex.

"Well, it may come to that. She's not happy so far at your place. She doesn't fit in at school. I thought you said you would have Mandy take her shopping for some new clothes. I think the other kids see her as retro or something."

Having Mandy take Fiona shopping no longer seemed a good idea. Even Alex had figured out that Mandy didn't exactly take to Fiona, and the one time he had spoken with her about helping Fiona get some new clothes had not elicited a warm response. A vein began to throb in his head, the precursor to a headache, no doubt.

"I'll have my assistant do it," he said. "She's pretty up on young women's fashions and will at least know where to go."

"And what about spending some time with Fiona this week?" Joan asked.

Alex sighed. He could feel a showdown on the horizon since Mandy complained constantly that he didn't spend enough time with her. And now that she was so freaked about the dog, Alex didn't think it wise to have her spend too many weeknights at his place, which meant she would want him to stay at her apartment more often. Yet he could also feel the stirrings of something pleasant in the thought of spending time with Fiona, maybe taking her to an event at the Getty, or to an opening of a film. He even experienced something like pride at the thought of showing up at one of those gatherings with his beautiful daughter in tow. She would, of course, need those new clothes—and pronto.

He made a mental note to phone his assistant as soon as he hung up with his sister and make arrangements for her to take Fiona shopping after school the next day.

"Okay, Joanie," he finally said. "I'll make some time for Fiona this coming week."

The following afternoon, Alex's assistant Linda picked Fiona up from school and took her to Melrose Avenue, one of the trendiest fashion hot spots of Los Angeles. One boutique after another lined both sides of Melrose and the intersecting streets with stores specializing in everything from clothing to turn-of-the-century vending machines. They visited stores with names such as Red Balls and Wasteland and within the first hour Fiona had tried on a dozen tops, pants, and skirts but had rejected all of them, even though, to Linda's eye, she looked terrific in everything. "What's wrong with that pink Michael Stars top?" Linda asked. Fiona didn't know how to explain. She felt like an imposter in those revealing and flashy clothes. And there was another aspect that was bothering her. Aware of what each item cost, she kept imagining what the Keatons could do with that amount of money. A T-shirt and jeans from one of those shops could feed their family for a couple weeks. And her school in Ireland worked hard in their fundraising efforts just to get the amount of money that had been designated to spend on her for nothing more than pieces of cloth with special labels.

"Is there another place we can go?" asked Fiona. "A place that isn't so expensive?"

Linda, a working girl on a budget, appreciated Fiona's concern.

"My dear, your father wants you to be one of the best dressed girls in your school and doesn't mind spending whatever is needed to make that happen, so go ahead and live it up a little."

"I know," Fiona said. "It's just that… I don't really like these kinds of clothes."

Linda thought for a moment and said, "What about Banana Republic?"

"What's that?" Fiona asked.

"It's a clothing store. Come, we'll go back to Santa Monica and check it out. We should find some nice things for you there. They're not too expensive, and they might be more your style."

Alex had just arrived when they returned home around eight that night. When he saw the bags from Banana Republic, he shot Linda a disapproving look. "I thought we decided you two weren't shopping in any chain stores," he said to Linda as Fiona ran up the stairs to find Blue.

"Fiona didn't like the boutique stores and didn't feel comfortable in the clothing from those stores."

"Hmmm. Well, I hope this will at least be an improvement from what she now has," he said, peeking into the bags. "Did you get something for her to wear for an evening out?"

"Yes, and wait till you see her in it. A simple silk and linen white dress, knee-length with a high scoop neck and sheer long sleeves."

Alex nodded noncommittally and after a few more minutes of discussion about the afternoon, Linda left. Alex called to Fiona from the bottom of the stairs. She and Blue came bounding down, happy to be together after a long day apart.

"I ordered some Indian food to be delivered in a few minutes," Alex said. "Tell me about your shopping adventure."

"Thank you for buying those clothes for me," Fiona said, with a quick bashful glance to her father while patting Blue.

"My pleasure," Alex replied. "But tell me, why didn't you want to shop in the smaller stores? You know, in those places you get things that are more original, stuff you won't be seeing on other girls."

"Well, I don't mind if other girls have the same things," Fiona said, not sure what was wrong with this idea. In her school in Ireland, it was common to wear the same clothes as other girls since there were a limited number of clothing shops in the region.

"You know, Fiona, I don't mind paying for anything you want. Why don't you try another go at shopping tomorrow afternoon?"

At this point, Fiona realized that she would need to explain the underpinnings of her discomfort to Alex and she suddenly had an idea. She stood up and faced her father.

"Alex, would it be okay if I gave my clothes money to some people who need it?"

"You mean make a donation to charity?" Alex asked.

Not quite understanding the distinction, Fiona replied, "Yes, our friends in Ireland need money. I could give it to them."

Alex hid his amusement. "Well, no, that is not done," he replied.

"What do you mean?" Fiona asked.

"We don't give money to our friends."

"Even if they're poor?" Fiona asked.

"Especially if they're poor," Alex found himself saying, although he started to sense a slippery slope.

"Why not?' Fiona asked.

"Well, it causes all kinds of problems. You might be too young to understand, but trust me, it's best not to give money to friends."

"But what is money for if you can't help your friends?" Fiona asked.

As though he were seeing through his daughter's eyes,

Alex suddenly became hyper aware of the circumstances in which they were having their conversation. The 8,000-square-foot house, the expensive cars in the garage, the museum quality art in nearly every room, the prime real estate on which it all rested. He thought about his periodic rental of corporate jets for long weekends in the Yucatan or Aspen, his three thousand dollars-a-day rooms and thousand dollar bottles of vintage Petrus. Just then the doorbell rang with the food delivery, and he was saved from these reflections and from answering Fiona's question.

20

Mandy stared at herself in the mirror. Shit, is that a wrinkle around her eye? She worried that she would need to start Botox soon. Maybe it's just the lighting in this damn bathroom. She wasn't about to spend a small fortune upgrading the lighting in a rental, but she feared that Alex would see her in this light and would notice *the beginning of old*. Well, there was no reason they had to be in the bathroom at the same time, and the next time he suggested that they shower together, she would make sure it was either in natural daylight or by candlelight at night.

It certainly didn't help that Alex had Fiona in his sight during the week. It grated on Mandy day and night that he might be comparing the two of them. And it was *so* not fair because Fiona was fifteen years younger! The girl was more beautiful every day and now that she had some decent clothes, she looked— what would be the way to describe her?—well, *elegant.* Yes, she looked elegant. What a bizarre way for a thirteen-year-old to look. They're supposed to look hip or sexy or tough or depraved or anything but elegant. There was something conservative about being elegant. Yeah, it was kind of old fashioned somehow. Look at all the pop stars Fiona's age. They would die if anyone described them as elegant. Yet, here is this gorgeous teenage rival who is also elegant. And elegant in that natural way whereby you don't care about such things but you are nevertheless endowed with having clothes drape your frame in nonchalant perfection, and your movements and the way you hold your fork or tilt your head are compelling for no reason anyone can pin down. A couple weeks previously, Alex had taken her and Fiona to a film premiere in Westwood. Fiona wore a white dress that on anyone else would have looked like it was meant for church communion but on Fiona conveyed the overall gawky grace of a young Audrey Hepburn. The photo in *People* the following week showed Alex with his "beautiful daughter" and she, who had hoped to be mentioned as an actress instead of a model, was cut out of the photo altogether! It was an unmitigated disaster.

But Mandy had a plan. Alex had recently told her about Fiona being unhappy at the school in Santa Monica so maybe he would now be willing to consider alternatives further afield. Mandy had been quietly researching boarding schools on the east coast and had a list that she was methodically checking out. She figured that she could sell Alex on the idea of sending Fiona away if she came up with a girls' school that specialized in arts and academics but was also known for a more gentle and traditional code of behavior. Perhaps Fiona would be happy to transfer to such a school. There was the problem of the dog, however. That damn dog. Mandy knew that Fiona would not want to leave the dog, and none of the boarding schools she had contacted accepted pets. Well, she would work that out later. Maybe Joan could keep the dog. First she would need to convince Alex of the wisdom of the plan. She would present it to him as being best for Fiona, first of all, and as a secondary benefit, best for his and Mandy's relationship. This had all been so stressful. She briefly wondered if Alex's headaches were a result of the added pressures in his life since the arrival of Fiona (and Blue).

Mandy's thoughts then turned to Rick Sole. Their friendship had deepened since they returned to Los Angeles. They had lunches and went to yoga classes together, and Mandy had recently invited him to attend the next chanting retreat three months hence in Santa Barbara with her. She had to admit she liked the idea of having some time with Rick without Alex around, and the one place she could be sure Alex wouldn't be was a chanting retreat. But she was also a little nervous about Rick's attentions and intentions. He had recently been making it obvious that he was interested in more than just a friendship. And there were moments when she caught herself wondering what it would be like to be with him. He was great looking and, being an actor who relied on his looks, he devoted much of each day to tai bo, Pilates, weights, jogging, or yoga, so he was in fantastic shape. Washboard abs and a hard body. Hard. She thought about the word and suppressed a giggle. Alex, on the other hand, while handsome in a more carefree way and pretty good about his workout schedule, couldn't really compete in the hard body department with someone whose job in life, like her own, was to look as good as possible. Plus Rick was a bit younger than Alex.

On the other hand, Alex was filthy rich. And he would stay rich and likely get a lot richer still, unlike Rick whose stardom would fade and who seemed to know very little about managing money. Mandy was well aware that even highly paid actors were just working stiffs compared to successful producers and that an actor's salary was eaten into by agents, managers, lawyers, and taxes. The thought of spending her life with an eventual has-been actor on a budget didn't appeal to her, no matter how hard his body or how many great conversations they had. Mandy sighed and went to the phone to make an appointment for an oxygen therapy facial.

Since their arrival home, Alex had been in disagreement with the studio over the music they wanted to use in the film and over several of the more complicated technical scenes yet to be inserted, which required technologies that had not been tried before. The film, a sci-fi thriller akin to a combination of *The Matrix*, wherein the characters are dreaming their lives, and the sixties' apocalypse movie *On the Beach,* when Australia is the last place life exists after a cataclysmic die-off everywhere else, needed some of the best special effects people in the business. With the elimination of several of the trickiest scenes and jettisoning the use of all experimental special effects, the studio could reduce the technical process significantly and save a fortune in what was already an overrun budget. Alex couldn't let that happen or—he and the director were in full agreement on this—the film would be ruined. It was a daily battle.

In addition, he was on an eight-weeks program of tests for food allergies in which each week he eliminated a new thing from his diet to see whether his headaches were an allergic reaction to a particular substance. One week it would be dairy, the next week wheat, the next week caffeine, and so on. He could barely keep track of it all as his health was the least of his concerns at that moment.

The most difficult situation he faced by far was the rising tension among the females in his life. Fiona was generally unhappy with school, her home life, and probably with him. Mandy was unhappy that Fiona was there. And Joan was unhappy that he didn't take a firmer stand with Mandy and keep her away from Fiona. "After all, you have the whole weekend to spend with Mandy while Fiona is with me. Why does she need to be over there during the week?" his sister had asked in open hostility.

The main reason he had to appease Mandy with some overnights during the week was that she was holding her friendship with Rick Sole over his head. "Oh, no problem if you can't see me Tuesday night. I'll hang with Rick and see a film," Mandy had said the last time he suggested they cancel one of their weeknight dates. And she now began their weekends together with about a day of pouting and silent treatment. His headaches forced him to increase his intake of Vicodin, and he had also started using Adderal to help clear his thoughts as a counter to the dulling effects of Vicodin.

Although Alex could find almost no sanctuary in either his home or work, to his unending surprise he was developing a pleasing relationship with Blue! It had begun on the third week of Fiona's stay. Alex had come home late one night while Fiona was sleeping to find Gwen watching television in the media room with Blue by her side on the floor. After Gwen left, Alex decided it might be wise to take the dog out for a walk and let him relieve himself. They strolled around the cool dark grounds of the estate under a starry sky, the dog dutifully spraying a bush here and there and catching up with him for the circumambulation of the house. When, on his arrival late the following night, Blue had bounded down the stairs to greet him with wagging tail, Alex understood that they should have another go at a walk together. It became a secret ritual for Alex at the end of his day, this stroll around the grounds with Blue, and one to which Alex began to look forward as the only time of peace in his otherwise stressful existence.

But as difficult as Alex's life seemed to him, he would not have been able to imagine the difficulty for his daughter in her new life. In the first place, she felt like a ward living in a big fancy institution with little connection to the other humans who came and went. The Equadoran housekeeper who spoke no English, the Mexican groundskeepers who said "Hola," then kept their heads down when she and Blue walked by, the various service people who delivered things throughout the day. She liked her minder Gwen well enough, but she knew that Gwen watched the clock for the minute it was time to leave. Being with Fiona was just a job for Gwen, no matter how much they liked each other, and Fiona knew that Gwen would soon move on since she often spoke about going home to Wales.

Her school was simply a horror. She felt as though she were locked up with a bunch of expensively dressed savages— mean, entitled, and greedy. Three hundred Lord Fountleroys with credit cards. And even though some of the girls invited her to sit with them at lunch the week after her picture was in People magazine, she didn't enjoy their company. They only wanted to know about the recent movie premiere and who was there and why she was photographed. It quickly became clear that being in People magazine was not reason enough for her to be included in their group, and Fiona drifted back to her place apart within a few days.

In addition, she felt uncomfortable with Mandy. It seemed to her that Mandy either looked in another direction when Fiona spoke, or tried to change the subject. After that unfortunate day with Blue at the pool, Mandy had never again seen the dog since Fiona was careful to keep him in her room when Mandy was in the house, but she often made remarks about the diseases that animals carry, and Fiona once overheard her telling Alex of an article she read about the germs found in a dog's saliva. Whenever she was in the house, Blue seemed uncharacteristically distressed.

And what about Mandy's refusal to sit next to Fiona, even when it was the only seat left? Fiona couldn't imagine why this was the case. At first she thought that it could be due to Mandy's allergy to animals and that she might smell Blue on her clothing, so Fiona had been careful to put on clean clothes and shower before Mandy came to the house or before they went out to a restaurant, but to no avail. It was embarrassing to Fiona, even though she was sure that no one else noticed.

Fiona's life with her father also produced a strange loneliness in her. In the rare times they were together, he was always in motion. Always doing, always busy. Ants in his pants, as they used to say back home. Even when he would sit still for a little while, sometimes in the breakfast nook or by the pool, it was only to read the paper. As soon as that task was done, he was up and on the move again. He played a jazz radio station that pumped music on speakers in all the larger rooms and garden every waking minute of his time at home, and his cell phone seemed to never stop ringing. Fiona's experience of him was that of a whirring top spinning in and out of the house periodically. They had never once sat down face-to-face or gone for a walk to discuss their day.

It was nothing like her time with her mother. And this was the hardest part of all, the part that she couldn't bring herself to talk about, even with Joan. She missed her mother every day. She would often have something that she couldn't wait to tell her, or she would wake from a dream in which she and her mother were together, only to remember that her mother was dead. She would try to go back to sleep to recapture the dream and stay there with her mother forever, but it was no use. Instead she would lie awake in her sadness, and there seemed to be no end to her tears in the middle of the night. In the first couple months after her mother died, Fiona's shock and the move to a new country served almost as a distraction from the finality of her mother's death. But with each passing month, Fiona's awareness of the uncompromising nature of death grew deeper. It was as though her body and mind needed time to accept the fact that death was irrevocable, and with this acceptance the missing grew stronger.

Her only real refuges were Joan and Blue, and she looked forward to each weekend with the desperation of one who was struggling for a gulp of air in turbulent surf. Joan had found homes for the strays that had been living with her so that she and Fiona were now free for outings and short trips with Hamlet and Blue almost every weekend. They went to Desert Hot Springs and soaked in steaming mineral waters coming from several hundred yards below the earth and to Joshua Tree Park, where Fiona marveled at the emptiness of the desert, the purple rock formations, and the strange hearty plants that grew there. They spent a weekend in La Jolla near San Diego and ate at lovely cafes by the ocean or walked along the boardwalk at night. They went to Yosemite National Park and saw the giant sequoias. And soon, because it was Thanksgiving, they would spend four whole days in San Francisco. Alex was planning to spend that time with Mandy and would spend Christmas with Joan and Fiona. Joan had offered Fiona the choice of a traditional Thanksgiving with friends at home in Topanga or a trip to San Francisco, and Fiona had chosen the trip. She looked forward to traveling, not only for the thrill of seeing new places but because, by being out of her usual routine, she thought less about all that she missed.

21

In the weeks before Thanksgiving, a new kid arrived in Fiona's school, a boy from South Africa with skin the color of rich earthy peat. Joshua Mosala had obtained a musical scholarship to The Santa Monica Academy and would reside with the school's music instructor, Fred Paley, and his family for the rest of the school year, an arrangement initiated by Paley after hearing the boy play solo cello at a concert in Johannesburg the previous summer.

In the first week of his arrival at the school, it was clear to Fiona that Joshua would also be an outcast there. It was not that he was black; the kids at school were too hip to be overtly racist. It was that he was poor. His white socks and scuffed loafers, his buttoned-down collared shirts and polyester pants, the worn leather book bag he toted to classes, and what Aine used to call John Lennon glasses signaled to the other kids that he was of no consequence to them. The fact that he was also a classical music geek made certain that there would be little he could do to gain his classmates' approval, even if he underwent a makeover. As a rapper he might have had a chance. But if he was aware that he was being ostracized at school, it didn't seem to concern him. He kept to himself, attended classes, and played his cello in the music room for hours at the end of every school day.

By happenstance, Fiona passed by the music room on her way out of school one day and heard Joshua practicing. She returned the next day and the next, careful to stay out of sight in the hall, enraptured by Joshua's virtuosity. He was very good, Fiona thought. His timing, his emphasis. Now and again she would sneak a peek at him through the doorway, knowing that his head would be bent over his instrument. He was lean and long-limbed with reed-like fingers that seemed to sense the pulsation in the air. But it was his face that was most arresting. With high cheekbones and forehead and gentle eyes that sloped upward at the outer corners, his face was a combination of refinement and ferocity, vaguely reminding her of photos she had once seen of Masai warriors. For several days he had been practicing the fifth of Bach's unaccompanied suites, and Fiona could almost hear a ghostly violin playing the same piece in the recesses of her mind. For reasons she didn't bother to analyze, she looked forward to these stolen moments after school and, without saying why, told Gwen to pick her up a little later than usual from then on.

One day, after a week of her eavesdropping, Fiona was surprised to hear Joshua playing a jazz riff! He was really jamming, as her father would have said. And she smiled, knowing Alex would have wholeheartedly approved.

After several minutes, the playing stopped.

"I thought you might like a change of pace, " said a voice, accented in an exotic form of English, from within the music room.

It took only a few seconds for Fiona to realize he was talking to her! Her tawny complexion turned crimson. Oh no! He knows I have been out here all these days! Grabbing her backpack from the floor, she raced through the halls as far from the music room as possible, all the while fighting tears of embarrassment. Fortunately, Gwen was outside waiting in the car and Fiona ran to it, jumped into the back seat next to Blue, and slammed the door.

"Gwen, drive away. Please go. Go!"

Alarmed Gwen put the car into gear and drove away from the school as fast as the legal limit would allow.

"Fiona, what on earth happened? Are you all right? Did someone hurt you?"

"No, it's not that," Fiona said, her neck and face flushed as if with fever. "It's something else. I can't talk about it."

"Are you sure? Was someone chasing you just now? We can put a stop to any harassment, Fiona. I can have your father contact the school authorities right away."

"No, nothing like that. It's really okay. Please, I can't talk about it," Fiona insisted.

Gwen surmised that whatever it was that Fiona could not talk about might involve a boy and wisely decided not to pursue the matter. Fiona concentrated on Blue, who was intent on licking her face and who could always make her smile. But she couldn't bear the thought of having to go to school the next day.

The following morning Fiona found a note taped to her locker. "Dear Fiona, I didn't mean to frighten you," it read. "I would be sorry to lose the only member of my audience." It was signed, "Joshua." Fiona folded the paper and put it in her pocket. Several times throughout the day, she re-read the note until it became a little dog-eared. Still, she wasn't going to lurk around the music room like some stupid groupie, no matter how nice this Joshua might be. Fortunately, there were only a couple days left before Thanksgiving vacation.

After spending a day and a night touring the sites of San Francisco, Joan drove Fiona and the dogs forty-five minutes north to Point Reyes National Park, a vast expanse of shoreline bordered by groves of pine and fir trees, where they checked into a nearby inn. Walks along the empty beaches in the cool foggy air reminded Fiona of Ireland, and for the first time since she had come to this new country, she didn't mind the memory of the old. Their few days passed both quickly and slowly. On the drive home, Fiona told Joan about the incident with Joshua and his subsequent note.

"But, Fiona," Joan said, secretly delighted that her niece was showing some interest in music again. "He likes you! He liked having you listen to him play. No need to be embarrassed at all."

"Well, I don't want him to think that I liked him! I just liked hearing him play the cello, that's all. He's a very good musician and…well, it was nice to hear someone my age who could play. That's the only reason I was listening. I don't even know him."

"Okay," Joan said. "But maybe you could get to know him. You probably have a lot in common."

"Not really," Fiona said, looking out the window. "Since I don't play anymore."

When Fiona returned to school the following Monday, she found another note taped to her locker: "There is a live jazz concert in Santa Monica a week from Friday. Mr. Paley invited me to go with him and his wife. Would you like to join us? –Joshua."

Fiona stared at the note as her heart began to race. She was aware that she was blushing again and hoped no one would notice. She spent the rest of the day in a kind of stupor, awaiting the final bell when she could go home and phone Joan. She needed consultation about what to do.

"Well, why not go?" Joan exclaimed. "Mr. Paley and his

wife will be with you."

"I don't know," Fiona said. "I feel funny about it."

"It can't hurt to go one time," said Joan. "If you don't like being with Joshua, you won't go out with him again. That's how it works, Sweetheart. That's how people discover whether or not they're going to be friends, by spending time together."

"But, that's not how it was in Ireland. I grew up with my friends. I knew them my whole life."

"Yes, I know," Joan said gently. "But now it's different. Now you have to make new friends, and it does take a little risk. Just a little."

Fiona thought about the risk. What if she didn't like him once she got to know him? What if he didn't like her? How would it be in school to alienate the only kid who was sort of like herself, an outsider? But although she was having the conversation with one part of her mind, the rest of her mind was made up. She would say yes to Joshua's invitation. A strange excitement welled in her such that a week from Friday seemed forever far away in time.

22

Alex and Mandy were on their way to her place after an evening with colleagues in the business. They had spent most of the night talking about distribution plans for Alex's film, which was now finally in the can after months of wrangling. Mandy could barely contain her excitement at dinner and managed to interject numerous glowing comments about how wonderful their time in Australia had been, how everyone working on the film had given their all, how great the picture had turned out. Alex felt that she was over-selling and took every opportunity to change the subject back to the business of distribution and marketing.

On the drive home, Alex complained of his standard headache and without thinking said, "Would you mind if we called it a night? I need to just go home and have a quiet walk with Blue around the grounds and then get myself to bed."

Mandy froze. Unable to restrain herself, she asked in an accusatory tone, her voice pitched uncomfortably high, "So, is that what you do every night? You walk around the grounds with that damn dog?"

Alex was in no mood to argue as his head was splitting, but he was also in no mood for nonsense.

"Don't tell me you're now jealous of *the dog*," he replied in a tone that said he was ready for a fight if necessary.

Don't tell me you're now jealous of the dog. Mandy held her tongue, but her breathing became more rapid. He means that I am also jealous of the girl. That is, of course, what he means. She felt her world collapsing. She was losing her hold on Alex. She would never be his Number One. She would probably not even make it to the top three. It wasn't his walking with the dog that bothered her. It was that she knew, even if he didn't, that bonding with the dog was his way of further bonding with Fiona. There would always be Fiona or Joan in first and second place, and now the damn dog would take third! She held back tears as she thought about never being anyone's Number One in her entire life.

An only child, she had been raised by a mother whose moods ranged from cruelty to indifference. Her mother worked nights as a bartender and left Mandy to fend for herself from the age of ten. They lived in relative poverty and received little help from Mandy's father who had left when she was five but who lived only thirty miles away. Over the years, he would sometimes visit, bearing expensive gifts and taking her to movies and the amusement park, which made him a heroic figure in Mandy's mind, her rescuer who would someday take her with him for good. But he never did. He had a new wife and children who were his primary family, and when Mandy showed up at his door, having run away from her mother's home at the age of sixteen, she was not welcome.

Her need to leave behind the life she had known had fueled her modeling career and had forged her relationships to both men and women. She kept hoping to find a man who would take care of her, for whom she would be the most important person in the world, but invariably she ended up with men who had other priorities. Women were only adversaries with whom she had to compete.

Defeated and too upset for further conversation, she simply said, "Yes, we should call it a night."

The evening of the jazz concert arrived at last and Gwen drove Fiona to the appointed spot near the venue where Fiona was to meet Joshua and the Paleys. With open seating tickets they were not able to get four seats together so the two young people sat a couple rows in front of the music teacher and his wife. Fiona had barely spoken except to say hello to everyone and to make arrangements with them to meet her aunt, who would be picking her up afterward at a designated place. She and Joshua settled into their seats in the hall, a place called the Jazz Bakery, named for its location in a large complex that had once been a baking factory and was now host to many of the jazz legends of the day. On its walls were large paintings of Billie Holiday, Charlie Mingus, Art Blakey, and other greats, most of whom Fiona recognized from her father's CD collection. On this particular evening, the Jazz Bakery featured The Jeff Gauthier Ensemble, a highly respected L.A.-based jazz quartet, there to promote their latest CD, "Internal Memo."

"I take it that you like music," Joshua began in his charmingly strange accent and slightly formal way of speaking.

"Yes, I do."

"Do you play an instrument?"

"Well, I used to play the violin… but I stopped when I was thirteen."

Sensing that Fiona didn't want to discuss anything further about her musical background, Joshua asked, "How old are you now?"

"Well, I'm still thirteen—and a half," Fiona said, immediately regretting adding the half . "How old are you?"

"Fourteen—and one eighth," Joshua replied, and winked.

With this they both giggled as the musicians walked on stage to the cheers of the packed house. For the next two hours Fiona, in her peripheral vision, could see Joshua moving in relaxed rhythm to the percussions, often with his eyes closed. But while she also felt the music throughout her body, she managed to keep perfectly still and only once turned to look directly at Joshua, who smiled and nodded in time with the beat.

At the appointed time and place, Fiona said good-bye to Mr. and Mrs. Paley and shyly shook Joshua's hand, thanking him for the evening as Joan watched from her car. She had rarely seen Fiona so aglow.

Fiona hopped into the car, all smiles.

"Well, I don't have to ask how it was," said Joan. "Looks like you had a pretty good time."

"Yeah, the music was great," Fiona gushed. "Very jazzy. Alex would have loved it. And the place was really brilliant."

"Uh huh. And was everything okay with Joshua? Did you get a chance to talk a little?"

"Yeah, we talked a little. He's nice," Fiona said, nonchalantly.

Joan just nodded and smiled.

Late into the night, Fiona, sleepless, walked out onto the porch of her aunt's home to gaze at the stars and trace the shape of the dark hills against the sky. A coyote howled in the distance and her imagination conjured up a wild animal in Africa calling across distant plains.

23

Joshua was also sleepless the night of the concert. He tried to read for awhile—a book on biology—but gave up after he had gone over the same page several times and not taken in a word of it. His mind was filled with music and, he had to admit, with Fiona. He had never seen a more beautiful girl, and he could hardly dare to imagine they might become friends. It was clear they shared a deep love of music, but he wondered why Fiona seemed no longer interested in playing an instrument. Maybe violin was not the right one for her. He might suggest that he teach her another. She had heard him play cello, the instrument dearest to his heart, but he was even more proficient in piano. Fiona seemed like a piano sort of girl, he concluded. When the time was right, he would offer.

But he was getting ahead of himself. Hadn't his father cautioned him before coming to this strange country that he should expect many disappointments in dealings with white people? His father had proven right for the most part, although luckily the Paleys, with whom he lived, were exceptionally kind and good to him. At home in South Africa Joshua had understood the whites better than he did there in west Los Angeles. At home, even though the black and white communities still lived mostly in segregated enclaves, they mingled easily. The whites, a minority and no longer politically dominant, had definitely lost their edge of superiority in the post-apartheid world of modern South Africa. They were better behaved as a result. But Joshua remained mindful of the life his father and mother had endured in the townships where they had once lived with no electricity, sewage system, or running water, and where an average of fourteen people shared a four-room house and all non-whites were required to carry a passbook of government documentation and produce it on demand. His father, in speaking of that time, would occasionally quote Desmond Tutu in saying that one of the greatest dangers of racial discrimination is that "you are brainwashed into an acquiescence in your oppression and exploitation."

He was too young to have known official apartheid, but he had nevertheless experienced racism in his own country. However, it was nothing like that of the U.S. He found that, more than anything else, white people seemed frightened by him on the street. Having seen enough TV to know how black teenagers were portrayed, he could sort of understand how a young black male would be a symbol of danger to the rich white society of west Los Angeles. Still, he was surprised by how consistent were the reactions to him—car door locks snapping shut as he crossed a street in the middle of the day; the watchful eyes of store owners that seemed to be interested only in *his* movements in a crowd of white shoppers. He had developed a habit of walking with his head down and his body held in so as to lessen the threat of his presence, but he often thought of Desmond Tutu's words when he did so.

The Santa Monica Academy was another matter. There were a number of other black kids, some of whom came from

wealthy families and a couple of whom were scholarship kids
from south central Los Angeles. They knew the language of the
street, the prison system, rap, hip-hop, gangs, and every other
stereotype of black culture in South Central and were
consequently part of the cool pack at school. They were *bad*, a
laudatory term in the minds of his schoolmates but exactly apt in
the context of his Christian upbringing in South Africa.

In his first weeks there he felt there was really no one at his
new school like himself. Maybe that was how everyone ultimately
felt. Maybe each and every person felt contained in the flesh they
inhabited and entirely alone there. It was a feeling he had never
known or considered in South Africa. He had always been
surrounded by people, his large immediate family, their extended
family of hundreds, their legion of friends. Just knowing all the
names of his cousins was a feat of memory deserving of a prize.
They belonged. They belonged to each other and to their land.
And he sometimes wondered if the gift he had inherited, the gift
of music, was a blessing or a curse, for it had infected his dreams
with a need to get out of the confines of his hometown. He wanted
to play music in the greatest concert halls on earth and from the
time he was a small child, easily picking out tunes on the ancient
piano in their local church, he was told by all who knew him that
he was destined for greatness, that South Africa couldn't hold him.
By the age of eight he played piano at both church services every
Sunday and by age ten had won a scholarship to Johannesburg's
prestigious Willoughby Academy.

It was there that he picked up a cello for the first time and
experienced effortless affinity with its feel, its sound, its weight,
and its resonance. Not a day had passed since that he had failed to
play a cello, and he had become pretty good, even by his own high
standards. His talent had not gone unnoticed, of course. After two

years of playing cello in local recitals with school-age children he was invited to play as a soloist for the Johannesburg Symphony. It was in his second summer of playing with the Symphony that Fred Paley heard him and arranged for a scholarship to The Santa Monica Academy.

Prior to coming to America, Joshua had researched Santa Monica online and, although he thought he had obtained a fairly good idea of the area through his study and through seeing numerous movies and TV shows set there, he found on arrival that it was not as he had imagined it. For one thing, the people in the movies and the articles online led him to think that America was a place where everyone was happy most of the time. There was almost a giddy quality to the shows he had seen on TV. The concerns of Americans were the concerns of people who had everything and could afford to whine over the tiniest of inconveniences, but even the whines were more like play-whines, not enough to keep them from their fun. It was a culture of spoiled children, it seemed to him, oblivious to the rest of the world, their only problem, the tyranny of excess, as his father liked to say.

But what he discovered soon after he arrived was something startlingly different from his expectations. People had happy facades but were miserable underneath. There was an almost palpable gloom that lurked a millimeter below the surface of many of the people he had met, as though one of their famous smiley face symbols were pasted on a corpse. Everyone wanted more stuff no matter how much they already had; there was a constant fear of terrorism among the general population, engendered by a cartoonish television news media; and the government did not take care of its poor and sick. Even its public education was one of the worst in the civilized world, far worse than public education in South Africa, which was so much poorer a country. So many people lived on the streets in Santa Monica that one became used to stepping around or over them as a matter of course. No, he had not found that people in America were happy, except in the most superficial ways, through their relationship with things and more things.

In Fiona he sensed the opposite. She had a slightly sad exterior that he attributed to the death of her mother, of which he had learned from Fred Paley. But underneath he felt there was a steadiness of spirit and an appreciation for what he, too, thought provided more profound forms of happiness—friendship, family, love of art, music, and curiosity about the world and its wonders. He didn't know how he knew this about her. They had barely spoken more than a few minutes at a time. But from the first day he saw her in school and learned that she was from rural Ireland, he had imagined that she was like him in those ways, and nothing since then had led him to think otherwise.

He could hardly believe his good fortune when he realized that the person who had been in the hall secretly listening to him play was Fiona.

24

There was only a week left before Christmas vacation. Joan, Alex, and Fiona were planning their family trip to Hawaii. Fiona had never been to a tropical island, and indeed, like many of her fellow Irish, didn't know how to swim, despite having grown up on an island. For one thing, the water off the coast of Ireland was almost always too cold. Fiona became concerned as she listened to Joan and Alex discussing the many water activities they had arranged. Snorkeling, body-boarding, whale watching—words that had never held any relevance for Fiona before.

"Um…listen," Fiona interrupted. "Did either of you know that I don't know how to swim?"

Alex looked at Joan as though this oversight were somehow her responsibility. Joan dismissed his glance and spoke instead to Fiona.

"God, no, Fiona. I guess we must have just assumed that since you grew up next to the ocean, you were an able swimmer."

"No, I've never been in past my knees," Fiona replied, worried about disappointing them or somehow spoiling the trip.

After a pause, Alex spoke up, "I'll teach you, Fiona. It's not hard at all. In one day, you'll be swimming like a fish."

Fiona smiled shyly and said okay. She doubted that

swimming could be that easy or everyone in Ireland would know how and hardly anyone she knew did. But she didn't want to make a fuss. She was so excited to be going to Hawaii she could scarcely contain herself. The only difficulty was in leaving Blue, but he and Hamlet would stay with some neighbors in Topanga, friends of Joan's who loved dogs and had a large property.

At lunch in the cafeteria the next day, Joshua asked Fiona if she minded if he joined her. Conscious that many eyes were watching, Fiona nevertheless beamed him a smile and, moving her books off the seat next to her, motioned for him to sit down. They ate together for a few minutes in silence until the others had lost interest in them.

"Will you be around for the holidays?" Joshua asked.

"No, we're going to Hawaii."

Joshua nodded as Fiona detected a hint of disappointment.

"Will you be around here?" Fiona inquired.

"Yes. I'll be with the Paleys and their family."

There was something in this exchange that made Fiona a little sad, but she couldn't put her finger on it at the moment. Only later would it would become obvious.

"I don't know how to swim," Fiona said.

"Well, I think Hawaii is probably a good place to learn. I hear the water is warm there, like South Africa's in the summer."

"Yes, I've never been in a warm ocean. It must be nice," said Fiona.

"It's very nice."

"I'll be back when school starts up again," said Fiona.

"Well, maybe we could go to a movie or something when you get back."

"I'd like that," she replied.

For the rest of the day, Fiona reviewed her brief conversation with Joshua. She relived each moment from every perspective she could conjure. When he said that, I said this. When I said that, he replied such and such. She tried out the conversation with different responses and made up entirely different subjects. She pictured them in fits of laughter and in moments of deep seriousness, with Joshua revealing his secrets and she her own. In her imagination, she wore different clothing; one moment, jeans and a jacket, the next, a royal blue skirt and sweater. She went over her sad feelings during the part of the conversation when she realized that Joshua would not be with his own family at Christmas, and she became aware that she reacted because she, too, would be away from home at Christmas—away from Ireland—and that this would be the first Christmas she had not spent with her mother.

Her thoughts then drifted to memories of Christmas in County Galway. Although her mother was not religious, she had loved Christmas. "It's an excuse for us to celebrate with friends and family in the middle of winter," Aine would say. It was a time of year when darkness came early so that Christmas lights seemed especially cheerful during the long wintry nights. They would decorate a small tree with tiny white berries, and Aine would place the traditional white candle in the window to "light the way for strangers" as a symbolic gesture of hospitality. She would prepare spiced beef and mince pies and Christmas pudding, and they would all meet at the Keaton's house for dinner, where Aine would let Fiona have a small glass of red wine with her meal. At home later that night, they would exchange gifts by the fire. Aine would have either purchased or made something that Fiona had dearly wanted—a particular CD, a sweater—and Fiona would have made something for her mother in art class or composed a special violin sonata dedicated to her.

Fiona contrasted these memories of Christmas to the holiday season in Los Angeles. Christmas in such a warm arid place hardly seemed like Christmas. Lights on palm trees and big red Santas dressed in inappropriately bulky costume, flying sleighs with reindeers over the boulevards through bright, sunny skies. A manger scene near the Santa Monica boardwalk, the beach and surfers in wet suits in the background. It just wasn't the same. Fiona wondered what Christmas would be like in Hawaii. Probably even more ridiculous. Well, it was just as well. She didn't want to be reminded of those cozy days and nights of winter holidays in Ireland.

25

As they checked into The Four Seasons on Maui, Fiona thought that heaven, if ever there was such a thing, could not be more beautiful. Flying in over turquoise water, ribbons of whitecaps streaming from the reefs below, the drive in the convertible from the airport to the hotel in warm tropical air that was scented with flowers. They entered the vast marble expanse of the lobby of the Four Seasons and a Hawaiian woman from the hotel put *leis* of tuberoses around Fiona's and Joan's necks. Intoxicated by the fragrance of the *lei,* Fiona gazed out over wide palatial steps that led to an outdoor series of pools, patios, café and bar, and finally the beach and ocean.

She followed her father and Joan to their two-bedroom suite in a sort of daze. She and Joan would share a room. They changed into swimwear, and Joan showed Fiona how to wear a sarong over her bathing suit. They had lunch in the open café by the sea, then strolled along a concrete walkway that rimmed the cliffs by the ocean for a couple miles. During this time, they spoke very little. They were happy to be there and to be there together. Fiona had never spent this much solid time with Alex and was beginning to feel more comfortable with him by the hour. She began to appreciate how well he had planned their trip and how, since their arrival, he had been taking care of things, making sure everything was just right. She and Joan had done nothing more than unpack their clothing.

After their walk, Alex announced that it was time for Fiona's swimming lesson. They spent the next three hours in the shallow end of the pool. Alex began by holding Fiona in a floating position and gradually taking his hands away for moments at a time so she would get a feel for her weight in the water. Next, while having her stand and practice in water to her chest, he showed her the crawl stroke and how to rotate her breathing during the movements, a skill she immediately picked up, having studied numerous breathing techniques in music. He then placed one hand under her belly to keep her afloat while she practiced the stroke and breathing, once again taking his hand away for moments at a time. At the end of three hours, Fiona could take four or five stokes on her own before heading into a sort of funny sideward nosedive.

"That's probably enough for a day," Alex said when he sensed Fiona was getting tired.

Breathless, Fiona nodded, "Thanks, Alex. I'm sorry I couldn't get all the way across."

"You did great. We'll have another lesson in the morning." He watched as Fiona exited the pool and scampered to where Joan was reading a book under the shade of a pool cabana. Grabbing a towel she jabbered to Joan just out of his hearing, but he could see that she was glowing from the swim and the sun, and she seemed happier than he had ever seen her. Something in him swelled with pride. This girl, this wonderful girl, was a source of surprising delight to him. His sister had been right, as usual. It was a privilege to have Fiona in his life.

That evening they sat on their balcony and watched as

unknown forces painted the sky in great swaths of magenta, purple, pink, and finally cobalt blue, sprinkled with a million stars.

By the next afternoon, Fiona was proficient enough in getting around the pool that Alex decided she was ready for the ocean. The three of them ambled down and gently waded in, Alex and Joan on either side of Fiona. The water temperature was just a tad chilly, it being December, and there was an even chillier current running about thigh level. Fiona had never felt a current before. She vaguely understood the concept, having grown up hearing about currents and other seafaring talk from the locals. But she had never imagined that one could actually feel a current. It was a strange sensation. She looked out to sea and suddenly had a moment of being overwhelmed by the immensity of it. This body of water, even though it had a different name than the one of her homeland, was nevertheless the same water. It evaporated into clouds and came down in the form of rain and went into rivers in remote mountain regions and still found its way back to its own source. It touched the shores of County Galway, where all her old friends would be getting ready for Christmas. She felt a sudden chill. The current was suddenly even colder, but it made the other water swirling around her seem warm, the two temperatures together producing goose bumps in the young girl. Standing there, shivers of excitement running through her, reminded Fiona of seeing her first violin concert in Dublin, of entering another world.

Over the next days, Fiona became more comfortable in the ocean and even let Alex push her on a body board to catch a wave while Joan waited in the shallows to spot her. They hiked through a bamboo forest to waterfalls and fresh water pools, went whale watching off the coast of a tiny nearby island, and drove the magnificent scenic road to Hana, an area on the other side of the island, where hints of old Hawaii still existed and where rainbows greeted them on their way. They ate exotic fruits with names such as lychee, guava, and lilikoi. They even went snorkeling, Alex swimming alongside Fiona and pointing out the wondrously colored fish. This was an experience that Fiona had never dreamed. She had seen a few shows of underwater diving, but it was an entirely different proposition to be among the ocean life itself. She felt like an enormous fish as she and Alex swam near a turtle half her size. Alex told her later that the creature must have been a hundred years old.

On Christmas day they exchanged gifts on the balcony of their suite. Having agreed that they would give small, easily transportable presents, Joan and Fiona had purchased two Tommy Bahama shirts of excellent soft cotton and subtle Hawaiian-style design for Alex to wear while on the islands but which he could also use for outdoor parties back home. Alex gave Joan a fine watch, one he knew she had admired, and Fiona, a spectacular pink shell necklace, interspersed with tiny white pearls. Joan gave Fiona a bottle of island-scented coconut oil and Fiona gave Joan the new Van Morrison album knowing Joan was a huge "Van fan," having many times joked with Fiona about someday running off to Ireland to find him.

Unbeknownst to Fiona, Joan had also brought along another gift for Alex, the book by Aine that told the story of their daughter, which Alex had not previously had time to read and which would become his bedtime companion as he was lulled to sleep each night by the sound of the ocean and the breeze of the tropics.

Mandy's holidays, on the other hand, were not going so

swimmingly. She had planned to go to Portugal for a yoga-lates (yoga and Pilates) workshop, but at the last minute the workshop was canceled, and she certainly didn't want to be alone in Portugal during Christmas. She decided to stay home and see who she could scare up to spend the holidays with, but everyone she knew was with their relatives or out of town skiing somewhere, or …in Hawaii.

Every time she thought about Alex being on Maui with Fiona and Joan, leaving her alone for Christmas, she had to suppress a sweltering rage. She knew she had agreed that she would have Alex to herself for Thanksgiving and the others would be with him for Christmas, but now she saw how completely unfair that was. This was a much longer time period and a more important holiday. She was always the one making sacrifices. Never Joan. Never Fiona. Only Mandy. She was so sick of it she could hardly have a single thought about the subject without feeling her blood pressure rise. And the thoughts seemed never to stop. She was even dreaming about the situation, dreams in which Alex, Fiona, and Joan were happily having poolside barbeques surrounded by many dogs while she was floating in outer space, alone and unhitched from her space capsule. Or she would dream of revenge. Alex would choose her and they would live an international high life based somewhere far away, like Australia, and Fiona would be sent to a strict eighteenth-century-style boarding school in Ireland and Alex would see Joan for the meddling retro she was and rarely ever speak to her again. She would wake from these dreams with her heart pounding, not particularly pleased with herself. After all, didn't Ramu always say that revenge was not an option for a true yogini? Once, she even considered the irony that she was in the stepmother role to Fiona just as her father's wife had been in that role to her. The only difference in her experience and Fiona's was that her own father had chosen his new wife and family over her, and now her boyfriend was doing the same. She was always left out, no matter which role she was in—stepdaughter or stepmother. Her therapist seemed never to tire of pointing out that we repeat our childhood traumas through unconscious attractions to partners who will enact the exact patterns of our childhood. Alex had barely phoned her since he arrived on Maui, and whenever she tried to reach him, she got his voicemail.

Mandy decided to contact Rick Sole. They had not seen much of each other of late because Mandy could sense Alex's growing impatience with their friendship. He had gone from being extraordinarily amorous, due to what she liked to think was a healthy possessiveness, to anger and indifference. "Maybe he's the one for you," Alex had offhandedly said on the phone one afternoon when she was off to see Rick for tea. From that moment on, Mandy had cooled her involvement with Rick. But now she needed him.

Rick was delighted to hear from her.

"I thought you were going to Portugal."

"No, the trip got canceled. I was just wondering…. what are you doing for Christmas?" A quiver in her voice.

"Just going to see my folks and my brother's family in Bakersfield. Uh…what are you doing now that your trip's off?"

"Well… I don't really have plans."

"Would you like to come to Bakersfield and meet my family, spend Christmas with us?" he asked.

"I'd love to," Mandy said with relief, even though Bakersfield, a dusty inland armpit of trailers, cheap hotels, and fast food chains was not exactly her Christmas dream come true, plus she had no idea how she was going to explain this to Alex.

26

Fiona slept with her head resting on a pillow on Joan's shoulder as they flew through the night from Maui to Los Angeles. Alex was reading a script by the small light illuminating his seat when Joan nudged him softly.

"You know, I was noticing...," she whispered, careful not to wake Fiona, "you didn't complain of a headache the entire time we were gone."

"Yeah, I noticed that, too," Alex said without looking up.

"Alex, maybe there's a message here. Maybe you're just working too hard. That's probably all that's wrong with you."

Alex shrugged, "I'm not going to quit working, Joan."

"Well, you wouldn't have to quit. You could just cut back."

"It's not that kind of business, Sis. It's full throttle or you're on the sidelines."

"So, what's so bad about the sidelines if you can live there without headaches?"

Looking up with a grin, he said, "You're not gonna give me one of those *Don't wait till you're dead to rest in peace* lectures now, are you?"

Knowing that Alex would at this point start making jokes

at her expense, Joan returned to her magazine. For all his smarts, he was so damn slow sometimes. But she thought about all that had been accomplished over the past ten days, the bonding between Alex and Fiona, the laughs and good times they had all shared, and contented herself with knowing that, though he was sometimes slow to see the important things, Alex would eventually come around.

Mandy was back in Los Angeles after her Christmas vacation with Rick Sole and his family in Bakersfield. She had stayed at the Bakersfield Holiday Inn, the worst hotel she had been in for many years, but nevertheless she'd had a pretty good time over Christmas. She was comfortable with Rick's family. They were working class people, the kind with whom she had grown up. Unpretentious, unworldly, and proud of being what they considered middle class (although Mandy couldn't help but think that the middle class was actually the new poor), they treated Mandy as an honored guest and gushed at every opportunity over how gorgeous she was. It reminded her of being back in Tennessee when she was the most beautiful creature for a hundred square miles.

And Rick had been so kind to her. Although they never spoke of it, he seemed aware that she was feeling lost and was at her service during their entire four days together, always solicitous of her needs and a perfect gentleman throughout. She could see that Rick's family adored him and seemed to think that no one on earth had accomplished more than their movie-star son/brother/uncle. He was somehow in his element there, a proverbial whale in a small pond, and it seemed to bring out in him an endearing humility. At the end of their days together, as they said good-bye in the parking lot of the crappy hotel where he had come to see her off, Mandy kissed him—a real kiss, a deep kiss, not just a quick peck on the lips. She had been thinking about that kiss ever since, not only because it was rather wonderful and her mind liked to imagine the rest of what might come after such a kiss, but because it had greatly complicated her life. First off, she now had to keep a big secret from Alex. And he would no doubt ask her if anything had gone on between her and Rick since she had left a voicemail message for him informing him that she was going to spend Christmas with Rick's family (and, of course, stay in a Holiday Inn by herself). Alex, for all his blustering about her friendship with Rick, had always seemed to take her word that there was nothing physical going on between them. She would now have to breach that trust and lie when he asked her.

The other problem was Rick. Prior to the kiss she had managed to maintain the semblance of being just friends. Sure, they would flirt at times, and in doing partners yoga Rick would sometimes place his hands on her thighs a bit higher than was absolutely necessary, but she had never before given him any reason to think there was a real chance for the two of them. The kiss had changed that. Rick had been calling every day since she left Bakersfield and had asked her to meet him for dinner when he got back into town as he wanted to talk with her face to face. She had agreed and knew that it was going to be a difficult conversation. She would let Rick down gently and take responsibility for misleading him because, for all her problems with Alex, for all the hell she now had to endure in her relationship with him, she was still in love with him. Oh god, she didn't know what that even meant anymore, but she at least knew that she still wanted him. She still wanted to marry Alex. It wasn't just the life he could provide, although she certainly liked that part. There was something wild and mysterious about him, like a rare animal from a faraway land. He was always on the move, just out of reach, and this exhilarated her, a response that her therapist felt derived from her wounded childhood but which she nonetheless felt powerless to resist. As handsome and kind and available as Rick Sole was, he didn't have that other thing, that *je ne se quois* that Alex had in spades, the love of which, Mandy suspected, would somehow be her downfall.

She now found herself feeling contrite about her behavior with Rick and desperately looking forward to seeing Alex. The time with Rick, along with the kiss, had the strange effect of softening her rage at Alex. She suddenly understood why some women don't mind if their husbands cheat a little because they come home so guiltily penitent, often with presents in hand. She would have her own present for Alex. He would arrive in the wee morning hours of December 31st and they would spend New Year's Eve together, just the two of them. Fiona would be staying with Joan for a couple days until school started. Alex and Mandy would have the house to themselves, and, though he would be none the wiser, she would make up for all her terrible thoughts and transgressions in all the ways she knew to please him.

27

During the week after their return to school, Fiona and Joshua began to sit together every day at lunch. The following Saturday, Joan took them to the Third Street Promenade for pizza and a movie, and by the following week Fiona was hanging out in the music room at the end of the school day, listening to Joshua practice and sometimes even making musical suggestions, ones which Joshua found to be highly sophisticated. He would tease her about her days of furtively lurking in the hall, "You're coming up in the world, Fiona. You're *in the room.*"

Everything about Joshua fascinated Fiona. Initially, she was captivated by the fact that he was African since she had never known a person of African descent. Growing up in the west of Ireland she had hardly even seen black people and then only in Galway or Dublin, not in the village where she lived. There were no children of color in her school, even though the administration would have welcomed them and, in any case, made sure to provide a progressive curriculum that included some of the histories of those peoples told from their points of view. She, therefore, had no prejudice, just curiosity.

Her arrival in America had exposed her to many encounters with people of color, but none of them led to any understanding of who they might be in a social context. Her father employed a dozen Hispanics of different nationalities: the workers and waiters at nearly every business and restaurant they frequented were mostly Mexican; numerous African American, Asian, and Latino kids were in her classes at school; her father had a few black and Indian colleagues who sometimes came by their house. But none of these encounters had ever led to a conversation that included Fiona.

Though Joshua being a different race may have initially intrigued her, Fiona soon forgot to even notice this difference and was only reminded of it when others stared at the two of them on the street or in school. What began to fascinate her most about Joshua was his breadth of knowledge about so many interesting things. First off, he was a brilliant musician, as proficient in the classics as any young person she had ever heard, and equally talented in jazz, ripping away on the strings of his cello or on the keys of a piano. And then there was his love of the natural sciences. He would patiently explain to her how important it was to understand biology since every living organism depended on the delicate interweaving of the life systems. He described to her, for instance, the Ngorongoro Crater, a twelve-mile-wide extinct volcano and one of the seven wonders of the natural world, located in Tanzania. Home to 25,000 animals including zebras, lions, leopards, cheetahs, impalas, rhinoceroses, and elephants, it provided a glimpse into an eco-system that approximated what much of Africa may have been at one time.

"Have you ever been there?" Fiona asked.

"Yes, I went there with my school once."

Fiona tried to imagine what it would be like to be among the great animals of Africa. Perhaps it would induce a similar sensation as when she snorkeled with the turtles and tropical fish on Maui, a feeling of entering an entirely different reality. Having grown up in Ireland, she had never seen a large mammal in the wild until she came to America and observed deer running free on the roads and trails in Topanga Canyon. The world was getting bigger and bigger in her imagination as her former life and that of her friends' in Ireland seemed to be shrinking. She thought of the Keatons and of her teachers in school back home. They hardly traveled and rarely even made it to Dublin. She felt a little guilty having these thoughts and the thoughts also made her feel lonely. Who would she be if she no longer felt at home in Ireland since she certainly didn't feel at home in America? She looked at her new friend and thought that, though he was a stranger to this country, he must at least be firmly rooted to Africa in his heart.

At that exact moment, as though reading her mind, Joshua said, "I like to think of the earth as my home. When I see photos of the earth from space, I think to myself, that looks like a good place to live. All that water and the shapeliness of the landmasses. What a beautiful planet. And then I think, I'd like to play music on every continent as a way of saying thanks."

Fiona laughed as her spirits brightened. She liked the idea of thinking of the earth as her home as well. It had never before occurred to her that one could be affiliated with the entirety of the planet rather than just one particular place.

"Fiona, I've been wondering…would you have any interest in learning to play the piano? It's relatively easy. I could teach you."

Fiona's happy mood darkened a little. "No, that's alright. I don't really want to play anything. I'm happy to just listen to you, if that's okay."

"Sure, no problem. I love having you as my extra set of ears," Joshua replied, once again puzzled by Fiona's reticence.

Some weeks after that conversation, Joshua broached the subject again. The previous night they had gone to the Walt Disney Concert Hall, Los Angeles's world-class venue for music and home to the Los Angeles Philharmonic. Alex had purchased four tickets to see the L.A. Philharmonic perform Beethoven's Seventh Symphony and invited Fiona and, if she wanted, Joshua, whom he had not yet met, to join him and Mandy for the evening. Fiona, though a little hesitant about spending the evening with Mandy, was nevertheless thrilled and immediately phoned Joshua.

The two young people had both seen photos of the Disney Concert Hall in magazines and newspapers but were unprepared for the beauty of its design and the perfect acoustics of the hall itself. Seen from afar, the building looked like a cluster of great white sails on a sea, as though an armada of ships were floating in downtown Los Angeles. As the music began, Fiona and Joshua sank into an atmosphere in which they felt entirely at home. They were so used to coping at school and at their respective living quarters, making do with their feelings of not quite belonging, that they had almost forgotten what it was to feel completely at home. But here, in the world of classical music, every note as familiar to them as the sound of their own names, they were at ease. Wide-eyed and eared Fiona and Joshua took in everything their senses could process. At one point, Fiona leaned into Joshua and whispered, "Maybe you'll play here one day."

"Maybe you, too," he said back into her ear.

Fiona looked straight ahead and seemed not to hear him although he knew she had. The following day Fiona and Joshua discussed the concert by phone, admiring the skills of several of the musicians and the gifted conductor, Esa-Pekka Salonen. At a lull in the conversation, Joshua said, "You know, Fiona, there are very few kids our age who speak this way about music."

"Ay, I suppose," said Fiona cautiously.

"I was wondering about your training. You must have been very good…. Why did you stop?"

Fiona was silent for a moment, feeling herself on a precipice, wanting to pour her heart out to Joshua yet afraid that the floodgates of grief would overwhelm her. Her need to share her story won the day and she told him everything, from the moment she first heard an Irish fiddle to the day she threw her violin off the cliff. At the end of her story, Fiona cried.

"I'm sorry," she said through her tears. "I shouldn't have told you this."

"No, please don't think that," Joshua insisted. "I'm so glad you did. I understand exactly, and we don't have to speak about it again. I'm amazed that you are even willing to listen to me practice or go to a concert, knowing what that must mean for you, how it could remind you of those…those sad things. I won't suggest anything about you playing ever again. I promise. Okay?"

"Okay."

"And I hope you'll still come to the music room after school. Okay?"

"Okay," Fiona said, comforted in knowing that there was now at least one other person in the world who understood her actions that day on the cliff.

28

"What did you think of Fiona's friend?" Mandy asked as casually as she could although it seemed that every time she said Fiona's name, it came out strained.

"Seems a nice enough kid. Quiet type, I guess. Why do you ask?"

"I was just wondering. You know, you told me how much trouble Fiona has been having in school and how alienated she feels there."

"Yeah, so?" Alex began to feel uncomfortable with where the conversation was heading.

"Well, I just wondered if being friends with this boy would cause her further alienation. Him being from South Africa and all."

"What do you mean exactly?" Alex asked, his tone becoming more strident.

"I don't mean anything about race, for god's sake," Mandy said defensively. "I just mean, he seems kinda out of it compared to other boys their age. Like he's from another century."

"Well, she's sort of like that, too. At least she's found a friend. And he's apparently a gifted musician. They probably have a lot in common."

"No doubt," Mandy said, unable to contain the sarcasm in her voice.

Alex didn't respond as he didn't trust himself to be civil much longer. But he also began to wonder if Mandy had a point. He didn't like the picture that was forming in his mind of his daughter being ostracized in school and reduced to hanging out with the scholarship kid from South Africa. The next day he broached the subject with Joan.

"Get a grip, Alex," Joan said, irritated as hell.

"Hey, I just want what's best for her, Joan," Alex replied.

"What's best for her is that she has a new friend, a kid who seems very intelligent and must be phenomenally gifted to have been brought halfway around the world on a full scholarship to that snobby school."

"Yeah, you're probably right, Joan." He was defeated once again, though relieved.

They hung up but within a few minutes Joan called him back. "I was just thinking about the conversation we just had and wondered if those were really your concerns or if someone else had planted them in your head."

"You're asking if it was Mandy's idea, right?" Alex asked without beating around the bush.

"Yeah, because it didn't make sense otherwise. You've known for weeks that Fiona had a friend from South Africa on scholarship. The only thing new in the equation was that Mandy was with all of you last night."

"She was just trying to help," Alex said weakly. A total cliché that even he didn't believe.

"What's her phone number?" Joan blazed, her fury unleashed.

"Joan, no way. Just let it go. Please. I can't handle all the women in my life at each other's throats. Please, just let this go. Mandy won't have any influence on anything I do about Fiona. I give you my word."

"Then keep her the hell away from both of us or I will personally go to her house and you'll wish to god that I had phoned her instead," Joan practically shouted. "I'll talk to you later!" With that she slammed down the phone.

How could Alex be such an idiot when it came to women? In fact, how can men in general be such idiots? The only thing that twerp Mandy had going for her was that she was pretty. Pretty to men, Joan scoffed. Women could see through her in three seconds and it wasn't a pretty sight. When would her brother realize that what you need in a woman is someone *you can talk with*, someone *you trust*, someone *who doesn't hate your children*. No matter how great this girl/woman's body is or how many tricks she knows in bed, the actual time spent in bedroom activities is negligible, minutes compared to the thousands of hours one spends talking and negotiating the details of life. How can Alex, a businessman par excellence, not have done the math on this fact of life? They really do think with their dicks, Joan concluded, and unfortunately their dicks don't think that well.

A few minutes after Alex hung up the phone, his head began to pound as though spikes were being driven into it. He popped several Vicodin and stretched out on the couch in his office, telling his assistant to hold his calls. His life was spinning out of control. He was suddenly white hot in Hollywood. There were at least three huge deals awaiting his attention, stalled until he could decide which of them to do. The town was buzzing about the release of *Entropy,* and the press were at him every day.

Entertainment Weekly was talking about putting him on its cover with the headline, "The Platinum Touch." There were not enough hours in the day.

And now he had to deal with the wrath of his sister and keep her forever more away from Mandy. Joan had also said to keep Mandy away from Fiona—"Keep her the hell away from both of us"—which was going to be impossible. Though they rarely saw each other, there were times when Mandy and Fiona were both in the house. God, what a mess. Well, Joan would have to get over it because it would be eternal war if he told Mandy that she couldn't come over when Fiona was there. He would do his best to limit their contact, and they wouldn't be going on any more "double dates" with Fiona and her friend.

The damn Vicodin was taking too long to kick in this time. He was probably building a tolerance to the drug. He tried to use some relaxation techniques he had learned from one of his alternative health practitioners who told him to picture himself in a serene environment in which he had once felt relaxed. He visualized himself walking his property late at night with Blue, the smells of the night-blooming jasmine and lilacs accompanying them on the breeze. He reflected for a moment on why Blue had to be in the picture—why not just have himself walking around the property in the fragrant darkness?—when he realized that Blue actually had a calming effect on him and was therefore a necessary part of the visualization. With Blue he had the benefit of having a companion (of sorts) but none of the responsibility of having to be anyone in particular. Blue accepted him for the most fundamental reasons possible, that he *existed* and that he behaved in a relatively benign manner. Alex didn't have to be the boss, the creative director, the brother, the lover, the provisional father, the lord of the manor. He could be himself, just as if he were alone in the shower, and that was fine with Blue, who was still happy to keep him company. Joan often quoted a line from some famous dog lover: "The more I know of people, the more I like my dog." He now chuckled to himself. When he had first heard the sentiment he found it kind of pathetic, but at this particular moment, he was beginning to agree.

However, as an immediate counter to the quote, his thoughts turned to Fiona. What a mystery the relationship with her was for him. What a remarkable girl. If even half of what her mother wrote in that book was true, and knowing Aine he had no reason to think otherwise, Fiona was not only one of the most lovely people he had ever known but also one of the most talented. He wished there were some way to encourage her return to music, but he didn't dare suggest it. They were still too tentative with each other. Though they had made a real breakthrough in Hawaii, things had more or less reverted to the old patterns when they returned home. They rarely saw each other and lived together almost as anonymously as would two strangers in a large hotel. They occasionally made plans a day or two in advance to have a meal or go to a movie, but Fiona's weekday evenings were limited due to having to be in bed at a reasonable hour and his by work and the demands of his relationship with Mandy. He had offered to take Fiona away for a weekend now and then, but she never seemed to want to go, always preferring to be with Joan on weekends. Yet, things were warmer with Fiona. Though she continued to call him Alex, she smiled at him more often and even teased him now and again, a sure sign of affection in Alex's mind.

"Alex, say now, what are you using to bribe my dog into becoming a creature of the night with you?" she had recently asked.

"I don't have to bribe him. It's the call of the wild; he

comes on his own free will," Alex had cheerfully retorted as the two of them giggled at the foot of the stairs.

Yes, things were better between him and Fiona and, though there was strife with Mandy about it, his caring for his daughter increased by the day.

29

Joan had to decide what to do about the impending premiere of *Entropy* on Easter weekend. This was going to be a big one if all the hype around it had anything to do with its success. It was being talked and written about as Alex's breakout film and predicted to put him in league with Ron Howard or Quentin Tarantino. His name attached to a project would henceforth get made and almost always with a big studio budget. She had never missed one of his premieres, and this was the most important one to date.

But Joan couldn't bear the thought of being there with Mandy, having to watch as she preened and gleamed on Alex's arm, desperate for the cameras. Joan had managed to tolerate her when she first came into Alex's life, but with Mandy's obvious ill will toward Fiona she had crossed a line and there was no return. She would make an excuse for Fiona's sake, but Alex would know exactly why his sister would not be attending the premiere.

Resolute and calm about her decision, Joan went outdoors to water her garden, Hamlet at her side. She had been reflecting lately on the meaning of motherhood for she felt herself more in that role than she had ever dreamed. First of all, though it was probably silly to many people, she thought of herself as a mother to

Hamlet. Sometimes her friends or Alex would chide her when she chose Hamlet's comfort or happiness over her own, such as being unwilling to leave him alone at home for too long a time. She found it hard to explain that if she were out for an evening and too many hours had passed, she would know that Hamlet was missing her and there would be no pleasure for her in staying out any longer. Most people could understand those feelings about children but not about dogs. Alex had often used the word *limit* when he expressed concern over Joan's caretaking of Hamlet: "I just don't like to see you limit your life for the dog," he would say.

But *limit* was not at all the word she would apply to taking care of Hamlet—and now to taking care of Fiona. Instead Joan felt she was experiencing life at last. Though she had not given biological birth, she nevertheless felt like a mother, and it was the most meaningful role of her life. Now she found herself fiercely protective, a mother-tiger for Fiona, worried that Mandy would find ways to make Fiona's life difficult and that Alex would be too oblivious to notice.

Joan was also worried about Alex. The headaches seemed to be worsening and the drugs unable to alleviate the pain. Though he'd had brain scans, blood work, and a battery of other tests, Joan couldn't quite shake her anxiety about what could be causing the problem. Their mother had worked and worried herself to death. Joan remembered with a shudder that her mother had often complained of migraines when she got home from work. If only Alex would cut back. He had plenty of money now. He could retire and live well for the rest of his life. But Joan knew that it wasn't just about the money. She knew her brother's need for being on top of things, whatever his passion *du jour*. He would play out this Hollywood success story until he dropped, and there was little she could do about it.

The bonds of love, Joan decided, while noticing the new sprouts in her garden, were both the sweetest thing that life had to offer as well as its most terrifying.

Mandy went to Barney's and tried on almost every designer dress in her size before finding something suitable, a low-backed Versace that showed off her lean yoga muscles. She resented having to buy a dress for the premiere (even if Alex was paying for it) when all the other young actresses were courted by the big designers and offered original gowns made exclusively for them. Well, it would probably all change with her debut in *Entropy*. It was almost unbearably exciting to think about all the ways her life might soon change, and she lived in a state of agitated anticipation. She had given numerous television and print interviews already, and the press seemed to love her. "From the Runway to the Screen—A Young Beauty Lights Up the Outback" gushed Movietime Magazine. And there were even a few rumors in the tabloids about a possible affair between Rick Sole and Mandy on the set, which made the entertainment press all the more interested in her. Alex didn't seem to much mind these rumors since he knew they weren't true and because it was good for the film. But Mandy found herself wishing he would mind a bit more than he did.

She couldn't shake the feeling that Alex was losing interest in her. He had been remote for the past couple months, ever since his trip to Hawaii. She tried to attribute it to the work involved with getting out the film, his almost constant headaches, and the added pressures he now had in having to care for Fiona. But in her heart, she knew that the problem was about the way he now felt about her. Strangely, he seemed unaware of the changes in his responses to her, and she didn't think it wise to point them out. Why call attention to them? But for one thing, he didn't seem to want to have sex as often, and when he did, it was usually at her initiation. She hated to think of the times he had pled off with a headache. God, it was all backward. And here she was, now twenty-nine, no closer to anything solid with Alex than the day they met two years before. In fact, further away from whatever that lovely day had promised.

They had both attended a late afternoon garden party in the Hollywood hills at the home of a young director. Alex had helped the host find money for his most recent film and showed up, welcomed as the Great Facilitator, just as the sun was setting and the guests were invited indoors to screen the director's cut of the film. In what would become a moment that Mandy liked to replay in her mind, Alex chose the seat next to her even though there were plenty of others, better seats, from which to choose. As the guests milled about in the room, finding places and talking shop, Alex and Mandy said only a few words to each other. But Mandy was aware of an intense electricity between them, so distracting she could hardly pay attention to the film. Alex walked Mandy to her car as though it were his right and, after opening the door for her, asked for her number. He called later that night and they talked for an hour before reluctantly hanging up. They went to dinner the following evening, and by the third night Mandy stayed with Alex until morning. Over the next weeks, he canceled all appointments that would have taken him out of town, forwarded his calls to the office on weekends, and seemed never to tire of saying that the world looked more beautiful with Mandy in the foreground of his sight.

Remembering those days Mandy sighed as she got in her car, Barney's garment bag in hand. At least she had the premiere

to look forward to, and this time she would not be upstaged by
Fiona.

Fiona was also anticipating the premiere but for different
reasons. Since word had gotten out about *Entropy,* her status at
school had risen, and she was now being pursued by the cool kids
again. Sara Baxter, whose father was head of Global Securities,
invited Fiona to her birthday gala, which would include
entertainment by several big name comedians and musicians
performing on an outdoor stage at Sara's family estate in Bel Air.
It was a coveted invitation. Nevertheless, Sara made a point to say
to Fiona, "Bring your friend from South Africa, if you want.
Maybe he'd be willing to play his cello during the breaks." Fiona
had a strange feeling that Joshua's and her attendance had a price
attached, but she couldn't imagine what it could be. Certainly Sara
didn't care whether Joshua played his cello in the periods when the
other entertainment was on break. And I have nothing Sara
Baxter would need or want, thought Fiona.

Fiona knew that Sara and others at school had once hoped
for tickets to the premiere of her father's movie. It had all the
elements of a film that appealed to both adults and teens, a sci-fi
thriller set in a post-apocalyptic landscape that challenged the
viewers' beliefs about reality, using the latest generation of special
effects. It was even rumored that many scenes looked three
dimensional to the viewer. But Fiona had already told the kids
who had asked, including Sara Baxter, that she couldn't get
additional tickets. She had only one extra ticket—only because her
aunt had decided not to go—and Fiona had invited Joshua. Fiona
knew that hundreds of people in the business were trying to get
tickets to the premiere and that Alex was under an avalanche of

requests from everyone who had the slightest connection to the film: studio execs and their families, actors, writers, the crew, even the caterers, plus all the friends of friends and the usual list of press, film critics, and industry insiders. Alex had even wondered aloud to Fiona if he could spare the extra ticket for Joshua. "But that was Joan's ticket," Fiona protested. "She gave it to Joshua."

Alex heard the dismay in Fiona's voice and immediately backed down. Plus, Joan would kill him if he reneged on the ticket for Joshua.

Watching her father deal with so many people who wanted something from him made Fiona think that perhaps it was better not to have what others were denied. Otherwise, it seemed to make everyone unhappy, even the ones who had the thing desired. She thought that her father, though charged on a strange force of energy, seemed unusually anxious and distracted. And Fiona was getting her own bitter taste of being a have in a sea of have-nots, pursued for reasons other than friendship and having to say no to her petitioners.

30

The Saturday of Sara Baxter's party in late March was cool and crisp. Fiona and Joshua arrived within minutes of each other, both of them seemingly early as they had come at the time listed on the invitation, unaware that the party would not really get going for another hour. Sara Baxter and her older sister greeted them wearing mini-skirts that barely covered the mounds of their buttocks, despite the cool of the day. Sara led Joshua to where she wanted him to set up his cello, a spot on the grass near the stage. "Would you mind playing as the guests arrive?" Sara asked.

"No, not at all," Joshua replied.

Fiona felt uneasy and hung around while Joshua took his cello and bow out of their cases and warmed up a little. He then began by playing the first and last movements of the Haydn C Major cello concerti, alternating them with jazz tunes of Thelonius Monk and Miles Davis. Sara brought the two of them punch from the largest crystal bowl Fiona had ever seen and winked as she handed two glasses to Fiona, one for her and one for Joshua when he got a chance.

"It tastes funny," Fiona said.

"It's spiked," Sara laughed.

"What's that?" Fiona asked.

"Oh god, you really are from the moon!" Laughing harder. "It's got a little rum in it. My sister punched it up while no one was looking. That's why it's called punch."

Fiona nodded and pretended to take another sip, knowing that she would toss the contents of both glasses into the grass as soon as Sara walked away. Mercifully, a group of kids arrived and Sara was off to greet them.

After about an hour, a band of African-American guys in sweat suits began to assemble on stage, a rap group whose name Joshua recognized from seeing posters around town. He stopped playing, put his cello in its case underneath one of the serving tables, and joined Fiona on the grass near the front of the stage as the band set up and began playing. Fiona and Joshua quickly realized that they were way too close to the speakers as the roar engulfed them. The music was nothing more than simplistic pounding on the instruments, and the lead rapper's words were almost incomprehensible, but what could be made out from them were sentiments Joshua wished Fiona didn't have to hear about the activities of "pimpin', niggas, and ho's." Worse still, the guy placed his hand on his crotch every time a new line came out of his mouth, as though he had to wind up his private parts to get a word out. Fiona averted her eyes, staring at the grass, and after a few minutes, Joshua spoke loudly in her ear, "Would you like to take a walk around the grounds?"

Fiona mouthed YES, relieved for a rescue.

They made their way through the crowd as other kids pushed in to take their places closer to the band.

"Let's get as far away as possible from that racket," Joshua said.

"To Japan!" Fiona laughed.

The two friends walked briskly to the opposite end of the large estate, down a series of steps into a rose garden, the sounds of the band fading almost entirely.

They plopped on a bench overlooking the garden, a little out of breath, and didn't speak for several minutes.

"I will never fit in here," Fiona said.

"Nor I," Joshua agreed.

"But you won't have to. You'll be going back to South Africa soon." Fiona didn't conceal the sadness in her statement.

"Not for two more months."

"That's pretty soon," Fiona noted. "Do you think you'll come back next year?"

"Well, the Paleys offered to host me until high school graduation. They're very nice to me and I'm grateful for all they've done, but I think I had better leave for good. Even though my opportunities for music are limited in South Africa, I don't think America's a good place for me. I've been meaning to talk with you about this. I haven't entirely decided yet, but I don't think I'll be returning here next year, although there is one thing about living here that I will greatly miss, something I could never replace no matter where I go in the world." He stole a sideways glance at the nicest and prettiest girl in the world.

Fiona sensed his gaze and felt the sting of tears filling her eyes but managed to keep them from rolling down her cheeks. Just then, the band stopped playing, the faint noise in the distance going to silence.

"I guess that's my cue to get out the cello again," Joshua said, mindful that he had agreed to play on breaks and that perhaps it was best to end their conversation. "It will probably be a most unwelcome change for the audience," he joked in an old world accent.

They returned to the original place on the grass, picking up the cello under the table on the way. As Joshua began to play, Sara, who was standing with a group of girls, caught Fiona's eye and motioned for her to come over. Fiona walked across the grass as the other girls backed a short distance away.

"Are you enjoying the party, Fiona?" Sara asked.

"Ay. I mean yes," Fiona answered awkwardly. The one thing she was enjoying about that party was Joshua, so she figured it wasn't a total lie.

"Good, 'cause I was hoping we could become friends," Sara said.

"Okay," Fiona said, wanting to be finished with this talk but feeling there was more to come. Fiona glanced behind her at the group of girls who were ineffectively pretending not to be watching but were clearly in on something with Sara.

"I was wondering, you know the ticket you were going to give to Joshua for the premiere…" Sara began.

"Yes?'

"Well, why not give it to me instead? After all, I've invited you to my party, and there were lots of kids who wanted to come and didn't get to. I think it would be only fair if you paid me back."

At first Fiona tried to accept the logic of this statement on face value, but she knew there was something terribly wrong with it.

"But I invited Joshua weeks ago. I already explained that to you in school."

"You could change it and take me instead. I mean, Fiona, when are you going to figure out that we don't hang out with the help? You've got a lot to learn about living here, and I could teach you."

At first Fiona didn't understand what Sara meant, but as it came clear to her, realizing the girls in the group behind her were now openly staring at them and giggling, she began to feel her entire body quiver. Without another word, Fiona turned and ran to Joshua, the tears she had held back in the rose garden now streaming down her face. Joshua saw her coming in the mid-distance across the lawn and stopped playing, putting down his cello.

"Please, can you leave with me?" Fiona gushed in panic. "I don't know how to get away from here, and Gwen is not due for two more hours."

"Do you have your cell phone with you?" Joshua asked.

"Yes, but it will take her too long to come, and I don't want to wait here," Fiona cried.

"Don't worry." Joshua quickly packed up his cello. Holding it under one arm and gently taking Fiona's hand with his free one, he walked her across the lawn, past Sara and the group of girls and out of the Baxter estate. As soon as they were through the gates, he phoned a cab on Fiona's cell phone. "Where shall we go? To your aunt's or to your dad's?"

"My aunt's house is too far to go in a taxi. We'll have to go to Alex's."

Once in the car, Fiona told Joshua about her conversation with Sara, the initial shock and hurt turning to anger. Joshua remained silent and held Fiona's hand as he thought about what Sara's words implied about him. His father had not been right about all white people, but he was right about some of them.

Alex was talking on the phone and gazing out of the window in his study when the taxi pulled into the driveway and

Fiona and Joshua got out, Joshua lugging his cello. From the look on Fiona's face, Alex knew that something must have happened and, ending his call, quickly went outside to meet the teenagers.

"I thought Gwen was picking you up and taking you to Joan's. What happened?" Alex asked, walking toward them as Joshua paid the cab fare.

"We didn't like the party, so we left early," Fiona said, not wanting to go into details.

Alex nodded, hands on hips, and decided not to press her. "Okay. You must take after me, Fiona. I hate parties." He turned to go back in the house. "I'll call Gwen and let her know not to go back for you. How 'bout a coke, you two?"

"Yes, thank you," Joshua replied. "I haven't had anything to drink for hours." Carefully standing his cello case against the wall in the foyer, Joshua followed Fiona and Alex into the kitchen.

Bill Evans's "Time Remembered" emanated from the speakers as Joshua drank his coke with one hand and drummed his fingers on the kitchen counter with the other.

"Do you ever play jazz?" Alex asked

"I do," Joshua replied.

"I'd like to hear you sometime."

Joshua didn't know what came over him; perhaps he wanted to brighten Fiona's mood or perhaps he felt obligated to Alex for the promised ticket to the film premiere. Whatever the reason, Joshua nodded toward his cello in the nearby hallway and asked, "How 'bout now?"

"Now's good," Alex said, smiling.

For the next two hours, Joshua accompanied some of the greatest jazz artists of all time as Alex played favorites from his CD collection on speakers throughout the house and danced with Fiona around the kitchen. Joshua, who turned out to be one hot cellist, jammed with the best of them, taking off on improvised riffs that reminded Alex of Eric Friedlander.

Wow!" Alex kept saying, shaking his head. It was the most fun he'd had in a long time.

31

Joan watched from her porch one morning as a DHL truck rolled down her driveway in a cloud of dust. The only other time DHL had come to her house was to deliver a box of garden tools that Alex had special ordered from Denmark. She suspected that this was another expensive European gift from her brother.

But she was wrong. As the driver handed her the long narrow box, asking for her signature, Joan noticed the return address on the label. It was from Maria Girardi. It's the bow, thought Joan. She brought the box into the house and set it on her kitchen table. It was heavy, made of wood, and would require tools to open. Joan heated a pot of green tea and sat down with the morning paper. She needed to relax before embarking on the project of getting into that box. She would approach it almost with reverence, as though she were opening a container of ancient spiritual artefacts.

An hour later, hammer in hand, she pulled all the nails from the lid of what turned out to be only the outer box. There was also an inner wooden box, surrounded by packing. Those Italians sure do know how to pack an instrument, Joan thought as she worked. Removing the last of the packing, Joan noticed an envelope taped to the inner box. "To Joan and Alex," it read. She opened and read the letter, hearing in her mind Maria Girardi's voice.

Now I send what is Fiona's back to her. Time will one day release most of her grief and she will again play the violin with the beautiful bow from her mother. This I am sure.
Maria Girardi O'Shaunnessy

At the end of the letter were the details of Maria Girardi's new address and phone number in Rome. She had returned to her homeland and family.

Joan phoned Alex and told him the news of the bow and of Maria's letter and prediction.

"I hope she's right," Alex said. "For now, let's just keep the bow in its box and safely hidden."

"Agreed," said Joan. "I'll drop Maria a note and thank her."

Joshua sprawled under a tree in the Paley's backyard, watching the sky through the branches. Lying under a tree was a favorite pastime of his at school in Johannesburg, a place for him to think. He now needed to make an important decision about his future. Fred Paley and he had talked until late the previous night about his options for the coming years. Fred hoped that Joshua would consider staying on for at least one more year at The Santa Monica Academy. "It is prestigious in the world of music, as you know," Fred had said. "From here, with your talent, you could easily get into Juliard for your final year if you wanted. I know that for a young person such as yourself, a few years seems like forever, but when you're a little older you'll realize that a few years' sacrifice for a long term goal is no big deal."

Joshua thought about Mr. Paley's words and considered them as deeply as he could. It was true that he was young and probably didn't fully understand the importance of decisions, how a turn at a juncture could influence one's life forever. Older people all seemed to agree on this point, and though Joshua was inclined to listen to his elders, he could find no peace in his heart at the thought of returning to America the following year. He didn't want to attend either The Santa Monica Academy or Juliard. He didn't belong in this harsh country. As he lay under the tree, he imagined his future in South Africa. He would likely be part of a company that played in Jo'berg, Durban, and Cape Town. He would probably teach music and biology, perhaps at his old school. His family would want him to marry one of the girls from their old township, someone whose family was friends with his own. These prospects did not uplift him; he felt only a quiet resignation. He would have preferred to study music in Europe and see where fate would take him, but opportunity had knocked in America and he doubted it would knock twice. He had to face reality as a poor boy from a poor country. He would probably never play in or even see the great music halls of Europe. He also knew in those moments under the tree that he would forever be haunted by what might have been.

What might have been. He closed his eyes and thought of Fiona. Sometimes he wished he had never laid eyes on her. No other girl would compare. And though he had not heard her play an instrument, he knew that she understood music as well as he. Her comments and suggestions were more brilliant and innovative than most of his teachers', their afternoons in the music room an enchanted world of the classics. They had become best friends but, of course, it was also something else, a feeling most mysterious to him. He couldn't bear the thought of saying good-bye to her. He would never be able to forget Fiona.

Joshua stood and brushed his pants. His father had taught him not to succumb to sentimentality and feelings of loss. "Keep moving forward, son. Don't spend too much time looking behind. Mostly only sadness there." Joshua would go to the premiere with Fiona next week and would enjoy her company as much as he could in the time they had left. But he would have to put her behind him when he returned to South Africa. Though they were as one in some ways, they would soon live in entirely different worlds.

32

Fiona heard the doorbell just as Giovanni, a makeup artist Alex had hired, put the finishing touches on her lips.

"I've kept it all as natural as possible since you hardly need anything. We've just enhanced your beautiful green eyes with a little shading and eyeliner and added a slight bit of color to your lips. You're gorgeous!" Giovanni stood back and admired his work.

Fiona, sitting in a green silk slip, her hair falling loosely around her shoulders, looked at herself in the mirror and laughed. She had never worn makeup, and at first the effect seemed almost clownish, but then she realized that it was actually quite subtle and made her look suddenly grown up. As if to second the opinion, Blue, who had been sitting at attention while watching the procedure, barked twice, prompting his newly transformed mistress to reassure him with hugs that she was still herself.

"Thank you, Giovanni," Fiona said shyly. She couldn't get used to all the fuss being made about her and how she looked. She thought of the few times she had seen her mother apply makeup, removing from her dresser the treasured little compacts, liners, and containers purchased from Boots Pharmacy on Grafton Street in Dublin. Fiona remembered the wonder she felt whenever her mother used the magical wands and colors and tried to imagine a time that she herself, when she was grown, would know what to do with those things.

As Giovanni left the room, Fiona carefully put on her dress, an emerald green velvet creation by a new young designer, fitted through the bodice, and flaring at the three-quarter-length hem. Alex had sent Fiona shopping with Roxanne, a stylist he had employed in several films. They found the dress at a boutique on Montana Avenue in Santa Monica, along with a matching raw silk shawl embroidered with tiny beads and pearls. Roxanne showed Fiona several ways to wear the shawl and had come by to practice one last time earlier that afternoon.

Facing the mirror, Fiona arranged the shawl on her shoulder. She looked to herself like a stylish fairy princess and twirled several times, making the flair of her skirt wave like that of a Greek dancer's before floating down the stairs to meet Joshua. Standing in the foyer and very handsome in a dark blue suit borrowed from Fred Paley, Joshua bowed and extended his hand to the vision on the stairs, "M'lady, may I escort thee to the ball?"

"It's just a premiere," Fiona laughed, suddenly realizing that she sounded in that moment a little too Hollywood for her own taste. Just a premiere, indeed!

The four of them emerged from the limo into a dozen flashing lights outside the Mann Bruin Theater in Westwood. Alex had prepped Fiona about getting directly to their seats in case he got hung up with reporters, which of course he did. Mandy made sure this time to stay snugly on Alex's arm and was grateful that the South African kid was along to keep Fiona company so that those two could go ahead of them into the theater. As she stood smiling her brightest for the reporters and cameras, Mandy caught Rick Sole in her peripheral vision. On his arm was Lola Lal, his co-star in *Entropy*, with whom he seemed unusually intimate that night. Mandy felt a pang of jealousy. She hadn't spoken to Rick since the night she'd had to let him down easy over dinner when he wanted to have the big talk with her. Still, seeing him with Lola stirred something unpleasant in her.

Everyone eventually took their seats in the theater and for the next hundred and twenty minutes were transported into another time and a very different place. The new special effects that approximated 3-D made the audience gasp each time they occurred, the setting was one of the most unusual ever seen on screen, and the story had everyone on the edge of their seats. At the end of the film, the entire audience leapt to their feet for one of the longest standing ovations anyone could remember. It was going to be a very big hit.

Alex could barely get out of the room through the deluge of people wanting to talk with him, shake his hand, congratulate him. Studio heads put their cards into his palm and said simply, "Call me." Beautiful women slithered by with "come hither" nods deliberately oblivious to Mandy's glare. People pressed in on him from all sides, and he felt as though at any moment they might lift him into the air like some jock who had just made the winning touchdown.

His head was killing him. He felt momentarily dizzy but tried not to let it show. They were due at the premiere party at the Beverly Wilshire Hotel in half an hour but Alex now doubted that he could make it. Helplessly he looked at Mandy, "I'm not feeling well," he managed to say. "Maybe we should skip the party and go home."

"Alex, don't be ridiculous. This is your night! It's only five minutes down Wilshire. You can take a Vicodin when we get there."

Alex could barely shake his head no as the pain intensified and blurred his vision, forcing him to focus instead on simply staying upright. Turning to find Fiona, he held his hand out to her to steady himself. Fiona immediately saw that her father was unwell and rushed to his side, discreetly using her weight to support him and saying to Joshua, "Tell them to bring the car right away."

As Joshua ran to the car attendants, Alex turned to Mandy, weakly: "You go on without me. I'll meet you at home."

The limo pulled up and Alex climbed into the vehicle, Joshua and Fiona blocking curious eyes around them and getting in behind. Mandy stood bewildered and alone at the curb just as Rick and Lola walked up to another waiting limo.

This really sucks, Mandy thought. Really, really sucks.

"Mandy, do you need a ride to the party?" Rick asked in a friendly manner as Lola snuggled into his neck and cameras flashed. "You can ride with us."

"Yeah, thanks, Rick," Mandy answered, unable to hide her frustration and mortified with embarrassment. "Alex has one of his damn headaches."

A few days later, on Good Friday, *Entropy* opened on over 4,000 screens, grossing $90 million during Easter weekend and remaining number one at the box office for the following five weeks.

33

At Joan's insistence, Alex agreed to take some time off and decided to combine it with fulfilling his promise to Mandy to take her on a trip anywhere she wanted. Unfortunately, Mandy chose New York City, not what Joan had in mind as a rest for him, but a deal's a deal.

Mandy was flying high on recognition from strangers and from anyone she had ever known who had seen *Entropy,* and she couldn't wait to be seen in New York. As far as Mandy was concerned, the only places on the planet that mattered were New York and Los Angeles, and she had already dazzled everyone in L.A.

She planned every detail of their trip. They would stay at The Mercer in Soho, attend the opening night of David Hair's new play, eat at Nobu and The Spice Market, take in some jazz at the Blue Note, and hang at Balthazar's till two in the morning. They would see "Yatra," John Bush's series of films on Asia at the Reuben Museum, and attend a Larry Gagosian gallery opening in Chelsea. And they would go shopping. Lots of shopping.

Knowing that Joshua would be going back to South Africa soon, Joan and Fiona made plans of their own. Joshua had once mentioned that he had never seen snow, so Fiona suggested that they take him to a beautiful snowy place.

"Well, it's early May," said Joan, thinking out loud. "But there's still plenty of snow in Alaska."

"That sounds wonderful," Fiona said. Visions of polar bears and dramatic icecaps. "I'm sure Joshua has never been anywhere that looks like Alaska."

"Unlike you, eh, world traveler?" Joan said, teasingly.

Fiona laughed and shook her finger at Joan. "I didn't mean I had been everywhere."

Although Fiona looked forward to the coming trip to Alaska with Joan and Joshua, she lived with deep foreboding about what was to become of her life in the coming few years. Since Sara's party the situation at school had further deteriorated. She and Joshua had retreated more deeply into the sanctuary of their friendship, spending not only afternoons in the music room but taking their lunches there as well. Because they couldn't talk of future plans or any context in which they would ever be together again, they spoke mostly of music, comparing notes on contemporary composers such as Lutoslavsky and Xenakis, or discussing famous recordings of *The Rite of Spring* by Igor Stravinsky conducted by Pierre Boulez for The Cleveland Orchestra versus the rendition by the Columbia Symphony Orchestra conducted by the composer himself. When the conversation about music had exhausted itself, Joshua would play something they had discussed or they would fall silent. It became a strange meditation for the two of them, these last days together filled with music, talk of music, and silence. Fiona knew that Joshua was pained by their imminent good-bye, but she wondered if he knew that she was the one who would most suffer. She would be left in this lonely place and have to endure it with no end in sight. She once asked him what he thought of the possibility of her attending public school the following year. His answer was similar to that of Joan's: "It seems to me the public schools here are nothing more than custodial institutions for the poor."

They chose Glacier Bay National Park as their destination in Alaska. Glacier Bay, a geologic wonder amid shorelines and islands, was completely covered by ice only two hundred years previously. Some of the glaciers had melted since that time, and now the land near the mouth of the bay was forested with spruce and hemlock. The area was known for its marine life of humpback, minke and orca whales, harbor seals, porpoises, and otters, as well as its land mammals of moose, bears, wolves, and coyotes. Fiona thought it the perfect place for Joshua to experience before returning to South Africa, "the polar opposite" she had joked with Joan.

They chartered a plane from Juneau to Gustavus where Joan had booked rooms in a lodge about ten miles from the park. Flying into Gustavus, straddling the 15,000-foot snowcapped mountain range, reminded Joan of the time she had flown with Aine and Alex into Nepal from Benares along the rim of the Himalayas. Now looking back on that time, only fourteen years past, she seemed to herself almost a youngster then. So much had happened in the intervening years. Fiona, here and fully formed, a budding young woman, did not even yet exist. Aine, then a full person in her own right, now ceased to exist. Joan gazed at the strata of the glaciers and considered the expanse of time stretching in all directions, bookends of infinity around every mark of existence. These glaciers, all that we are seeing, all that we are, will someday be gone, thought Joan. A shiver ran through her. It was a bit chilly in this small plane.

She glanced back at her two young charges sitting on opposite sides of the aircraft in the two-seated row behind her. They were peering out of Fiona's window, excitedly pointing at a herd of mountain goats at the foot of the snowy peaks below, just as the plane dipped into its descent for the runway.

Prior to his trip Joshua had read up on Glacier Bay in particular and Alaska in general. He had a vague understanding of its delicate and complicated eco-systems and the threats to the local wildlife and their habitats. Some areas, such as Glacier Bay National Park, were protected, but much of Alaska was open for business for the oil-hungry hoards below. Joshua put these thoughts behind him as he emerged from the plane into one of the most spectacular natural environments he had ever seen. He stood with eyes closed facing the sun, feeling a strange icy wind that seemed to carry on its wings snowy essence from the mountains nearby.

They checked into their rooms and within an hour were bundled up and on their way to the National Park. Joan hired a boat to take them around the bay. Within minutes in the open water they saw a moose on the shore, its large network of antlers indicating that it was male. Their guide cut the engine and let the boat drift as closely as possible before the moose ambled away. Fiona had never seen such a large creature in the wild and couldn't decide if she should be excited or alarmed. They had come fairly close to him and in somewhat shallow water. Could he attack? Joshua squeezed her hand in quiet assurance; she imagined this was no big deal for him since he was used to elephants and lions roaming around. But, in fact, Joshua was pretty impressed with the moose.

The guide parked the boat at a small tie-up near a trailhead and they disembarked and entered a nearby trail in single file, the two females in the middle. After a time they were in deep forest with no sense that water was nearby. The treetops were still covered in snow and the underbrush was wet and in some places muddy. Fiona imagined herself in an enchanted forest, and as they silently walked she entered a world of fantasy, far back in time, Joshua and Joan, her beloved fellow journeyers and their trusted guide leading them to a Holy Grail. When they arrived at their destination, Fiona popped out of her reverie, almost embarrassed by her thoughts. Blimey, they are the thoughts of a child, she chided herself.

But Fiona also knew that many of her thoughts of late were certainly not those of a child. More often she found herself in strange territory within her mind, especially with regard to Joshua wherein her imagination had been activated in unfamiliar ways. She often daydreamed of the sensations she felt whenever he held her hand, the curious way that his simply touching her fingers produced shivers throughout the rest of her body and in places she had never experienced such sensations before. She thought about the way he always smelled, like fresh laundry, like a spring mornin', as her mother would have said. She imagined slow dancing with him. She imagined kissing him.

Bartlett Lake stretched before them. Neither Fiona nor Joshua had seen a glacier lake and were astonished by its color. "Crystal blue, just like the guidebook says," noted Joshua. The guide lowered his pack and took out sandwiches and bottles of water to share. They were all hungry by this time and though the food was not up to Joan's organic standards (in fact it seemed to consist of commercial store-bought sandwich meat of dubious origin), they wolfed it down and helped themselves to seconds.

Suddenly a small brown bear appeared on the other side of the lake. The guide pointed it out for them and then kept his eye on it, even as they asked him questions. As a larger bear appeared, the guide said it was time to go. "Don't rush or panic. They're on the other side, at least a mile away. And I do have a stun gun, if needed."

It was thrilling. As they quietly walked back through the forest to the safety of their boat, Fiona at one point tickled Joshua and whispered in a playful growl, "You have lions, *we* have *bears.*"

After dinner that night they sat by the fire in the main lodge, talking and laughing about their day in the wild. As it was early spring in Alaska, there were few guests in the lodge and all the others had retired to their rooms. After an hour or so, Joan began to yawn.

"I think I'll turn in," she said. "Fiona, I'll leave a light on in our room if you want to stay down here a little while. But don't be too long. We're getting up early tomorrow for another hike."

"Okay," Fiona replied. "I'll be up soon."

Joan figured she would go to the room, get ready for bed, and wait until she heard Fiona come in before letting herself fall asleep. She trusted the two youngsters but had a great respect for the power of teenage hormones. She would also keep a sharp listen out for any movement in Joshua's room adjacent to their own. How ironic that she, who had always been a champion of sexual freedom, found herself in the awkward role of guardian and, in a sense, third wheel to Romeo and Juliet downstairs. They don't know it, they don't understand it, but these two young people are in love, she thought. What a poignant and impossible match. He would return to South Africa and it was unlikely they would meet again, at least in any context like this, where the rest of the world was only a backdrop for them. Fiona, almost fourteen, and Joshua, going on fifteen. They were so very young. Is it possible that at such tender ages they could be for each other what no one else ever would?

At that very moment, Joshua and Fiona, by the fire downstairs were laughing at Fiona's fright at having just seen a mouse scurry across the floor near their feet.

"You were more scared of the mouse than you were of the bears," Joshua teased.

Fiona playfully shoved him. Even that, the touch associated with a shove, was electrifying to both of them. They soon stopped giggling and looked quietly into each other's faces, realizing the full significance of their situation. Alone in a cozy room by a fire in a faraway snowy place. Their faces drew closer to each other until their lips were almost touching. Joshua hesitated, then surrendered. They kissed for a full minute, a timeless eternity that left both of them dizzy.

"I guess we'd better go up now," he said afterward, not trusting himself to kiss her for a second time, not wanting to ever stop kissing her.

"Ay. Joan will be waiting for me," Fiona said shyly. She reached out her hand, and they went upstairs to their respective rooms.

34

Joan phoned Joshua at the Paley's the evening after they returned from Alaska.

"Josh, I wanted to talk with you about something. I overheard you and Fiona on the way home talking about when you would be going back to South Africa."

"Yes, I have to leave two days after school ends. My father has arranged a job for me, and I am also due to start school there."

"Josh, is there any way you could delay your departure by a week to be here for Fiona's birthday? You probably know that Fiona's mother died the day after her last birthday and, well, her life has been in such upheaval this year that we wanted to make this birthday as wonderful as possible. I was hoping you could attend a party for her, a very small one, just the family, really."

Joshua immediately agreed. "I'll email my father and work it out. I'm sure he will let me postpone a week."

Relieved, Joan hung up and then called Alex who was home recovering from his New York vacation with Mandy. Lying in bed with closed eyes and an ice pack on his head, he heard the special ring that had been programmed for Joan and Fiona's exclusive use. Since Fiona was outside on the lawn with Blue, Alex knew it was his sister and hesitated before answering, something he had never done before. He was in too much pain to talk, and he also didn't want to hear about the stupidity of using his precious vacation time to run around New York with Mandy and further exhaust himself, even though Joan was right.

He sat up and looked at the Caller ID. Sure enough. Joan.

"Hey Sis, my head is killing me," Alex said, hoping to ward off unpleasant big-sisterly recriminations.

"Oh, Alex. Have you taken anything?"

"Yeah, I'm virtually pickled with drugs. A vial of my blood in some poor sucker's car would probably be enough for a drug bust, except, of course, they're all legal drugs in my system— or mostly. What's up?"

"I wanted to start making plans for Fiona's birthday party. I think Joshua will stay an extra week to be here, and I thought we could do something special. Just wanted to brainstorm with you a little."

"If I had a working brain, that would be fine, but I don't. I'm open to whatever you want to do. Make it grand. Just tell me what you need," Alex said, wanting to hang up.

"Well, I had hoped you'd help me plan it, but okay, since you've exhausted yourself, never mind. I'll figure it out on my own."

"Tell you what, Joan. Leave the presents to me. You do the party side,"

"Okay, done."

Fiona threw Blue's tennis ball into the shallow part of the pool and watched as he leapt in to fetch it. Blue loved the water (it's the Lab in him, Joan always said) and Fiona knew that Alex liked for Blue to get into the pool on a regular basis to stay clean.

No matter how many times she threw the ball, Blue was happy to leap into the water. Fiona sometimes wondered if he would do this all day, but she was never inclined to test him longer than it took for him to get out of breath. He seemed to so love the game that even when he was tired, after half an hour of constant pool fetching, it was only with reluctance that he would give up the ball and let her towel dry him.

Fiona plopped onto a lounge chair and Blue curled up next to it in the sun, his fur still damp. Within minutes he was snoring as Fiona dreamily noticed the bursting garden that surrounded her. She hadn't been to Alex's in a week, and the plants and flowers had filled in dramatically since that time. Summer was almost here. Her thoughts drifted lazily to Ireland. It might still be very chilly there, even rainy, but the impending summer would permeate the air and everyone's mood. *Top of the mornin', Moira Keaton, may the road rise to meet ya*. Fiona could almost hear her mother's voice. But she mustn't think about her mother right now. She had best concentrate on the living.

Yet even thoughts of the living could be troublesome. She pictured Alex, lying sick in his room. He was getting worse. The night of the premiere had scared her more than she could let on to anyone. She didn't dare mention it to Joan as she knew her aunt was already so very worried. For some reason, she found it hard to discuss anything personal with Alex, plus she sensed that he didn't want to talk about the headaches. She was vaguely aware that he was seeing doctors, and knowing Alex, he was seeing the best in the world. But doctors didn't know everything. She was sure of that. She felt frightened and forced her thoughts elsewhere. To Joshua, her best friend in the world, the smartest, most talented, and, yes, most handsome boy she had ever met. Their time in Alaska was brilliant. Even Joan said it was one of the best trips of her life. And Joshua had been so appreciative, thanking them over and over and writing an eloquent letter to Alex in appreciation for his sponsoring the trip. She would never forget their last morning in Glacier Bay when he lingered after breakfast to speak his solemn words to her, as though he had rehearsed them in his mind: "I will always remember how beautiful you are against a backdrop of snow, Fiona. Like a rose in a field of white."

But Joshua would be leaving her as well. There was no safe place for her thoughts to land. She had to let them go as they came. She stretched her arm from the lounge to rest her hand on the warm sleeping Blue, her eyes moist with memories and forebodings.

35

Alex was about to make a large expenditure and for that he would do the research himself. He began his homework by studying eighteenth-century violinmakers of Italy, France, and Germany and settled on the Italian masters whose skill, it was agreed by all in the know, was unsurpassed. Naturally, the Italian violins of that period were the most expensive in the world, a Stradivarius in excellent condition, for instance, now going for about $2 million.

Eventually he phoned Maria Girardi in Rome for consultation. Though they had never met, they talked for over an hour about Fiona, violins, and life transitions.

"Places one has known or lived in long ago grow smaller when one has been away. But in time, smaller is better, I think," she had mused. Alex assumed this meant that she was happy to be back in Italy.

Suddenly Maria had an idea. "Call me in two days," she said mysteriously, and hung up.

Two days later, Alex phoned back. "I've found the violin," she said excitedly. "It is a Tononi made in 1715 and rumored to have once been played by Vivaldi himself. It is expensive—about

€200,000—owned by a dealer in Paris. If you are interested, I will go and play it before you purchase."

"I'm interested," said Alex. "How can I thank you?"

"I do this for Fiona. Ciao," Maria said unceremoniously, and once again hung up the phone.

Alex liked the no-nonsense quality of this woman.

In the next couple weeks, he read everything he could find on the violinmaker Carlo Tononi and Tononi violins. Born in 1675, Tononi grew up in Bologna, Italy where he worked in his family's business making stringed instruments until 1713. He then moved to Venice, the center of stringed instrument workshops and what was known as the new Venetian School, of which Tononi was one of its foremost masters. In current time a Tononi was regarded by other violinmakers as one of the finest and most artistic instruments and was favored by chamber music players for its "introspective" qualities. That certainly fits Fiona, Alex thought when he read the words.

He phoned Joan after he'd made the purchase and arranged for shipping from Paris.

"I'm having it sent to your house," he told her.

"Good, I'll wrap the bow and violin in separate boxes. I've pretty much organized everything for the party. And Joshua is offering us a private concert."

"Fantastic." Alex looked forward to hearing Joshua play again.

"Wouldn't it be amazing if Fiona joined him in playing?" Joan wondered out loud.

"Hmmm. We'll just have to see." Alex, ever the pragmatist, didn't want to inflate his sister's hopes. But, of course, he too was counting on something just like that to happen. After all, he hadn't just spent €200,000 on a whim.

Meanwhile, Joshua pondered what he would give Fiona for her birthday. It had to represent how he felt, but that was impossible. It had to remind her of him when he was gone, but that was also impossible. He had once studied Tibetan religious principles in his school in South Africa. Some of their most sacred art was made to last only a short while in the form of large images called *mandalas* made of fine grains of colored sand, carefully dripped from dispensers, a few grains at a time, and taking months or years to complete. After a relatively short period on display, a high lama would ceremoniously brush through the image, and other monks would then sweep the entire thing away. This custom signified the impermanence of all things. When Joshua learned of the practice, he felt confused and thought it an exercise in pointlessness. But he was beginning to understand the wisdom of it.

He decided he would compose a musical piece especially for Fiona. He would convey his delight in knowing her, indeed, his relief. He would tell her through music how lovely she was, and he would want the sounds to lift her and remind her of her own strength. He would let the strings offer his gratitude for making him laugh and think and cry like no one he had ever known. And he would let her know that though they would be a world apart, he would never forget her.

Joshua took his cello into the Paley's backyard. Setting up an encampment under the tree, he worked for five straight hours, producing one of the most beautiful cello compositions that would ever be played only once. He made no written notes but let his body record every movement as though he had played it a hundred times. When he finished practicing, he went inside to dinner, letting the music continue to refine itself in his mind as new and deeper feelings emerged.

Fiona knew something was afoot for her birthday. On the last day of school Joshua told her that he was postponing his departure in order to attend her party. Joan had said it was to be a small family affair, but Fiona sensed that Alex had something up his sleeve. Whatever it was, she would be gracious. As hard as this time would be—she didn't think her birthday would ever again be a happy occasion—she didn't want to burden the few people who loved her with her unhappiness. And she also didn't want her last time with Joshua to be a sad one in his memory. In a moment of generosity, she even suggested to Alex that he invite Mandy, though she knew it meant keeping Blue in the bedroom all night, which would greatly displease him.

"That's very nice of you, Fiona." Alex replied. Very politic as well, he thought. He had been worried about recriminations he faced from Mandy if she was excluded from Fiona's party. Of course, he might face Joan's wrath over Mandy's attendance, but since Fiona had invited her, Joan would have to go along with it. He made a mental note to talk with Mandy about behaving herself.

"I'd also like to invite the Paleys," Fiona added. "If that's okay."

"Absolutely," Alex replied. She's so considerate, he thought. Must get it from her mother, or her aunt.

36

Cynthia, the party planner, hung small blue and white lights on tree branches and bushes as one of the caterers set the table. Earlier in the day she had attached a hundred large white balloons to stones on the grounds in front and back. She was putting party favors of orange-scented soap and candles next to each plate when Joan arrived.

"It's lovely," Joan said in admiration. Cynthia thanked her and said she would be on her way. The caterer went back inside, leaving Joan alone in the yard to cast her eye on any last minute details they may have missed. Fiona watched from her window upstairs. What a lot of fuss this was. She thought of the simplicity of all her previous birthdays and of her last birthday when her mother had found the strength to make a cake. Sighing, she made her way down the stairs just in time to let Joshua and the Paleys in the door. Alex came down the stairs as well and seemed in good form, Fiona was happy to note. He warmly welcomed everyone and showed them to the back lawn. Mandy arrived a while later in a very sexy black dress carrying a small beautifully wrapped box and made her way out to join them.

"Hello Fiona. Happy birthday," Mandy said softly, mindful of everyone watching her. "And nice to see you again,

Joshua."

Damn, she looks good, thought Alex. He put his arm around her to make her feel welcome and sort of reward her for being pleasant to Fiona. He also just wanted to touch her. They hadn't had sex since New York due to her travel schedule and his headaches on the few days she had been home, and he looked forward to later in the evening. Glancing at Joan, he tried to gauge her mood. She seemed nonchalant about his affection toward Mandy, concentrating instead on Joshua who was setting up his cello. Joshua had arranged with Joan to give Fiona her gift before dinner; the others would give theirs afterward. As the group quieted, Joshua looked at Fiona and simply said, "I composed this for you, Fiona. Happy birthday."

The piece began in trills that for Fiona evoked images of birds hopping or babies bouncing to music. She almost laughed out loud. After a while, the trills became a melody—and what a melody it was. It took them each on a journey to faraway places, to Africa and beyond. To Fiona it spoke of Joshua's history, of where he came from, and who he was. A boy of Africa but a citizen of the planet—or maybe of the galaxy. Her spirit soared. The musical journey then segued into sadness, but only briefly. A touch, a hint of loss before it went rollicking into more trills alternating with the haunting melody in a chant-like effect that mesmerized the group. He concluded with beauty. The sounds of the cello first whispered, then fairly shouted the feeling of beauty to Fiona. And in those moments Fiona felt beautiful and whole.

When he finished, the group sat in silent reverence and gratitude for several minutes before bursting into applause.

"My god, boy," Fred Paley said, taking him by the arm. "You must produce that composition for publication. I'll help get it known in the music world."

Joshua shook his head. "It was intended to be played only this once—for Fiona. I didn't even write it down." Paley stood stunned. As a mid-level musician Paley could only appreciate greatness, never possess it himself. From the first time he had seen Joshua in South Africa, he had known he was possibly in the presence of greatness. As of this evening, there was no longer any doubt. And now he was to understand that the masterpiece they had just heard would never be played again. A tragedy, he thought, and yet it happens. There are beautiful blooms of the rarest of flowers that occur only once in a hundred years and are never seen by anyone. Paley considered himself a lucky man to have been present at this performance; he could only hope that there were more to come from this young genius in his unforeseeable future.

Fiona had not moved from her seat. She didn't dare speak and instead willed her eyes to express what her heart longed to say. Joshua shyly glanced at her several times and finally winked to let her know, he got her message. When Fred Paley eventually let go of his arm, Joshua made his way to his seat next to Fiona. Under the table she took his hand and squeezed it, then relaxed her grip but gently held on. Joshua would have preferred to forego eating rather than let go her hand, but manners required otherwise.

They lingered over dinner while the sun set and the temperature dropped. Champagne flowed for the adults and sparkling cider for the teenagers as they toasted Fiona's birthday and Joshua's music. Soon the caterers brought out the cake and everyone sang "Happy Birthday" to Fiona with Joshua accompanying on cello. As they ate their dessert, Alex discreetly disappeared into the house and returned with two large boxes. It was time for the presents.

Fiona opened Mandy's present first, a silver and turquoise

bracelet from Mexico. Not too bad, thought Joan. As Fiona admired the lovely bracelet, putting it on her wrist and warmly thanking Mandy for it, Alex gazed at Mandy with what she took to be pride. Even Joan flashed a smile Mandy's way, and for a brief moment, a strange golden flutter passed through Mandy's body. In that moment, she experienced the possibility of being an integral part of a greater whole, of belonging to others not merely as a beautiful woman the way she had sometimes felt she belonged to a man, but as a family member who might be loved and accepted for the incontrovertible reasons that families love one another. The brightness of this feeling was so foreign to Mandy that within a few moments she grew frightened by it, and it quickly passed as the familiar shadows of her aloneness gathered to take up their usual places in her heart.

Fiona opened her next present, this one from the Paleys, a CD of instrumental Hawaiian music by Kapono Beamer. Joan then handed Fiona a box containing a few small things she knew Fiona needed: hair barrettes, camisoles, and a new watch. Then Alex placed the two large boxes on the table in front of Fiona as everyone else became silent.

Fiona opened the smaller of the two first, revealing the violin bow her mother had given her one year ago to the day, swathed in expensive packing, obviously having been on a long journey. She swallowed hard and kept her eyes lowered. She could also now guess what was in the other box. Nodding and trying to smile, she began opening the other box. As soon as she saw a portion of the violin she knew that it had been made by one of the great Italian masters, but when she revealed it in its entirety and saw that it was a Tononi, in perfect condition at that, she knew that she held in her hands one of the music world's great works of art, in a class of perhaps only a couple hundred others at most. She had no idea what something like this would cost; she could only judge its value by its rarity in the art world. For an instant, she longed to play it. But as soon as the thought came, she was swept back to Ireland, to the hours of playing at home with her mother in the kitchen, to the times at the county fairs and her mother's face beaming in the audience, to the day that her mother lay dead in their house as she flung her violin off the cliff.

Fred Paley and Joshua stared openly. "Good lord, that is a Tononi, and looks to be in mint condition," Fred said as Joshua whistled in astonishment. "Where did you find that? Good lord!"

"Paris," Alex replied, eyes on Fiona. Just then Mandy rose from her seat saying that she was going in to get her shawl. Joan noticed that Mandy's mood had predictably darkened. She can't control her jealousy no matter how hard she tries, Joan silently concluded.

Fiona held the violin in her lap as though it were a newborn. "Thank you, Alex," she said quietly, managing a smile in his direction and another one to Joan. Although Alex might have wildly hoped that Fiona would pick up the instrument and burst into Irish jigs with it, he contented himself with the fact that she hadn't thrown it into the pool, a paranoid vision he had entertained several times since buying the violin. She could take all the time she needed to play again. If she never did, well, that Tononi would be a damn good investment.

Later that night in her room, Fiona examined the exquisite violin and bow and, sighing, carefully put them both in their cases and placed them on a high shelf in her closet.

37

The Saturday Joshua left was entirely overcast with what is known in Los Angeles as "June gloom." Joan drove Fiona to the airport to meet up with Joshua and the Paleys for breakfast and final good-byes. Fiona sat silent and sullen in the car.

"I've been looking into some marvelous camps for you, Fiona," Joan said, trying to lift Fiona's mood a little.

Nothing.

Joan continued: "There's a wonderful summer camp in northern California, a place where they focus on the arts but in really fun ways. They put on plays and a big festival with music and dance, and the younger children learn to juggle and do magic tricks. Kids from all over the country go there."

Fiona looked out the window. Non-responsive still. Finally she spoke, changing the subject entirely: "Bad things come in threes, some say in Ireland. First my mother, now Joshua. I wonder who's next."

"Is that what's worrying you, some superstitious saying?"

Fiona wanted to lash out at Joan. Against her better judgment and knowing that Joan wanted only what was best for her, she wanted to punish her aunt. It was irrational and unfair, but she had no other outlet on whom to vent. She managed not to scream and instead spewed sarcasm. "No, nothing is worrying me, nothing at all. My life is great. All the fun of the fair. I like being taken away from my home and having the only people I care about die or leave me."

As soon as the words were out of her mouth, Fiona wished she could take them back but she was too far gone to offer an apology or any expression of regret. She sulked in deeper fury— and shame.

Joan was naturally hurt by the comment even though she knew that Fiona was not in her right mind at the moment. Nevertheless, Joan was in no mood to indulge Fiona's anger any longer and drove in silence the rest of the way to the airport. They got out of the car and Fiona slammed the door. Joan had had enough. She came around to where Fiona was standing in defiance and putting both hands on the girl's shoulders gently said: "Fiona, get hold of yourself."

Fiona collapsed in tears into her aunt's breasts as Joan stroked her hair. "We'll get through this," Joan said repeatedly. Fiona nodded wordlessly, grateful for Joan's forgiveness.

They stopped in at a restroom inside the terminal so that Fiona could wash her face before meeting the others at the designated food hall. Joshua stood as Fiona entered the area; she could see that he had been crying too. The adults made light conversation over the meal as the young people picked at their food in the fluorescent-lit Mexican airport café. When it was time for Joshua to go to his gate, they hugged good-bye at the security check line and watched as Joshua removed his shoes, belt, and change from his pockets for x-ray screening before disappearing into the secure part of the terminal. It was an unceremonious ending to what had been a glorious seven months of friendship, and love, for Fiona and Joshua.

That night Joan made a salad of baby lettuces from her garden and grilled two pieces of salmon. She then poured a glass of wine for herself and half a glass for Fiona and, winking, said, "Don't tell anyone or the child welfare authorities will be knocking at my door."

After dinner, a little tipsy from the half glass of wine, Fiona pensively wondered aloud to Joan, "Do you think Alex would help Joshua?"

"How do you mean?" Joan asked.

"Well, do you think he would give him some money? Because Joshua would continue with his music if he had another scholarship somewhere, like in Europe. But those are so hard to get for a poor person from South Africa."

Joan thought about it for a moment. Doubtful. She knew Alex's feelings about these kinds of things, but why not ask him? "I'll talk to him about it," Joan said.

Later that night when Fiona was asleep, Joan phoned Alex on his cell phone. He and Mandy were in the car on their way home from a fundraiser. It wasn't the best time to talk with him, Joan knew, but she so wanted some good news for Fiona by morning that she figured it was worth a try. What a great surprise it would be to tell Fiona over breakfast that Alex had agreed. And if he didn't, well, Joan wouldn't mention that she had phoned him and would work on softening him to the idea over time.

"No way, Joan," Alex said. "I'm not in the adoption business. And besides, the boy had a scholarship that he blew off. He could have continued at Santa Monica if he really wanted to study music. He's got a scholarship in South Africa at a very good school there. He's made his own choices."

"The school in South Africa doesn't have a good music program, only a mediocre one." Joan pressed on, explaining

Joshua's reasons for leaving The Santa Monica Academy and reminding Alex of his talent.

"His talent is not in question, Joan. I just wouldn't be comfortable doing this. It's too entangled, his friendship or whatever it is with Fiona, the expectations that would arise if we helped him. When would it end?"

Joan was frustrated with her brother once again. God, he could be so dense. Plus, knowing that Mandy was in the car, overhearing every word of Alex's side of the conversation, she figured his resistance to any charity for Joshua was doubled.

"Just out of curiosity, Alex, what fundraiser did you attend tonight?" Joan asked, baiting him.

"Okay, Joan, we're not going to have this conversation right now. I'm hanging up. We'll talk in the morning. Good-bye." He waited for her to say good-bye.

"Good-bye!" Joan hung up the phone. She would have to work on him about this.

The next morning, having no news for Fiona about Alex helping Joshua, Joan instead again brought up the idea of Fiona going to the camp in northern California.

"I don't want to go away this summer," Fiona said softly, hugging Blue and not looking at Joan. "I'd like to just stay here with you and the dogs…and Alex…, if that's okay."

"Of course, it's okay, Fiona! I only suggested the camp because I thought it would be fun for you to be with kids your age instead of us old fogies. But there's nothing that would please me more than spending the summer with you. So let's figure out what we'd like to do, okay?"

"Okay," Fiona said, relieved that, at least for the time being, she wouldn't be saying good-bye to anyone else.

38

Despite the attention she had received from her small role in *Entropy,* Mandy was not being offered any other parts. Well, not any decent ones. The only offer she had received was for a role in a low-budget horror film, which involved mostly a lot of screaming. No way, of course. But it was so depressing! She had thought that her acting life would simply take off after *Entropy*. After all, the film was a worldwide phenomenon. It was so unfair that Alex's life, which was already flush with everything good, had now gone into the stratosphere with the success of *Entropy* and hers had hardly changed at all. She would have to accept a series of modeling assignments that would take her to New York and Europe over much of the summer. It was also beginning to bug her that Alex didn't offer to support her or help her again in her acting career. He could at least cast her in his next film or ask any one of a hundred people in the business who were in his debt to put her in their films. But it was too demeaning to mention any of this to Alex, and she was reduced to dropping hints. Not that he seemed to pick up on any of them.

She was also keenly aware of an unpleasant shift in their balance of power. For the first year of their relationship, she felt equal to him in their attraction for each other and in their willingness to make accommodations. In those days he was solicitous of her opinions and desperate to see her if they were apart too long. He was amorous and would show up at her door with little gifts for no reason; sometimes the little gifts contained diamonds.

But now all of that had changed. First of all, Fiona's presence in Alex's life had alleviated a great deal of the loneliness he would otherwise have felt being in that big house by himself. Now he was virtually never alone. And he seemed to delight in Fiona's company in homey ways that reminded Mandy of his delight in times past with her when they would make breakfast together and read the paper by the pool before heading off for work, something they now did only on Sundays if they were both in town. Fiona had largely replaced her in Alex's home life.

The other issue for Mandy was that of other women. No doubt about it, Alex's stock had gone up. Handsome, young, powerful, and very, very rich, Alex was a catch. Even if he and Mandy had been married, women would be coming on to him. With him not married, he was considered fair game by every beautiful and available woman in Los Angeles, and there were plenty of those. Consequently, Mandy had be to on her best behavior at all times, go along entirely with what Alex wanted without parity for her own needs, and keep her mouth shut about all that bothered her. It was a continual strain.

Alex, too, felt the ongoing strain in the relationship with Mandy. True, he had been enjoying the attention he was getting from all sorts of women. Some very desirable creatures had made clear their availability to him and, had he been a free man, he may well have sampled some of those delicacies. But Alex, at this point in his life couldn't handle any more high drama. Having an affair or even a one-night stand of which Mandy might get wind counted as very high drama. It gave him a headache just to think about it. The problem really wasn't that he was likely to cheat. The problem was that Mandy was in a constant state of fear about it. She would turn to ice when a beautiful woman, most often an actress, came to their table to say hello. "How do you know her?" Mandy would hiss as soon as the woman had walked away. Usually he hadn't known the woman except by having seen her in film or on TV, but it would be enough to freeze Mandy for the rest of the night. He started to subliminally repel women when Mandy was around for fear that it would create a fight later but this also had the effect of making him more friendly to the beauties when Mandy wasn't around. Mandy's repression of him was creating the very thing she feared. If only he could explain this to her. But he knew she would blow up if he tried.

Meanwhile, he was working on an exciting new project due to be shot in the Philippines during the coming winter months, six months hence. Mandy had been angling for a role in it and he had deftly pretended he didn't get her hints. The truth was that she was not a natural talent as an actress, at least not from what could be gleaned from her role in *Entropy*. Fortunately it was a small part and he didn't take too much heat for casting her in it, but it was clear from everyone he worked with that they saw it as nepotism. This was another source of difficulty between them. He dreaded the day when she would confront him directly rather than drop any more easy-to-ignore hints, a day that he knew loomed in his future.

The other problem between them, of course, was his affection for Fiona, which seemed to exponentially grow by the week. Fiona was simply a delightful human being. He sometimes wondered if, had she not been his daughter, he would have found her quite so charming and concluded that indeed he would. True, she was perhaps a somewhat acquired taste for others. She was no extrovert and took time to get to know, but there was a depth in her that he had never seen in a fourteen-year-old and had rarely seen in an adult. Plus, there were times when she was witty and playful. A real rascal of a tease with an irreverent Irish humor. Why would Mandy deny him this joy in life, the love and appreciation of his daughter, a daughter who had suffered the loss of her mother? He was growing weary of Mandy's jealousy.

And yet, he and Mandy had something together. Sometimes when she wasn't looking he saw the young woman who had swept him away the day they met at the afternoon party, the bright and beautiful Tennessee girl, playing at being a sophisticate but exuding animal heat. She would be gone much of the summer for her work, and because the Mandy from the party on the day they met was the one who lived in Alex's mind, he had a brief moment of missing her, even though she had not yet left.

39

Fiona gazed out of the kitchen window at the little cove on Catalina Island where Joan had rented a summer house for them. Catalina was only twenty miles off the coast from Los Angeles, but it may as well have been a thousand. It also existed in another time, "something like the fifties or sixties," Joan had said. Fiona loved the place. Quiet and surrounded by ocean, she felt at home. Joan had chosen a large rambling old house, one of the few nice rental places that allowed dogs, and they settled into a gentle daily rhythm of rising whenever they happened to wake up, walking on the beach, having breakfast on the porch, reading or swimming until lunch time, and then going into town, a place called Avalon, which Fiona considered a hopeful omen, its namesake the mythical island in the British Isles where legend had it that King Arthur was buried. They would eat fresh fish and salad at one of the seafood restaurants and then wander around town a bit after lunch before heading back to the quiet of the cove and more swimming or an afternoon nap. Dinner was usually a simple meal at home. As Mandy was mostly away, Alex sometimes joined them on weekends, greeted with yelps, vigorous tail wagging, and many kisses from his old friend Blue.

Though Fiona did not mention Joshua much, Joan knew

that she was in touch with him by email. On that morning,
knowing Alex was about to arrive later in the day, Fiona suddenly
said:

"Joan, did you ever speak with Alex about helping
Joshua?"

It was a conversation Joan had dreaded for weeks, and
here it was, just like that. She had indeed spoken with Alex. After
the initial discussion with him, Joan had broached the subject
several more times, to no avail. Alex was adamant. We just don't
do that, Joan.

"What *we* are your referring to?" Joan had snapped back
the last time.

Joan paused before replying to Fiona, mindful of the
delicate relationship between father and daughter.

"Yes, I've spoken with Alex about it, Fiona. It's something
that he doesn't feel comfortable about doing. It's not at all about
you or about Joshua. It's just, well, Alex is in a position of wealth
that makes it difficult in all kinds of ways in his personal life
and…"

Joan stopped here as she could hear that none of this was
making much sense and sounded as flat as it felt in her heart.

"What if we sold my violin?" Fiona asked. A plea.

Joan looked down at her feet, noticing the veins that
seemed to have sprung up in the last few months, some crumbs on
the floor, a crack in the kitchen tiles.

"I don't think that is a good idea, Fiona," Joan said quietly.
"It's not about Alex being able to afford help for Joshua."

"Then what, what can we do?" Fiona again pleaded.
Frustrated, she walked out of the kitchen and onto the porch, Blue
at her heels. "I don't understand," she said, her back to her aunt.

Joan came and stood next to her, putting her arm around

Fiona's shoulders. "To tell you the truth, I don't either," Joan said. And they stared at the sea, letting the mystery of things be as it was.

When Fiona saw Alex paying the taxi fare in the driveway a few hours later, she went to her room and closed the door. Joan took Alex by the hand and walked him down to the beach. In the late afternoon, there were a few places in the cove that provided shade. Joan spread a large beach towel and the two of them flopped on it. She told him of her conversation with Fiona, leaving out the part about selling the violin.

"It's ridiculous," Alex said, slightly annoyed. He had developed an extreme headache on the helicopter ride over. "First off, Joan, it is really nobody's business how I spend my money and who I give it to, wouldn't you agree?"

Joan could find no rational reason to disagree but her heart told her otherwise. She said nothing.

"I'll talk to Fiona and try to make her understand," Alex said, getting up and extending his hand. "Come on, Sis. And let's you and I drop this subject once and for all."

Joan shook her head and said, "What am I going to do with you?"

Alex laughed and said, "It's a little late to worry about how I might turn out. Even though you are the *older* sibling." He grabbed her and swung her around until she squealed. It was hard to stay mad at him when he was in such a playful mood, which was more and more rare due to his headaches and the pressures of work.

A few minutes later Alex knocked on Fiona's door, calling to her: "Fiona, could I talk with you?"

The door opened and a sleepy Fiona appeared, evidently having just woken from a nap. She was wearing some sort of beach *mumu* covered in images of small purple cocktail umbrellas that looked like it belonged in an old Sandra Dee movie. God, where do Joan and Fiona get this crap, he wondered. I've told them a thousand times that she can go with a stylist any time she wants to shop or just let the stylist bring her things to the house to try on. But despite the silly *mumu*, his daughter was a sight to behold. Tanned and taller it seemed by the week, her green eyes even more translucent than usual against the dark of her tanned skin, Alex thought as he often did upon seeing her that she had gotten what had to be the best genes from him and Aine, a one in a thousand in the genetic lottery. He even had a few superstitious thoughts now and again about the fact that Fiona had been conceived next to the Ganges, India's holiest river.

"Would you go for a walk with me on the beach? We could watch the sunset."

Fiona nodded and put on her sun hat. Blue, of course, was delighted and went tearing down to the water, ball in mouth, hoping someone would take it from him and throw it in. Hamlet followed but was afraid of the water, leaving Blue with the entire ocean to himself. When they were by the shore, Alex explained his situation to Fiona and tried to reason with her about why they couldn't help Joshua or any of their personal friends.

"As I've told you, there are some things that you will better understand when you are older, some things that come only with experience, especially when it involves wealth," Alex explained.

Fiona looked at her father with a calm steady gaze. Once again, he appeared as a child to her. It was strange how many times it happened that the adults she met in this country seemed like children. Joan might be the only real adult she knew. She thought about Ireland, about her mother's friends, how hard they worked, how much loss they had all known. She pictured Maria Girardi's face, the sadness in her eyes. She saw the same sadness when she looked in the mirror. Maybe this was the difference. Maybe most of the people here didn't understand that some losses are forever and happy endings are more rare than the movies and television shows lead a person to believe. But Alex had lost his own mother. Wasn't that enough to have made him understand? Apparently not.

"So, what about it, Fiona?" Alex pressed. "Will you just trust me and know that I am looking out for all of us as best I can?"

Fiona nodded. It was true enough that he thought he was doing his best. She was not in any position to make demands of him, it was clear. Her thoughts flew to Aine. She desperately missed her mother, who, though they never had much to spare, would share anything she had with those she loved. Fiona sighed and stood to go back to the house. Alex walked down to the water and threw the ball in once for Blue. For the rest of the weekend, Fiona was more quiet than usual and several times remained in her room when Alex and Joan went down to the beach.

Over the next six weeks, Joan noticed that Fiona and Alex returned to being polite with each other, no longer playful. Alex came to Catalina less frequently, focusing instead on work or flying to New York to see Mandy on several of the remaining summer weekends. Joan, dismayed by the subtle rift between father and daughter, marveled at how alike they were, both so stubborn and dedicated to being right.

40

Joan stood in her garden shaking her head as Topanga Canyon sizzled in the late August heat. The plants had withered and turned into a field of brown and brittle leaves and stems. It depressed her to look at it. Before leaving for the summer, she had arranged for a Mexican waiter from the restaurant to water for her, but he had been suddenly deported two weeks before her return. She had not bothered to find a replacement for him figuring the garden could make it for two weeks without entirely dying off, but she hadn't counted on a record heat wave.

Fiona was spending the week at Alex's in order to begin school again. Joan felt it would be good for Alex and Fiona to get back to their old schedule of being together during the weekdays. Further, Joan needed to return to work at the restaurant, having taken off the second summer in a row and promising she would be back on the job immediately upon her return. She hoped they would all resume their routines as seamlessly as possible and that the good will between Fiona and Alex would re-establish itself.

That night Joan made up the porch couch with sheets and a pillow. It was too hot to sleep in the house. She had never had air conditioning installed as there were so few times it would have been needed at night. She drifted off to sleep under a galaxy of stars, Hamlet snoring by her side.

Alex dropped Fiona off for her first day of school since it was on his way to a meeting in Santa Monica and he thought it would be good if he drove her on the first day instead of leaving it to Gwen. Although in some ways he felt that he and Fiona were no closer than when she had come to live with him the year before, he also knew the possibility of their closeness, having experienced it in the interim, and he had to admit that he missed it.

A few hours later, Alex picked Mandy up for lunch and was cruising up Sunset Boulevard in his Porsche convertible when his assistant called on his cell phone.

"Alex, turn on the radio," she said breathlessly. "There's a big fire in Topanga Canyon."

As he fumbled for the radio dials, trying to find a local station, Alex's heart began to pound.

"What are they saying?" he asked his assistant in panic.

"They're saying that some people are trapped inside the fire ring. Alex, I called Joan at the restaurant as soon as I heard. The owner said she had gone home two hours ago to get Hamlet and they haven't heard from her since. I haven't been able to reach her on her cell or home phone. And your cell has been out of range for the last few minutes."

"Oh god. Oh god." Alex hung up the phone and pulled off the road, his eyesight blurring, his head throbbing, his mind temporarily gone.

"Mandy, you have to drive. To Topanga Canyon! God, Joan went into a fire for the dog!"

They got out of the car to switch seats. Trying to clear his head, Alex grabbed Mandy's water bottle and splashed his face.

Taking the phone again he called his assistant and told her to dial
Joan's cell phone every minute and call Mandy's cell as soon as she
reached her; meanwhile, he would call her home line on his own
cell phone. He instructed her to get one of the other people in the
office to contact the police and fire departments in Topanga and
get as much information as possible. "Who do we know there?"

"You give donations to the Los Angeles police and fire but
I think Topanga Canyon is serviced by departments in the valley,"
his assistant informed him.

"Then get our guys on the phone and see who does
Topanga! All the cops and firemen know each other."

Mandy drove in silence as Alex repeatedly hit the "redial"
for Joan's home number, a number that had never held any
significance until now but had suddenly become the entire focus of
his universe. Three. One. Zero. Four. Five. Five....Each time he
heard Joan's familiar voice on the outgoing message telling her
callers to leave their name and number. Inside he was screaming,
though no words came out of his mouth. Answer the phone,
Joanie. Oh god. Please don't leave me, Sis—please don't leave me.
Me—and Fiona. His thoughts raced to numerous possibilities
wherein Joan would not be reachable, but something in him,
something deep and sickening in his gut, knew that of all these
possibilities, there was one that most stood out.

An official roadblock kept all traffic from getting into
Topanga Canyon from both possible directions as fire sirens blared
in the distance and great plumes of black smoke filled the skies
only a couple miles away. People were screaming, panicked,
desperate to get home to their loved ones. Chaos reigned and
police began using bullhorns to control the crowd. "Turn back.
The road is closed except to emergency vehicles," they shouted to
the throngs. Alex was on the phone with a helicopter service he

frequently used, trying to persuade them with bribes to take him into the area of the fire when he got the call on Mandy's cell from Linda. "It doesn't look good, Alex. We just heard from our police guys that the firemen in Topanga radioed from inside the fire line. They found the bodies of a woman and a dog—at Joan's address. The fire seems to have been contained in Joan's area, but they won't let anyone in until tomorrow when they're sure there is no further risk. It started in the hills by her house and swept downward. It appears that everyone else on her street evacuated in time and have been accounted for."

Linda continued talking but Alex could no longer hear whatever else she said. The phone fell out of his hand and he slumped to the ground, retching the contents of his nearly empty stomach. Mandy came around and helped him into the car, not knowing where to go and gently asking where he would like her to take him. After some minutes, Alex answered, marveling that he could summon anything like practicality, that life could go on and others would still have homes to go to and living bodies to go into the homes, bodies that were not charred and laying in a house or a field. "Let's take you home. I have to get to Fiona before she hears from someone else," he replied, his voice strange and faraway. But it was not only that. He had to be with the one other person left on earth who loved Joan as much as he did.

School was just letting out when Alex arrived. Fiona was surprised to see Alex's car since she expected Gwen to pick her up, but on seeing his face she knew something terrible had happened. At first she thought it was about Blue. A quiver in her throat. As she climbed into the car and got a closer look at Alex, the entirety of him frozen in pain, she knew that this wasn't' just about Blue.

"Fiona," Alex began, hands out to her, palms upward, a gesture that she would remember in years to come, a resigned gesture, one that said that something horrible had happened and there was nothing to be done about it. For the rest of her life, a chill ran through Fiona whenever she saw that gesture again. "Joan died in a fire today near her house, trying to save Hamlet." It took only a few seconds to register. She asked no questions but fell into her father's arms. Alex and Fiona held each other in the car for an indeterminate time, both of them trembling, Fiona's tears soaking his shirt.

41

A doctor friend of Alex's came to the house that night and administered mild sedation to Fiona who, after they got home, went eerily catatonic for several hours and then began to whimper and eventually wail.

Alex spent the following day identifying his sister's body and beginning the arrangements for the cremation of what was left of her and for her memorial services. At Fiona's insistence, they intended to mingle the ashes of Hamlet and Joan once they had possession of them. Alex carried out these gruesome tasks as though sleepwalking. He couldn't feel anything. It all happened at a great distance. Unresponsive to the suggestions and offers of help from friends and co-workers, he found his own form of sedation in motion. He would stay busy, ahead of the pain, not stopping for a second. There were so many tasks—obituaries to write for the Los Angeles Times, the local papers in Topanga, and the Animal Shelter Newsletter; the planning of the memorial and letting Joan's friends and colleagues know; her financial affairs and the insurance claims on the house; the legal paperwork required for the deceased. He could stay connected to Joan by taking care of these things, as though he were just helping her with some business arrangements, tidying up a few details while she was away. But late at night, in utter exhaustion, he fought sleep for fear that the truth would catch up with him in dreams. After five days Alex no longer looked or seemed himself.

Five hundred people attended the memorial service for Joan, held at a Unitarian Church. Diverse groups of friends from Joan's work with animals, her twenty years in Topanga Canyon, the restaurant where she worked, as well as Alex's close friends and colleagues sat in the large chapel hall, the altars and every spare corner filled with magnificent white Casablanca lilies as ten of Joan's friends took turns in their eulogies to her. When it came time for Alex to give his eulogy to Joan, he stoically read a letter addressed directly to his sister, thanking her for all that mattered in his life, for being his beacon in the storm, for always knowing the highest good. His (and Mandy's) were the only dry eyes in the room.

In the days to come, something strange began to happen to Alex. Completely beyond his control, he started to see through Joan's eyes. He could almost hear her familiar tones giving voice to thoughts in his head. As a result, it was becoming difficult for him to be in the company of Mandy. Throughout their ordeal on the day of the fire, Mandy had been calm, too calm. Alex was too distraught to give it much notice and managed to dismiss the few thoughts that arose about Mandy not seeming very upset about what was happening that day, but now he realized that she seemed to have no sad feelings whatsoever about his sister's death and if anything, he sensed in her a kind of…hopefulness…yes, that was it. Always angling for herself. Even though she had not particularly liked Joan, couldn't she imagine what his sister's death would do to him? Didn't she care anything for his well being at all? As these reflections took hold, he saw Mandy as Joan had always seen her. Damaged—and consequently, manipulative and dangerous. He had been blinded all this time. Blinded by her beauty and his desire. The vision of Mandy at the party on the day they met had been merely a projected image for fantasies that lived in his mind. It had nothing to do with Mandy the person. He could not blame her. God knows, she had it rough as a child. But he could no longer see her through his projection of desire and fantasy. He could now only see her through Joan's eyes, an unsentimental picture of a selfish and superficial young woman. And with that new vision, he admired his sister's restraint in not hammering at him more than she did about Mandy. Joan had instead tried for the most part to maintain peace between herself and Alex, all the while having to worry about his choice in relationship and about Fiona, who was unfairly subjected to Mandy's pettiness. He had been such a fool.

The only person he could bear having in his presence was Fiona, though they could not find many sources of conversation. Everything they discussed seemed to lead to unspoken thoughts of their loss. So they would instead eat their meals quietly and at night walk the grounds with Blue. After two weeks of sorting Joan's affairs, which had involved a great deal of activity, Alex canceled all work for the foreseeable future. He then went to the suite in his house that contained his bedroom and study, pulled his Hella Jongerius chair to the window that overlooked the garden, and spent his days staring blankly into space.

Mandy knew it was over with Alex. He wouldn't see her and made excuses to hang up each time she phoned. He never gave a reason for his sudden loss of interest, but then he didn't have to. She knew that he no longer loved her, that the loss of his sister had made him see her in a different light, as though in loyalty to Joan. Well, she couldn't help any of that now. She had done her best. It just hadn't worked. Perhaps she had overreached in her hopes for the two of them all along.

Still, sometimes she thought about the last time she saw him, the day she decided to just show up at his house, use her key for the front door, and go to his room where she knew she would find him, sitting in his chair. What struck her that day was not the depth of his grief, though it was formidable to witness. What struck her were her feelings of envy. She realized in seeing him that she had never loved anyone enough to grieve as he did for his sister. She had never bonded with a family member, a lover, a friend, or even an animal such that she would end up in the kind of despair she witnessed in Alex. And though there was freedom in that for her, it was lonely and hollow.

Alex did not turn around though he knew she was there. She was not someone, the loss of whom, he would grieve. Mandy left the room and went quietly down the stairs, leaving her key on the table in the foyer.

42

Two weeks after Joan's death, Fiona went back to school. She, too, felt lifeless and would have liked to stay home and stare out the window, but the school had phoned and said she would need to get back in order to maintain her assignments. School assignments. As if they mattered. At night Fiona would sometimes think about her cruel words to Joan in the car on the way to seeing Joshua off. *Bad things come in threes. I wonder who is next.* She felt sick to her stomach at the memory of those statements and how much her subsequent words had hurt Joan's feelings. Had she somehow caused this? Was she a girl of bad luck, as some said of certain girls in Ireland? Her mother would have disapproved of her thinking this way. Superstition is for the weak-minded, Aine used to say. But how was it possible that both her primary caretakers—her mother and her aunt—the people whose main thing in common was that they loved her had died just over a year apart?

Fiona's main relief came in the form of emails from Joshua. He wouldn't hear of her self-recrimination or of her giving up on life. In desperation one night, when they happened to be online at the same time, she asked for the public phone number in his dorm so that she might talk with him directly. It was against the rules at his school to have personal calls on the dorm phone, reserved for emergency use only, but within minutes, Fiona dialed the number Joshua provided and heard the melodic sound of his voice.

"Fiona, tell me," he said. "What do you think your mother and aunt would have wanted for you?"

"I don't know."

"Hmmm, I think you do," Joshua replied gently. "I think you do know. They would want you to live. To have a happy life. To do all the things they dreamed for you. You must be strong, and it will come about. Do it for them."

Fiona hung up the phone and thought about what Joshua had said. It was true that Aine and Joan would have wanted her to keep going, to have a full and wonderful life. They were both powerful, independent women who sought to impart their strength to her. Just then Blue nuzzled her as if to second her thoughts. She patted his head and scratched his torso the way he liked. Aside from their evening walks, he had been somewhat neglected in the past few weeks. Everyone around there had been so gloomy, and now that she thought about it, Blue had been strangely subdued as well. She wondered if he missed Hamlet— and Joan. Fiona stroked him for another few moments before undertaking a resolve within herself. She went to her dresser where she kept photographs of her mother and aunt, now side by side in a double frame, and looked at their images for a long time. She would try to dignify their lives by dignifying her own. As the minutes passed she was aware of a surge of confidence, as though the aspects she most admired in those two great women took deeper hold in her own embodiment. She inhaled and released a slow, steady breath from her abdomen, the first of its kind in many weeks. She would let her mother's fierce intelligence and her aunt's great heart guide her from now on. They would live, the best of them, in her.

The following morning Fiona went into her father's bedroom to talk with him in private. They usually met for breakfast downstairs before Fiona went to school, but the housekeeper would be milling about by then, and Fiona wanted to have a few words alone with Alex. He was still in his pajamas; he hadn't shaved since the memorial the previous month and could have passed at that moment as a homeless man who had landed in some very nice digs. In the first week after Joan's death, Alex had been a whirlwind of busy-ness. The next week he had seemed to be in a kind of silent shock. But in the last couple weeks, he had been bitter, his few words of communication being those of frustration about little things around the house. And he seemed especially upset this morning. Fiona was glad to see that he held a towel in his hand and that he was about to shower. Maybe it would refresh him a little.

Fiona stood at the door for a minute before speaking, "I was wondering if you would like to go somewhere this weekend."

Alex threw the towel on the bed. "You know what I don't get?" His headaches had now spread to his shoulders and upper back. He lived in constant pounding pain from his head to his chest, as though his upper torso were in a vice. Without waiting for her to answer, he continued. "I don't get why she went back for the damn dog. Goddamnit, she was ridiculous about that fucking dog. Why? Why did she do such an idiotic thing?" He flopped on the bed in frustration, shaking his head downward, not looking up. As though he were talking to himself.

Fiona came and sat on the bed next to him. After some time she put her arm around him and said quietly, "She had to go back, Dad. She wouldn't have wanted to live if she hadn't tried to save him. Her life would have been over anyway if she didn't at least try. Hamlet was like her child."

Two things penetrated Alex's fog in those moments. One was the sublime truth of what Fiona said. He had been so outraged by Joan dying for what he considered a reckless and foolish act that he had not stopped to consider what her life would have been had she not gone back. It was true, Joan would have not been able to live with herself. He was struck by the simplicity of it.

The other thing he noticed was that for the first time, Fiona had called him *dad* (which came out sounding more like the Irish *Da*). He turned to search his daughter's eyes. He blinked. For a moment he thought he saw Aine staring back at him, the cool intelligence gleaming behind the pupils. He nodded slowly, letting the truth rip open his heart. And now he knew that the rage he had been experiencing, perhaps unconsciously holding onto, was only a protective superficial layer over the ocean of sorrow that was waiting underneath.

"I'll meet you downstairs for breakfast," Fiona said, squeezing his hand.

"Okay," Alex replied, but he sounded even more weary than usual.

That afternoon, Fiona tiptoed into her father's study to peer into his bedroom. She had hoped to find him up and about, that perhaps their talk that morning had lifted his spirits such that perhaps he understood that there had been no other way. But she found him still sitting in his chair, staring out the window, slumped and disheveled. He turned to face her, and the sight of him caused her to draw in her breath. He had gone from bitterness to gloom and seemed further away than ever. He shook his head as if to say he didn't want to be disturbed. In fact, he didn't want her to feel obliged to lift him out of his despair or be pulled down with him. Fiona left the room.

A few hours later, at dusk, something wondrous—almost magical—occurred while Alex watched the last of the light in the garden. From behind him in the dimly lit study adjacent to his bedroom came the most magnificent violin music he had ever heard.

Without planning or knowing even moments beforehand, Fiona played Schubert's *Ave Maria,* its familiar melody reaching into her father's heart to release the knots that grew there and Fiona's clearest way to tell him, "I will grieve with you today." After a short while, Alex began to weep. They were his first tears since hearing of the death of his sister, in fact, the first tears he had shed in years. As the melody crested, his sobs grew stronger. He cried for the losses of his life. His sister. His mother. He cried in recalling his confusion the day his father had picked him up before leaving forever and had buried his head into the young boy's chest, saying the words, "My son, my son," a long-forgotten image, which now soared through his mind on wings of forgiveness. He cried in remorse for the hurt he had caused, things he should have said when he had the chance, things he never should have said and did. He cried for the pain and fear that Joan must have known in her last moments of life. He even cried for Hamlet. He wept for Fiona, for all the sadness she had known and all that she would know. He cried for Mandy, whose childhood conditioning prohibited her from ever feeling safe. He cried for himself and he cried for the world.

As the last notes faded into silence, Fiona quietly left the room. She had not known she could still play and was surprised to find that her facility had, in fact, improved. She decided that her months of listening to Joshua practice had kept her in form, but she was unaware that there was something else as well. She could now express a greater emotional depth born of her life experience over the previous year and a half.

The following afternoon at dusk brought the first movement of Sibelius's violin concerto in D minor. Again, tears streamed from Alex's eyes and at the end of the movement, his headache and upper body pain began to dissipate.

The next afternoon came Bach: Chaconne in D minor from Partita No. 2 for solo violin. The music washed through him, lifted him, baptized him. This time Alex smiled into the glass of the window, seeing his reflection momentarily happy, not daring to turn around to look at his wondrous muse.

Over the following days the last movements of Mozart and Mendelssohn concerti and Beethoven's Spring Sonata graced his rooms each afternoon with bright and virtuosic alacrity, leaving Fiona in a filmy perspiration, her cheeks flushed crimson, and Alex in a state of peace.

On the last day of an extraordinary week of solo violin concerts, Fiona played her own arrangement of Von Weber's *Invitation to the Dance.*

43

Alex shaved his face, put on a clean shirt and baggy khakis, and left the house. For the past month, since the extraordinary week of Fiona's concerts, he had made a few plans and wanted to nail the final details before discussing them with his daughter that afternoon. After completing the last of his errands, he drove to her school with Blue in the backseat to wait for her to emerge. He had been in the habit of picking her up from school for the previous few weeks and looked forward to their afternoons of walking along the boardwalk or into one of the canyons, having ice cream on The Promenade, or taking in an early movie. The one part of this ritual that he found difficult was the beleaguered look on her face as she emerged from school. It didn't last long; she would cheer up as soon as she had hugged Blue and kissed her father on the cheek. But it pained Alex nonetheless. How had he never noticed this before? Joan had been telling him the entire last year how unhappy Fiona was at that school. It had been merely a piece of information that he didn't think had much relevance since there was nothing to be done about it. Now, because he continued to see things through Joan's eyes and heart (a habit to which he was adapting with some difficulty), he was forced to feel the pain of it.

"Fiona, I've been making some plans for a trip," he began. "I'm thinking of going back to India, to Benares. I want to put Joan's ashes in the Ganges River as we did my mother's, and I wanted to know if you'll go with me."

Fiona's heart quickened. She imagined India as the most exotic place in the world and had grown up on stories from her mother that reminded her of the tales of Rudyard Kipling. And Benares seemed the most exciting of all. Fiona was also aware that Benares was the place where she had been conceived. Quickly checking with Joan and Aine in her imagination, which she often did these days in times of decision, Fiona found them to be in enthusiastic agreement that this was an excellent idea. But it was a very long trip. When would she have time off from school?

"You mean, over Christmas?" Fiona asked, though it was only one of a hundred questions that came to mind at that precise moment.

"No, I mean next week."

"For how long?"

"Oh…for a month maybe," Alex answered casually.

"What about Blue—and school?" Fiona asked.

"It's all taken care of. You'll be on a sort of home school program for a while. I don't think there will be any better education for you than seeing India. And I have arranged for Gwen to take care of Blue at her place. So what do you say?"

It was hard to think of leaving Blue for a month, but Fiona knew that he would be very happy with Gwen, who loved him and with whom he had spent his days while Fiona was in school the previous year.

"Brilliant!" she exclaimed.

Their arrival in Benares coincided with the final week of Ramlila, a festival of ancient rituals, and the streets were filled with pilgrims from all of India. Fortunately Asi Ghat, where their hotel was located, was on a quiet section of the river, a good distance from the center of town and the main activity of the *ghats*. But on the drive from the airport, Fiona gawked with eyes the size of saucers as the taxi made its way, honking virtually nonstop, through the narrow streets filled with the sounds of cymbals and drums, painted elephants, and what seemed to be millions of people occupying every square inch of space.

They checked into their rooms at Asi Ghat. New owners had taken over, but otherwise the place was virtually unchanged. Alex took the room he and his sister had originally occupied; Fiona stayed in Aine's old room. Memories and familiar feelings of things he had not thought of since his last time there flooded Alex's awareness within minutes of entering the room. The feel of the cool tile underfoot, the smell of mothballs in the armoire that stood in the corner. An experience of himself as someone entirely different, new, slightly intoxicated with a sense that anything could happen. These feelings and memories stood in contradiction to the way he had held India in his mind during the years since he had last been on her soil. They were more as Joan would have again experienced India.

Although she had heard dozens of stories from her mother about Aine's time in India, Fiona was surprised and dazzled by the place. The colors of the women's silk saris, vibrant as peacock feathers, fluttering along narrow stone alleys five thousand years old. The smell of incense and wood-burning that permeated the city and drenched its every crack and corner, the songs of the pallbearers carrying bodies to the burning *ghats* day and night. The burning *ghats* themselves, where Fiona and her father would go every night and watch as six or seven bodies on the pyres disintegrated into ash and bone. The only difficulty was that it seemed that Alex had little interest in anything other than the *ghats*. Although his despair over his sister's death had lessened, he had a newborn fascination with death itself. Because existence was so forcefully the only experience he had known, it was impossible to imagine not being at all. And yet, there in Benares, seeing bodies burn, knowing that each one had lived a story that no one else could really ever know, evidence of the inevitability mounted.

Another reason the *ghats* drew Alex was to witness the irrevocable effects of fire. Since the demise of his sister, he had imagined her final moments thousands of times in his mind. Standing at the *ghats* was a way to burn into his own awareness what those moments might have been for her, his way of sharing her burden, if only in his imagination. It always brought tears to his eyes. On one such night, Fiona turned to her father and motioned for him to walk with her away from the pyres out of respect for the silence at the *ghats*. She wanted to talk with him. They walked along the shore of the river until they were out of hearing range of the *ghats*.

"What was it like—you and my mother? How did you meet?"

Alex smiled in the darkness, a sad smile.

"You know the stoop by the river at our hotel?" he asked.

"Yes."

"Well, I first saw your mother sitting on that stoop, reading a book. I thought she was beautiful, and I could tell she knew her way around because she was dressed in Indian clothing that looked like it had been on the road for a while. I found a way to strike up a conversation and we hit it off immediately. Then

Joan came by, and well, since we were all staying at the same hotel, the three of us—my sister, your mother, and I—began to spend all our time together."

"What did you all do, spend a lot of time at the burning *ghats*?"

"Oh no, not just that. We went to all kinds of places around here."

"Will you take me to some of those places?" Fiona asked.

Alex nodded, putting his hand on her shoulder in the realization that spending every night at the burning *ghats* may not be as fascinating for his fourteen-year-old daughter as it was for him.

Over the next weeks, they visited temples, ancient forts, and the Deer Park in nearby Sarnath. They attended concerts at the Benares Hindu University, famed for its Indian music department, and saw the Ramayana performed as a play in an outdoor theater there. They went to all the places Alex could remember that he, Joan, and Aine had visited. In each of these places, long forgotten images and scraps of conversations unfurled themselves in Alex's mind like dancers in shadow on a stage, suddenly coming to life, and as they did, he shared them with Fiona. They walked along the riverbanks for hours, sometimes animatedly talking about something they had seen or learned that day, sometimes in silence. They were peaceful and happy in each other's company, and the time passed lazily until it neared its end.

On the night they were to put Joan's ashes in the river, they wore cream-colored silk *kurtas* and pajama-like bottoms. Alex told Fiona the story of his mother's ashes blowing back on him the night they put her remains in the river.

"I hope that doesn't happen to you again," Fiona laughed. "Don't forget Hamlet's ashes are mixed in!"

Alex laughed and poked her playfully. He loved her irreverence. Just like her mother. They walked to the river where the hired boat waited. Another full moon, this one turning the dark river into a giant serpent of sparkles. The boatman rowed them out to the approximate place where his mother's ashes had been released. Alex then read passages from the *Tibetan Book of the Dead,* as Joan would have wanted. They sang Indian *bhajans* they had learned for the occasion as he and Joan and Aine had done before. Then Fiona sang the Gaelic song that Aine sang all those years before for the woman who, unbeknownst to her at the time, was grandmother to the unborn child she carried.

Alex and Fiona cried together for a few moments and then turned to the task at hand. On this night there was no wind. Alex took up the heavy urn and solemnly poured the ashes as Fiona tossed garlands of flowers into the holy waters. Afterward they sat in silence, holding hands and looking at the moon and stars while chants from the distant *ghats* filled the sky.

As the boatman rowed them home an hour later, Fiona experienced a puzzling urge to tell her father something she had wanted to say for a long time. The setting demanded truth telling.

"Da?"

"Yes, Fiona,"

"I wish we didn't have to go back. If it weren't for Blue, I wouldn't mind if we never went back."

"Hmmm. Well, who knows what will happen," Alex said cryptically and winked at her, his face clearly lit by the full moon.

He wouldn't need to tell her anything more that night as she would find out soon enough. During the weeks before leaving Santa Monica, Alex made a few changes in their lives to come. He was a producer, after all, and this had been one of his most satisfying productions. For they would not be returning to

California. Their plane would instead take them to Rome, where Maria Girardi would wait with flowers and play something of her choosing on Fiona's violin. She would drive them to their rented villa only two blocks from her own home, where Blue and Gwen would greet them, having crossed the Atlantic with several crates of their belongings on a ship friendly to dogs, and where Joshua, already in attendance at Fiona's new school, the Conservatorio S. Cecilia, would join them for dinner.

"Okay, Sis," Alex whispered to Joan as her molecules mingled with the river, the air, the moonlight. "We'll do it your way from here on." His sister was always right in matters of the heart.

Printed in the United States
78587LV00005B/94